The Ink Slingers Guild

Presents

On the Verge

A Collection of Short Stories
Volume Three

Contributing Authors

Nicole DragonBeck

Erika Lance

Rhiannon Matlock

JM Paquette

Lisa Barry

Robert Broughton

Laura Price

Desiree Matlock

Angel Woolery

Witching Hour Publishing, Inc.

Witching Hour Publishing, Inc.

ISBN-10: 0-9885799-8-7
ISBN-13: 978-0-9885799-8-9

Ink Slingers Guild crest: Nicole DragonBeck
Ink Slingers Guild crest digital artistry: Desi Matlock
Cover Design: Lisa Barry
Editor: Courtenay Dodds www.CourtenayDodds.com

Introduction

The Ink Slingers Guild is a group of writers who come together for support and encouragement. We give each other inspiration and the occasional kick in the arse.

This collection of short stories is based on a writing exercise done at every ISG meeting. The exercise is to have three members each pick one word. Members have five minutes to compose a story with the chosen words. As with any creative outlet, members take each other into new worlds the way only writers can.

And the concept of these books was born.

On the Verge is the Ink Slinger's third anthology based on that exercise. As with the first anthology, *Beyond the Threshold* and the second, *Into the Abyss*, the authors had several months to create their stories.

The words that were chosen this year were:

• Destiny
• Rogue
• Sarcasm

Each story is a journey created just for you, so sit back and enjoy as the Ink Slingers Guild keeps you *On the Verge* of your seat!

www.InkSlingersGuild.com

Dedication

As always, this book goes out to all those who are chasing a dream. Keep ripping away the barriers, keep jumping over those obstacles.

There is light at the end of that tunnel and we look forward to feeling its warmth on our faces.

Cheers!

Contents

The Huntsman's Sword

By Nicole DragonBeck

A tall, broad-shouldered man with a restless tendency, clothed in the browns and greens of the forest, made his way down the narrow mountain path. The Sword was warm and heavy at his side, the glow of the red stone in the hilt pulsing to keep the Shadows, still bold and empowered from the night, at bay. His name was Haden Darrenson, and he was the Huntsman of the Cordun Mountains.

In Cordun, spring had sprinkled white and yellow flowers through the meadows of the upper valleys and pale new leaves vied for place with dark fir needles. The morning sun had turned the sky pink and the air golden. At first glance it looked peaceful, the last vestiges of a child's dream, yet the chill was not entirely from the breeze blowing off the icy peaks above and the light undulated in weird patterns that made the stomach protest.

On mornings like this, when the fragile beauty of the land glittered like a glass painting, Haden's thoughts crowded close and refused to leave him in peace and memories of his parents would come to visit him. Before he'd been killed, Haden's father had begun to teach him the paths of the forests, the paths closest to the house, in preparation for the time when Haden would become the Huntsman.

Because the mountain folk were too scared to leave their valley, they assumed young Haden had died with his parents. So it was rather a surprise when, one winter six years before, Haden showed up, unplanned and uninvited, in the town of Shrim.

The Advisors had not liked him, and still didn't. They seemed to quickly forget that it was Haden who had kept the Shadows at bay with the Sword and made sure the dwindling stores of firewood lasted until the longer days came. Even so, Shrim had to burn some things to keep the fires going.

It was a small price to pay for their lives, but the Advisors were not happy about it and fought bitterly to keep their possessions. As the benefit of the fire's protection was shared by all equally, Haden made sure all paid equally to sustain it. They had been adversaries since, even though Haden continued to walk the trails his father had shown him, and kept the towns and hamlets of Cordun protected.

Haden quickened his pace to shake the memories loose and turned his attention instead to the problem facing him that morning. The King's Advisors had neglected to notify Haden of the Gathering in the town of Shrim. He had his own eyes and ears in the village however. So, Haden came down from his mountain home to find out what they were up to, for his gut told him the fact they hadn't summoned him was a bad sign.

His hand rested in a familiar grip on the hilt of the Sword at his side as he walked, his sharp green eyes swept both canopy and underbrush for the things that would be lurking out of reach of the sunlight. The heartbeat in the red stone was counterpoint to his own and the vibration sent both the chill and the Shadows scurrying from him. He broke out of the pine trees and saw the valley spread out below him.

Within the snow-crowned peaks lay Shrim, a town so old the meaning of the name had been lost. The rough wood-and-stone dwellings huddled close, taking comfort from each other. In the center of town stood the Gathering Hall, a tall building of stained wood, that rose up into four spires tipped with a Crystal.

The invaluable stone multiplied and trapped the light from the sun and sent a thousand beams of light to embrace the town in a protective light. It could also store the light for the night, when it kept the Shadows away. The days were lengthening now that winter was over. Feren and Scire, the nearest villages, had firecrystals of their own but the outlying hamlets had to make do with fire.

Seeing the Hall and its protective light eased the constant tension in Haden's stomach a little. A different kind of tension gathered as he walked through the empty streets to the Hall. At the door to the Gathering Hall, he paused and pulled his cloak around him, enough to obscure his face yet not too much to draw attention. Hunching his shoulders, he slouched inside.

The sight of an agitated mass of roughly half the townspeople gathered before the King's dais greeted Haden as he stepped into the warm interior of the Hall. Haden kept to the rear of the crowd, arms crossed and eyes narrowed as he listened to the loud, unclear shouts.

Rill, the small, wiry Healer of Shrim was trying hard to calm the rapidly deteriorating crowd. Though Haden knew the Healer could tell the difference between a moss-spider bite and the first signs of dryfever in one glance, his gentle voice was suited to a sickbed, not a Gathering Hall. "It seems to center around the chest. I cannot say anything for certain, but my ginger and hartwort poultice is showing promise..."

No one was listening to him and he stepped back to stand against the wall opposite Haden, wringing his hands. Haden caught his gaze and raised an eyebrow. The Healer rolled his eyes and Haden gave a half smile in response. His eyes moved from face to face as the shouting grew ever louder.

"...my son grows worse...!"

"...stare through me as though I'm not there!"

"...we have made it through the winter, but...!"

"...nothing is working! We must do something!"

"...the eyes, the black eyes! What can we do?"

The last cry stilled the crowd at once and it parted to show a young woman with blood-shot eyes that glistened with unshed tears, her hands bunched in fists in the fabric of her dress.

"They turned black overnight," she said, her whisper loud in the silence. "He...he..." she gasped and choked as she buried her face in her hands, her shoulders shaking.

Hands reached out to comfort her and the shouts started anew, some directed at Rill, some to the Advisors on the dais. Haden pursed his lips as his eyes moved from the crowd to the Advisors. All seven were seated, lined faces touched by simpering concern. The throne beside them was empty. The King had not appeared. Another bad omen.

The faces in the Hall were filled with dread and bewilderment. Haden might have felt something similar, but he was a Huntsman and didn't have that luxury. Besides, Haden wasn't entirely certain this wasn't some ruse of the Advisors, making much of nothing to some end known only to them.

The Advisors did their job of nodding and giving soothing reassurances in many words with little meaning. Any input the Healer attempted to give received the same nods and empty words. When the people filed out of the Hall an hour later still muttering among themselves, nothing had been solved. Haden pulled his cloak tighter about him and made certain the Sword was hidden beneath the cloth before he stepped into the departing crowd.

"Stay, Huntsman."

The voice, commanding with wheedling undertones, belonged to the First Advisor Styro. Haden could have obeyed or not as he chose. He stopped and deliberated for a moment. His hand automatically fell to the hilt of his Sword. The Advisor waited until the last townsperson had filed out, and the Hall was silent.

"We would speak with you."

~~~

Turning around slowly, Haden offered a perfunctory bow to the seven men on the dais. Each was of varying old age, with silver hair and robes in the colors of their families that looked too heavy for their frames.

None looked pleased, but First Advisor Styro was positively livid when he spoke. "Well?"

"Well what?" Haden said.

"What have you got to say for yourself?"

"I'm afraid I don't..." Haden began, preparing for a long and arduous session of debate with the King's Advisors.

"*You* are the Huntsman. It is your charge to *do* something about this situation!" Styro said, pointing at Haden. "What are you doing about this plague?"

Haden blinked. The absurdity of the question was so great he felt stupid trying to think with it. It left him gaping at the Advisor.

"I think perhaps you are confusing me with the Healer," Haden said at last. He couldn't help adding a small barb. "Besides, I received no summons saying a Gathering had been called. Fortunately, I happened to be passing through."

"The impudence! I could have you removed..." Styro began.

"Styro!" a tired voice came from behind the line of old men. "There is no need for that."

The Advisors stepped away to reveal the young King walking with careful steps towards them. He had only seen fifteen or sixteen summers but he wore the crown as though he had seen forty. His eyes were fighting dullness and he looked as though he had not eaten or slept in some days. If what the townsfolk were saying was true, he probably hadn't. Haden began to lend just a little more credence to the possibility the situation was more dire than an Advisor's plot.

10

"Your Majesty. You should be resting," Styro said, hurrying forward to offer his arm to the King.

"Alas, sleep escapes me," the King said.

Haden watched as the King dropped Styro's arm and came down from the dais, shaky but unassisted, to stop in front of Haden. "Greetings Huntsman."

Haden bowed deeply. "Your Majesty."

They had a unique bond, the Huntsman and the young King, sharing the trait of being very young when forced to take up their fathers' mantles. The King had been barely eleven when Haden appeared in Shrim. He was one of only three who treated Haden with something other than over-awed diffidence or barely concealed contempt. Haden sometimes imagined they might have been brothers in a different world.

"Thank you for coming with such promptness. I must speak with you, as I said."

Haden blinked. Rill had said there was a Gathering, but had mentioned nothing of the King desiring an audience. "Indeed?"

The King frowned. "You did not receive my message?"

Haden shot a sidelong glance at Styro before answering. "Of course, your Majesty, but...it was very vague."

Haden's words were the right ones.

"I did not wish to spread panic if it fell into unintended hands," the King said with a sigh, and rubbed his eyes. "Something is wrong, Huntsman. Very wrong. My heart tells me so."

Again, Haden looked at the Advisors. Only two met his gaze, Delmit and Hualt. Haden made note of that. No words were needed to tell of the simmering resentment in the remaining Advisors. None were needed to explain that Haden was the one with power, power that no man could overrule, not even the King.

Haden didn't know how he came by this incontrovertible influence, only that he possessed it. The Advisors knew it as well, and it kept the fire of their discontent smoldering.

Haden bowed his head. "What would you have me do?"

"You have not found anything strange in the mountains recently?"

"Nothing out of the ordinary, nothing worth mentioning," Haden said. "The Shadows keep to the night, where they belong."

"Perhaps you missed something," Styro said.

"Perhaps you'd like to look yourself, see if there is anything I missed." Haden's sarcasm was lost on the Advisor, but not on the King.

The King put a hand on Haden's arm. "I don't doubt you are very diligent in your duties, but strange things abound. This sickness in town, it has something to do with the Shadows. Why else would our Healer have such trouble, even when he has the help of the green witch?"

"I can pay her another visit," Haden said. "Perhaps if I tell her of the new developments, there is something more she can do."

Styro sneered. "Your fondness for that charlatan temptress blinds you, Huntsman. She had never done so much for this town as her words will have you believe. Her herbs are useless, as the Healer said."

Haden could have defended the witch, but to do so would only defeat the purpose, so Haden simply favored the Advisor with a cool glare.

"Do you have a better suggestion?" Haden asked.

"Please," the King said with a tired frown. "We must work together."

"You are right, your Majesty," Styro said, hurrying down from the dais to stand beside the King. "We will send messages to Feren and Scire to see if the people of those towns have fallen prey to this Sickness and if they have solved it. Meanwhile the Huntsman will go to visit his witch." He turned to Haden. "How soon can you leave?"

Haden ignored the latent slight in the Advisor's voice. "Immediately, but the journey will take at least two days," he said, mapping the fasted route in his mind.

"Hurry back, Huntsman," the King said. "I fear there is not much time."

"And until we discover what is happening, you are to leave the Sword here," Styro said.

The order was so unexpected Haden thought he had heard wrongly. It was only after a long look at Styro's lined face that Haden saw an answer was necessary. "No," he said.

"It belongs to the people of Cordun and their King," Styro said. "It must stay in Shrim and protect them."

"It belongs to the Huntsman," Haden said, infusing his voice with a subtle power. "It stays with me."

Styro foamed at the mouth as he fought to utter a word counter to Haden's. "*Un...acceptable...*"

Once again the King stepped in. "It is yours to wield Huntsman, but Advisor Styro is right to want it here. Something is drawing close and I do not think the light in the firecrystal will hold it off. The people here cannot defend themselves against the Shadows like you can."

"With due respect Your Majesty, who will wield it? One of your Advisors?"

"Your mother could wield the Sword in your father's absence. I remember well seeing her in the streets of Shrim, carrying it as brazenly as you do," Styro sneered. "You can share the power - do not deny it, Huntsman - you simply choose not to."

Haden fought to stay calm, refusing to rise to the bait. His mother had carried the Sword it was true, for less than a month before it claimed her life. "Perhaps my mother was simply stronger than you, Advisor."

Styro's voice was low and dangerous. "You should not be so ungrateful, Huntsman. This town took you in..."

"I will carry the Sword," the King said, silencing Stryo with a look.

Haden had no wish to insult his ailing King, but he saw by the light in the young man's eyes that he had little choice. He shrugged and offered the Sword to the King. The King held it for less than half a breath before his arm dropped and the Sword clattered to the floor. Four Advisors, Styro first among them, dived upon it but none were able to lift it. Haden waited a long moment before pushing his way through them. He picked it up, his fingers molding to the hilt.

"I'll take my leave then. Your Majesty."

Haden bowed to the King and walked away without looking back.

~~~

A small chalet sat on the mountainside, invisible to the idle eye until the fourth or fifth glance. Smoke curled from the stone chimney, flowers adorned the thatched roof and the green door was the exact shade of the new leaves.

Within, the cabin was a curious mix of homey and stark.

13

Fresh flowers on the table perfumed the air, but the furniture was bare of covering and no pictures graced the walls. When Haden stepped inside, he felt family in every wall and corner though he'd lived alone since his parents' death.

Haden's guest sat at the table, a basket covered in yellow cloth in front of his folded hands.

"I wondered if you'd be here," Haden said by way of greeting as he shook off his cloak and laid the Sword beside the basket.

"I wondered if you'd ever make it back," the Healer Rill said. "Trying to hold any sort of meaningful conversation with those twits could take half a lifetime!"

"Fortunately it did not take me that long to put them in their place," Haden smiled. "That smells wonderful."

"A present from my wife," Rill said, lifting the cloth to reveal an overflowing basket of honeyed fruit buns. "She was pleased with the flavor of the herbs you brought last time. I assumed you would be going again?"

The question was filled with layers of meaning, which Haden tried to ignore. "I will be sure to pass her compliments to Da...the green witch," Haden said and grabbed two buns. He shoved one into his mouth whole as he began gathering supplies for his journey.

"You still dislike calling her by name," Rill said. "Why?"

"It feels...disrespectful," Haden said, talking around the bun in his mouth.

"Yet you have known her for years now. Surely you have become more than...acquaintances? I know you visit her when you have no need for herbs."

Haden swallowed the bun. "Perhaps, but still, she is a witch." He grimaced at the unspoken question in Rill's eyes. "She teaches me things about the green and we talk," he said, and then added, "and she still calls me Huntsman."

"Probably because you call her witch." Rill smiled a knowing smile. "She is a woman like any other. Don't let the townsfolks' superstition cloud your eyes, boy."

"My eyes aren't clouded," Haden muttered as he stuffed a woolen shirt into his pack. "I can see just fine. And I'm not superstitious."

"Indeed," Rill said, more to himself than Haden. "You know, she would make a good wife for you. At eight and twenty years, it's past time you found one."

Haden shook his head. "No woman should have this life."

"To what life are you referring?"

"The life of a Huntsman, always looking for Shadows, always this close to being taken. The Sword repels them, yes, but it also draws them closer. A woman would never choose to live that way."

"Your mother did."

"And she's dead."

Rill paused, frowning as he searched for words. "I knew both your mother and your father. They were good people and they left us too soon, but I doubt either one of them would want for you to spend your life alone on their account."

"It's not because of them," Haden tried to explain. "It's just...something inside me is better off without anyone else. I don't know what it is but I can't share it with anyone..."

"You don't have to make your excuses to me." Rill stood and clapped an affectionate hand on Haden's shoulder. "But just know that what can be too heavy for one person to carry can be carried with ease by two."

Haden nodded and tried to be grateful for the advice but he found himself irked by the inadequacy of words that did nothing to help him.

"So you'll be paying her a visit then," Rill said, his tone turning businesslike.

"Is there anything more we can do?" Haden asked and ate the second bun in one bite.

He put rope, a tinderbox, three knives, a blanket and tin cup on the table, ticking them off a mental list. He added a canteen.

"There is something strange afoot here," the Healer said.

"The King said as much," Haden said.

"My wife thinks it's the new moon," the Healer continued. "I love her dearly, but sometimes she has very strange ideas."

"Unlikely," Haden said, his mind on his packing. "The Shadows have been scarce, practically nonexistent..." he trailed off, no longer thinking about the packing.

"Well, that's good," the Healer said. "That's good, isn't it?"

"I don't believe it," Haden said to himself.

"Believe what?" the Healer asked.

"Styro was right!" Haden slapped his forehead. "I missed something!"

The startled look on the Healer's face prompted him to explain.

"The new moon! Usually the Shadows grow bold at that time but they haven't bothered me for three days!"

"What does that mean?" the Healer asked. "The Sickness started before winter."

"True," Haden admitted. "Still..."

"Still, you must be careful," the Healer said. "Do not let your guard down."

"I never do," Haden said as the supplies went into a satchel along with dried meat, bread and a dozen of the fruit buns.

The satchel went over Haden's shoulder along with his hunting bow. Two more knives went into his boot. The Sword hung at his side, warm and heavy. His cloak slid over his shoulders.

"There is something else," the Healer said. "Once the eyes turn black, I do not think they can be saved."

"How many?" Haden asked.

"Seven more already," the Healer answered, his voice subdued. "The quickest was only a month before they turned."

Nothing Haden could have said would have made the distraught Healer feel any better. He clapped a hand on Rill's shoulder and gave him the most comforting smile he could muster. "Don't go out at night and keep the fires burning. I'll return as soon as possible, and with answers."

~~~

Haden walked out and set out down the mountain path. It ran into the valley, up the other side and around. As he walked, his keen eyes took in everything.

The highest peaks of the Heart of the Mountain rose as sentries to their valleys, watching over the green meadows. Farmsteads, fields of oat barley and orchards spread under a clear sky. Darker stands of pine and the blue-black water of still lakes gave depth to the otherworldly beauty. Black clouds on the horizon heralded a storm, and Haden thought it was going to be a monster.

There were Shadows as always, of course, but in the light they kept more or less to harmless mischief. Haden was tempted to deal with those Shadows he did see, but he was on a different mission today. The witch's home was a half a day's brisk journey toward the Heart of the Mountain.

Shielded from the sun by branches covered with new spring leaves, Haden was still sweating by the time he crested the last peak and beheld the small sylvan house tucked into a cleft of the mountain, a hidden valley of breathtaking beauty, illuminated by the rays of the setting sun.

The house was the picture of spring delight. Blue flower boxes under white window-frames were filled with rosebud and bluebells. A small garden in the front bloomed with bright flowers. Smoke curled from a stone chimney perched crookedly on the thatched roof and a cheery red door beckoned visitors forward.

Haden started towards it, tired and glad the journey's end was in sight. The path his feet followed was little more than a faint deer track in the lush valley floor but it led him true. Half way down, as he stepped into the cool shade pooling at the bottom of the valley, the back of his neck started to prickle and he looked behind him, up the mountain.

His heart stopped briefly and then sped up. In the tree line Shadows gathered. They did not dare to advance into the light yet, instead edging forward as the sunlight retreated. Behind them, lightning flashed silently in the dark clouds. He had never seen so many shadows in one place, not even when he had ventured out at night or when his father died.

Haden looked up at the sky. Only the barest sliver of fire on the western peaks remained of the sun. The witch's house sat in dusk and a slim rope of sunlight remained on the ground between Haden and the Shadows. He started to run. Flying down the mountainside, he used his momentum to hurtle himself towards the house and the safety of its firecrystal lantern.

Like an avalanche of darkness, the Shadows rolled down the mountain after Haden. A faint rustle of snarling, shrieking and howling built behind him, pressing close on his heels. Cold breath and claws tried to snare him. Teeth almost closed on his leg, but he kicked out, stumbled, regained his balance and struggled to push himself faster, muscles burning and vision blurring. Then he was over the fence and at the red door. Like crashing into a stone wall, the Shadows stopped at the edge of the light. Red eyes stared at him, their yammering fading as they disappeared.

Haden let himself in without knocking and breathed a long, slow sigh of relief. The house smelled like the witch, the earthy sweetness of a vineyard in summer, and it calmed his frazzled nerves. The rooms were as small and quaint as the house. The foyer led to a cozy sitting room, which led to the kitchen. A long wooden table dominated this last, leaving the sink and the black iron cook-stove just visible behind it.

The woman inside stood at the sink, washing deep green leaves in a pail of water. Her green dress shimmered when she moved and ringlets of dark hair fell to her waist. Her name was Daela, but to the people of Cordun she was simply *the witch*. She half turned and when she saw who it was, she smiled.

"Greetings Huntsman," her voice was warm. "You are in luck. I just put tea on to steep and you'll join me for dinner, of course. You'll be hungry after your long trek."

Haden immediately relaxed in the familiar presence of the witch and her homey kitchen. The memory of the Shadows dogging his heels slipped further into the back of his mind and he wondered if he'd imagined it. The witch turned to him and her green eyes widened.

"You look like you ran the whole way."

Haden grimaced. "I may have run a little."

The witch looked down and exclaimed in dismay. "You're bleeding!"

"I guess I didn't imagine it," Haden said, when he saw the lower leg of his trousers soaked in blood. Though he hadn't been aware of it before, now his leg began to throb with hot pain.

"Imagine what?" the witch asked as she made him sit on one of the stools and raise his leg.

"The Shadows," Haden said and winced when his trouser leg was pulled back to reveal puncture wounds from serrated teeth in his hamstring.

"I thought I heard something," the witch said, gently cleaning the wound with a warm, damp, sweet-smelling cloth that Haden swore magically appeared in her hand. "I assumed it was the wind. A storm has been brewing all day."

The witch put a salve on and bound the wound as Haden drank tea. After her ministrations, all that was left of the pain was an itchy warmth. He set out plates while she brought out the food.

Dinner was simple, stew and then dried fruit for desert. Polite small talk distracted Haden from the worries of the world outside the witch's kitchen. The witch poured small glasses of sweet nectar.

"So. What brings you to my door this day?" she asked.

"I'm sorry to bother you about this again," Haden said. "But the sickness still holds Shrim."

"When has it ever been a bother when you visit?" the witch smiled. "What do you need this time? Thyme or willow? Feverfew? Bloodmoss?"

Haden shook his head. "I don't think any of those are what I need."

"It's become worse?"

Haden shook his head. "The Sickness has changed. At first Rill thought it was Wetfever, but it's not, nor winter chills or Chestcough. It's...not something he's seen before," he said before she could ask. "Fever and chills, weakness and trembles. Sometimes delusions..."

"That doesn't sound incurable," the witch said.

"...but there is something else," Haden continued. "The eyes, eventually - after a month or more, according Rill - they go...black, unblinking..."

The witch fell still.

"That does not bode well," she said. "And it is not unfamiliar to me, though I do not recall where I heard it..."

She frowned, then stood and waved Haden to follow her into a dim study behind the kitchen. A triangular desk full of books, papers and quills stood in the middle of the room. The back wall held shelves of dried herbs and bright powders in glass jars. The remaining walls were full of books with titles in languages that Haden didn't know.

He waited patiently as she pulled out several books of varying sizes and shapes. She flipped through them but spent no more than a moment on each before she discarded it to continue searching.

Haden's mind had started to wander to the early storm and his encounter with the Shadows when her cry of triumph brought him back with a startled jump. The witch held up her prize with a smile.

~~~

The book in the witch's hand was slim, only a finger's

breadth in width and covered in dark leather. A gilt design of complicated lines graced the front and symbols danced across the top, twining and falling over each other in haste to get away. Haden noted with discomfit that the symbols *were* moving - it wasn't a trick of the light.

"This book is very old, many of its secrets are lost," the witch said softly. The look she gave the book was half awe, half fear as she laid it on top of a much larger and more cheery tome.

She opened it with two fingers, using a quill to turn the silky paper. She was careful not to touch the pages. Somewhere towards the end of the book, she found the page she wanted and pointed. Haden fought the urge to take a step back. Instead he forced himself to walk to her side and peer over her shoulder. The writing on the pages shifted depending on how he looked at it, but it didn't matter. He couldn't read it.

He could however see the picture and it made his skin crawl. The black, sunken eyes on the skeletal figure were eerily lifelike.

"What does it say?"

"It tells of an illness named Darkeye..." she bent closer, her finger hovering over the page as she read, "...it is very old..." her finger brushed the paper and she uttered a sharp scream of pain.

The tip of her finger was raw, red and bleeding. As he watched the wound grew, as though something was eating her hand. She clutched her wrist, jaw clenched in pain as tears leaked from her eyes.. "My herbs...lavender, comfrey..."

Haden went to the back without question or hesitation. His eyes flew over the labels and his hands snatched up the jars.

"Myrrh, silverwort and shadowbane," the witch said and moaned.

Haden nodded and pulled those off the shelf as well. Grabbing a mortar and pestle and the jug of carrier oil, spilling a little, he hurried back. The raw redness had traveled down the witch's finger and into her palm. Haden cleared a space for the herbs on the desk by sweeping a stack of books and papers to the floor.

Working feverishly, trying not to pay attention to the fact that the red was now to her wrist, Haden threw the herbs together with the oil and ground it to a paste. Scooping it up with his hand, he smeared it with indelicate swabs onto the witches skin. A hissing came and Haden could feel the heat with his own skin. Covering her arm almost up the elbow, Haden watched the witch's visible relief and he started to breath properly again.

He bound up her arm with fresh cloth, not half as neat as hers had been, and fashioned a sling for her.

"Thank you," the witch said with a rueful smile. "That was careless of me."

"What is that book and why does a green witch of the mountain have it?" Haden asked roughly, as he put away the herbs and picked up the books from the floor.

The slim black book fell from the stack and landed at his feet. Haden jerked back.

"It's safe to touch the cover, just not the paper," the witch said.

Despite her reassurance, Haden took a piece of parchment and used it as a barrier between his flesh and the sinister book. He noted that the witch had not answered his question. He gazed at her sternly and her eyes slid away like a blade glancing off armor.

"I took it off some traveling rogue who had stolen it from the library in Charneth and wanted to get rid of it," the witch said. "I looked at it only once, and perhaps destiny intervened, for it was that page that I read."

"I've never heard of Charneth..."

"The black city by the sea. I spent some months there a time ago."

Haden held the book out. "This came from a place called the black city of Charneth? And you kept it? Why didn't you burn it?"

Daela smiled. "Sometimes you sound very much like the superstitious folk who never venture beyond the reach of the mountains. To them everything is trying to eat them, hex them or ensorcell them."

"I *have* never ventured beyond Cordun," Haden said, eying the book distrustfully. "And it *did* try to eat you."

"Put it back on the shelf," the witch said. "There is nothing in there that will help you."

"You know this from one page?" Haden raised an eyebrow.

The witch gestured to the book. "You saw the labyrinth on the cover, yes?"

Haden nodded, recalling the confusing swirl of lines that crossed and knotted on the front.

"It means this is a book of information, not answers. It tells what the sickness is, not how to cure it."

"So it is a book of riddles." Haden did not try to hide is disgust.

"Yes," the witch nodded. "You will have to see someone more knowledgeable that I if you wish to find answers."

"And you know of someone?"

Her eyes flicked up towards the Heart of the Mountain and unseen peaks towering above them.

"Yes."

~~~

The light from the stove in the kitchen helped to banish the incident in the study from Haden's mind.

"You must stay the night; you can go on in the morning, when it's light," the witch said.

Though he was quite uncomfortable with her offer, tonight the thought of traveling in the dark did not appeal to him. The witch set out pillows and blankets on the couch and Haden collapsed, sleep taking him without delay.

In the morning, Haden awoke to the sound of soft singing in the kitchen. The witch had removed the sling and put a new bandage on her finger, the rest of the wound practically healed. She served hot porridge for breakfast and would only vaguely hint at where and who the person was when Haden questioned her. It did not take long for him to realize she thought she was going with him; Haden disagreed.

"No," he shook his head for the tenth time, watching helplessly as the witch prepared for a journey. "You don't have to do this."

"Yes I do," Daela said as she pulled a thick wool cloak over her shoulders and hefted her pack onto her shoulder. "Besides, I know where to go."

"You said it was less than a day's travel. I can climb a mountain, follow the rock and the sun," Haden said. "Just tell me the way. I'll remember, but if it will make you feel better you can draw me a map."

"That won't be necessary. Let's go." The witch walked past him and held open the door with a bright expression.

His fingers fiddled on the hilt of the Sword, an unconscious action, but the witch knew exactly what it meant. She gave him a stern look.

"You'd better not pull that 'I'm the Huntsman, and everyone has to do what I say' routine with me. It won't work, you won't make it without me and you don't have a choice anyway," she said. "Are you ready?"

Haden sighed, but the corner of his mouth turned up and he gestured for her to lead the way. The sun was out and no harm would come to her in the light. He would make sure of that.

~~~

The witch led Haden much deeper into the Heart than he'd ever been. They climbed slopes of gravel, scaled cliffs and crawled up ravines that a child would feel claustrophobic in. The Sword weighed heavy at Haden's side and even his pack felt like he carried provisions for a small army.

They were worming their way through a passage of stone that became narrower and narrower until it was more of a crack than a passage. He stopped to breathe, the rock pressed close around him, the blue sky crowded out. The witch's gentle touch on his shoulder convinced him to continue.

Eventually the passage ended in another sheer rock face and the witch began to climb. Haden looked up and then glanced away from the sight of her shapely calves. He followed her, testing each hand and foot hold before he put his full weight on it, which made the climb slow and exhausting. When he pulled himself out onto a mountain ledge, all he did was lay on his back. He did not even move to shift the pack that dug into his side.

"Almost there," the witch's voice prompted him.

Haden gazed around, his eyes wide with wonder as he took in the free, open space. He was on top of the entire world, the mountains' snowcapped teeth below them. Above, a craggy face of stone gazed down like a benevolent giant and the sky was a silver and blue curtain.

The witch did not give him long to admire the view, and he staggered up the precarious mountain path behind her. When the path started sloping downward, Haden paused to massage a stitch in his side.

"How much further?" he asked.

"Almost there," she said again.

The path continued to slope down, then up, then down and Haden lost track of whether they were ascending or descending. He just doggedly put one foot in front of the other. A forest appeared suddenly, springing up around them as they rounded a cliff wall. A measure of Haden's fatigue melted away as he stepped onto the carpet of leaves.

The huge trees protected a deep green silence, their boughs sheltering a timeless stillness. Haden imagined it would be peace unimaginable but for the fleeting glimpses of Shadows in the undergrowth.

As Haden walked through the forest, he noted that the Shadows were for the most part predictable and usual, but one or two started to get too close for comfort as they followed him. *It's nothing, I'm still just hung up from yesterday*, he told himself, but something about these Shadows rose the hair on his nape.

"You should keep close," he called out to the witch as he unsheathed the Sword and held it up in front of him.

The Shadows fell back, but only for a moment. They began to dog his heals and Haden sped up to catch up to the witch. He was tired. A fight was the last thing he wanted. A Shadow darted in front of Haden and he had to sidestep rapidly. He spun around and put a tree at his back. The Shadows crept closer and started to gather in front of him.

Haden's breath grew ragged as he danced on his feet. He tried to get past the Shadows to the witch who was barely visible in the twisting darkness. Fortunately, the Shadows were concentrated on him, writhing as claws snaked out. The Huntsman swung the Sword in graceful arcs and it slid through them, sending swaths of them fading in the air.

The red stone in the cross-guard flickered and some of the color bled away. It leached the warmth from Haden's hands and he almost dropped the Sword. Shadows flew at him and bit with mouths of ice. He felt teeth sink into his leg and shoulders. Regaining his grip on the Sword, he brought it up in time, slashing savagely. The Shadows fell back, right into the witch.

"Haden!"

Her cry doubled Haden's efforts, and he broke though the clutching Shadows. Moving as fast as he could, each step shot fiery pains up his limbs. He reached her and pulled her close, shielding her with his body and the Sword. The green witch was trying to control her own terror and she did an admirable job, the only sign a slight tremble in her breathing. An uncertain fear wormed its way into Haden's chest. The Shadows had never come out in the day and they did not move in packs.

"What do we do?" she asked him.

"We have to get into the sunlight," he said.

They took two steps together, but Haden saw he was going to slow her up. The Shadows advanced. She looked at his new wounds, bit her lip then closed her eyes. Haden opened his mouth to ask what was wrong when movement nearby caught his attention. It wasn't the Shadows.

Plants were pulling out of the ground, moving toward the witch. Haden saw why the mountain folk said what they did about her. Here in the forest, where the plants came alive at her command, she was as fierce and wild as any wolf or badger. Fortunately, she was on his side. Plants began to batter the Shadows and sent them scurrying in a fury of thrashing branches.

Haden limped along beside the witch and dealt with any Shadow that came within reach of the Sword. He had to favor one leg as cold fire shot through his veins with every movement.

Then the Shadows did something Haden had never seen.

~~~

The Shadows came together, some forming giant limbs, others claws. Some coalesced into a head with burning eyes, others into huge wings and more strung themselves into a razor edged tail until a monster four times as tall as a man reared in front of them.

Haden gaped while the witch redoubled her efforts and called the leaves up from the ground and turned the shrubs into spinning weapons. Haden stabbed the Sword at the snapping maw coming down at their heads and received an angry roar. Gusts of wind from dark wings buffeted them and the thing clawed the air in front of them, keeping out of reach of Haden's thrusts.

When he stumbled, the witch caught him with one hand and he held onto her shoulder for support. Leaves flew like demented green darts, only to be shredded in the teeth of the Shadow. Still, the Shadow seemed less somehow, almost ragged around the edges like an old coat.

"What do we do?" she asked him, her fingers trembling with

the strain as she called a heavy oak bough down on the head of the Shadow-beast.

It squealed as the tree used every limb to batter it, but the gentle giant of the forest could not hold forever. Little by little, the Shadow wrapped the tree in limbs of its own and though the oak struggled to free itself, the Shadow sank deeper and deeper, teeth gnawing until the tree fell still, white and withered, pale flakes of bark slough off like snow. The witch gasped for breath, pale and sweating.

"It is too strong," she said. "I...cannot...hold it."

She tried to hold her hands aloft, shaking with the effort, but they dropped to and it was Haden's turn to catch her as her knees gave out. They stood, holding each other for support as the Shadow, sensing weakness, pressed in.

Haden squeezed his eyes shut. The witch's clean scent filled his nose, and he felt her body warm against his one side, the Shadow cold on the other. This was how his father had died, standing in a circle of Shadows, the Sword shining silver in the darkness as he tried to protect Haden's mother, yelling for Haden to run, go back inside the house. When his mother had appeared in the doorway, pale and bloody, but alive, dragging the sword behind her, the young Haden hadn't needed to ask what had happened.

Haden opened his eyes. "You must take the Sword."

"None but a Huntsman can wield it!" the witch said.

"It is easy," he told her, offering her the hilt. "Take it."

"I cannot..."

"Daela," he said and her eyes widened at the sound of her name carried on his voice. "You must go."

The stubborn look he was coming to know well entered her eyes. "Not without you."

Once again, Haden had no choice and only one chance. *I will not let her die.* Her hand around his gave him added strength and he swung the Sword up in an arc of silver light. The blade bit into the Shadow monster and its scream reverberated through the air.

The breath was sucked from Haden's lungs as the Sword drank in the Shadow in a moment of total stillness. The metal heated, searing his palm. A blinding flash of light burst from the Sword illuminating everything, and sent Haden flying back.

The world went dark.

~~~

Haden woke gagging under a feathered cover that smelled of garlic and sulfur. He pushed it away and found himself naked, his numerous wounds covered in a thick, dark purple paste, which smelled worse than the feathers. He was alive however, and could move with ease, so he reconciled himself to smelling terrible for a while.

Outside the window, giant trees stirred in a gentle breeze. The sleeping room was unfamiliar, his clothes were nowhere in sight and neither was the Sword. A slight panic set in and he began thrashing around in the bed. Searching the corners and shadowy places of his room disclosed the Sword was not there. Then he heard voices from another room that grew louder as the owners moved closer to the door.

"...attacked by Shadows..." It was Daela, her voice worried. "He collapsed."

"He will be fine. He is the Huntsman." A voice Haden didn't know and wished never to know. Within the soft tones was a latent power, sinuously wound through the words and kept in check by a will even greater than the power. Haden found his skin covered in gooseflesh as the voice continued. "I had wondered where he had gotten to. Time runs short for him."

"What will you tell him?" Daela's voice.

"Everything," the powerful voice said. "Everything I know. The fate of all depends on it."

"He's going to leave, isn't he?"

"He is the Huntsman. He will do what he must..."

The voices faded and Haden tiptoed across to the door. He poked his head out into a large sitting room. Everything was upholstered in black or the skins of animals. A dozen large mirrors with ornate frames hung on the walls.

Haden walked back to the bed and grabbed the feathered coverlet. Swinging it around his shoulders, he walked out into the second room. Two doors stared at him, one closed, one just open. Through the crack, shadows moved and as Haden walked closer, he heard voices again.

"...early for spring showers."

"Many things are changing. They are only symptoms."

A long pause and then a few whispers and rustles. Haden

edged closer and gently tapped on the door. It opened immediately. A figure stood on the other side.

~~~

The woman, who could only be a sorceress, was robed in mirage and the lines of her face were one moment that of a grandmother and the next a young girl. When Haden looked straight at her, his eyes began to water and his muscles twitch so he stared at her feet. He knew of sorceresses of course, but never expected to meet one. The wise-women were reclusive and enigmatic.

"Greetings, Huntsman. I am glad you are here."

Haden gave a nod and glanced up at Daela. She gave him an uncertain smile.

"We were afraid you wouldn't make it," she said. "How do you feel?"

"Alive," Haden said, feeling every bruise and cut protest when he shrugged. "A little sore. How did I get here?"

"I half-dragged, half-carried you. You were delirious, but thankfully not unconscious," Daela said. A hysterical giggle escaped and she clamped her lips shut. She was pale, her eyes grim with something she was trying to keep hidden lurking in their green depths.

"Thank you," Haden said. Something had changed, and it stood between them like a brick wall. "I'm sure you saved both our lives."

"I could have done nothing else," Daela said and though her lips smiled, her eyes were still dark.

The sorceress held up her hand, beckoning Haden closer, but directing her words to the witch. "Perhaps you would be so kind as to get the Huntsman his clothes, my dear."

Daela bowed her head to the sorceress and slipped by Haden without meeting his gaze. He ignored the cold clenching in his stomach and instead turned and tried once again to look into the sorceress's eyes, but her even gaze made Haden's head ache.

"So you're a sorceress," he said to her feet and winced.

"I am," she said, traces of amusement in her granite voice. "And you are a Huntsman and we are running out of time for stating the obvious. What did you come here for?"

"Daela brought me here," Haden said, shifting uncomfortably under his makeshift cloak. "I need help."

Her voice sent pale ripples through the air. "What do you think I can do for you, Huntsman?"

Haden swallowed. "A sickness has taken hold of the town of Shrim. Daela said it was called Darkeye."

The sorceress barked a mirthless chuckle. "That is a name I have not heard in a very long time."

"But you know of it?"

"Something like it, called by a far fouler names in older vernaculars. It does more than turn the eyes black. It turns the very soul black."

Haden shivered. "Can you cure it?"

The sorceress looked at him. Out of the corner of his eye, Haden could see her features were of a middle-aged woman, with hints of feline features - slitted pupils and fine silver whiskers. When she spoke, her voice had the aspect of a purr.

"This sickness can be cured only by Light, or the wielder thereof." She did not give him time to understand the cryptic answer, nor did she offer further explanation. "Do you know what sickness is Huntsman?"

They were interrupted by Daela's return carrying a pile of clothes over her arm. She handed them to Haden, who took them while attempting to hold the cover about himself with one hand.

"Thank you," he said.

Daela nodded and the two women turned away while Haden dressed himself, puzzling over the sorceress's question. When he was clothed, he laid the feathered cover over the nearest chair and seated himself in it. When he looked at Daela he saw with surprise she had also brought the Sword. She came over and offered it to him. He took it and smiled at the familiar metal under his hand.

"Well Huntsman? Do you have an answer?"

With the sorceress watching him, Haden thought for a moment more and realized that though he could recognize a hundred ills, he could not explain the word itself. He shook his head.

"A sickness, Huntsman, is the fighting of a malevolent outside force. If there is no sickness, the person is immune to it *or...*"

Haden's heart sped up in the brittle silence her incomplete sentence left. When the sorceress finished the thought, her voice was more akin to a feral hiss than anything human.

"...the person has succumbed to the force, *offering no*

resistance at all."

A picture of the seven Advisors flashed to Haden's mind, then a picture of the young King.

"I have left him with the wolves," Haden said, standing to leave before the words left his mouth, the Sword ready in his hand.

The sorceress's sharp laugh stopped him. "You think those men are wolves? You have never seen a true Wolf, Huntsman. His teeth are sharper than knives, his stench acid and his claws poison. His reach is far and he bears no love for light or goodness."

The words conjured images of the monster in the forest. Haden's grip on the Sword grew tighter and tighter until his knuckles were a pale extension of the metal itself.

"I must return immediately," he said.

"Wait."

Her sharp command made him pause and he looked straight at her, determined to go to the rescue of the people of Shrim and all of Cordun if necessary. It was his duty as Huntsman and he would not forsake it even at the behest of a sorceress.

For a moment he thought he would have to fight, but somewhere behind her iridescent eyes was the recognition and silent acknowledgment of the fact that she could no more control him than the Advisors of Shrim could. Confusion muddled his determination and he faltered. *What power do I wield that even a sorceress cannot hold me?*

"Why do you bear the name Huntsman?" the sorceress asked, her voice surprisingly gentle.

"It was my father's and his father's before."

"And the first Huntsman? Why did he take that name?"

"He didn't," Haden said with a frown. "It was given to him by his King."

The sorceress stared at him and Haden knew at once he was mistaken.

"Haden son of Darren, I don't know what history you were taught or by whom, but the Huntsmen predate any kingdom of men by thousands of years."

Haden blinked. His father had taught him the lore of the Huntsman as a matter of course. Haden remembered listening with rapt attention to the tales his father painted with the color of words, but Haden had been very young and there were many blanks in his knowledge. When Haden had come to Shrim, the young King had filled in the spaces.

How much of that knowledge had come from the Advisors? Haden thought with a sinking feeling. "I don't understand..."

"How did you come by that Sword?"

Haden opened his mouth and then paused. "It was my father's, handed down from father to son, given to the first of our line by King Cordun himself, but I venture that is not accurate."

The sorceress smiled. "You learn quickly, Huntsman. The Sword is heartiron, forged in fire and starlight by three. The first was the Fae King, Emorail of the Silver Sea. Second, a Wizard most knew as Neral and third was Perspe, youngest daughter of Light himself. For it is only Light that can slay the *Dark* young Huntsman, and it is the *Dark* you face and the *Dark* you must defeat."

The way the sorceress spat the word painted all in ice. The walls leaned closer and the air grew thicker. Haden fought to breathe as his lungs froze in the sorceress's wrath.

So much weight pressed on him that he was flung free of fleshy raiment. He saw to the far ends of the world, from the horizon and the Skyrealms to Underland and the Silver Sea. Everywhere the Dark crept onward and inward, enveloping the Light to send it spluttering to an inky death. In his mind's eye, the Dark took the aspect of a wolf, its black eyes devoid of the spark of life, the claws like obsidian spears and his razor-tooth maw the final blackness of the grave opening to swallow Haden as he retched against the stench of blood and decay...

As quickly as he had seen it the vision disappeared, leaving Haden in a small chalet perched on a stone finger pointing to the sky in the mountains of Cordun.

"How..." he gasped out, "how can such a thing be defeated?"

The ice melted and Haden could breathe again.

"With Fire, of course."

~~~

"So I should set the trees of Cordun alight?" Haden said. "Burn everything?"

"Your Sword," the sorceress said with an impatient shake of her head. "The Sword called Fire."

He looked down at the Sword in his hand. With a start he noted that the fire had gone out of the jewel on the hilt. Haden hadn't realized how much the pulse of the red stone had made the presence of the weapon. Now it was ordinary, the stone just a clouded ruby. The Sword looked so unremarkable that it took Haden several moments to find the faint engravings that marked it as his Sword.

He frowned. "I don't understand what happened to it. The Shadows have never done that to it before."

"That is because you have never tried to wield it that way before," the sorceress said.

Haden remembered how the Sword had drawn the Shadows in and spat them back out as lightning. His hand had blistered from the heat, but when he looked all that remained of the wound that should have taken a month to heal was fresh pink skin and a white outline scarred into his hand.

He lifted the Sword and held it to the sunlight from the nearest window. It was still his Sword. He could feel it in the weight and the balance, in the warmth that flowed into his arm. The blade had seemed so brittle against the power of the Shadows.

Even now, Haden could see fine hairlines across the metal, but in the pit of his stomach, he could feel the power within the weapon. He tested the edge with his thumb, wondering if it was still sharp. It bit into his flesh and red blood flowed down the blade. The blood stood for a moment and shimmered on the blade, and then it disappeared into the Sword. The ruby at the hilt began to glow with an eager light. His skin was unbroken.

"What just happened?" Haden demanded as he examined his hand.

"The Sword has acknowledged you," the sorceress said. "You are your father's heir, heir to the Sword of Light and now it truly belongs to you."

Haden could feel it. The Sword no longer felt heavy; it felt like air. He knew he could make it fly with less than a thought and it would dance like a hummingbird. It felt good, strong and invigorating, like a shower under the falls swollen with snowmelt, but at the same time Haden felt as though he were a small child, thrown into the deepest part of the lake for the first time.

"Why is this the first time I have heard of this?" he asked.

"You were a boy when your parents died. I do not know what happened, but I lost sight of you and it was not my place to come looking for you."

"You were watching me?" he asked, incredulous.

"Of course not," the sorceress said. "I do not need my eyes to tell me everything, Huntsman. As you should learn to do as well." The reproving look made Haden feel as though he had failed to learn some school lesson to a satisfactory standard and he shuffled his feet like a boy.

"It is of no consequence now. We go forward, for we cannot go back. There is much I must tell you. The three who forged the Sword did so out of a great need brought about by their knowledge of and deep respect for Man. Man is much more powerful than he knows, and the potential for greatness lies within him. Great construction, yet also great destruction. The Wolf would have a terrible weapon should it win Man over. But - there were those who wanted Light to fill the world, and so they gave Man a weapon to use against the Darkness: a Sword, sister to flame, forged in the same. It was given to a man strong enough to wield it and passed down from parent to child, father to son, mother to daughter."

"Who was the man?"

"The one man able to wield the power of the Sword. His name was Risin, youngest son of Perspe."

"Wait...Perspe, the daughter of Light?"

"The same."

"But how...I mean, she was the daughter of Light...is that even possible?"

"It is. She wed a man, the wizard Neral. According to legend, they had six children. Though none of his siblings could wield it, Risin took the Sword as a babe and took the name Huntsman."

"When was this?" Haden asked.

"A thousand, thousand years ago."

"Then there must be hundreds, *thousands* of descendants of Light," Haden said.

"Yes," the sorceress said. "There is a portent: all the sons of Light will fight a great battle against the Wolf for the fate of the world, led by the one who can wield it as Risin did."

"And what exactly do I have to do?" Haden said.

When she answered, the sorceress's voice brooked no argument, and Haden felt deep inside, in the same place he felt his own strange power and the comforting power of the Sword, that the words she spoke were true.

"You carry the Sword, Huntsman. That means you trace your ancestry most directly back to Light Himself. The Sword has awakened for you, so it is you who will lead them."

~~~

Haden's thoughts froze at the magnitude of the statement. After a moment, he regained the power of thought and speech.

"I wield the same power that the Sword is imbued with. That is why the Advisors or even the King cannot hold me," he said slowly. He lifted his gaze to the Sword and felt the truth of the remark as solid as the metal in his hand. "Yet you also have power...?" He left the unspoken question in the air.

"It is true," the sorceress said. "I have power over the bodies and minds of men, of space and time, and yes, even over souls. But there are different kinds of power, Huntsman. And it is your power that will defeat the Wolf, not mine."

"Even if I don't know what to do? My father never told me how this is supposed to work," Haden said as he realized that if he failed, more than just a sickness would take hold of the world. "Where am I going to find the sons of Light? Will they listen to me? What if the..."

"One step at a time, Huntsman," the sorceress said. The shifting form went for a moment into what Haden suspected was her true self, a woman of great age whose beauty still shone in moonlight hair and timeless eyes. "You have Fire, the Sword of Light. And you have a great many friends who will aid you when you need it, and there is one who will be of untold aid right at hand."

Haden only had to think for a fraction of a moment to figure out who the sorceress was referring to. He looked at Daela and the thing that lurked out of sight in her eyes became evident in her stubborn gaze. She was afraid, afraid he was going to go off on his own and she wouldn't be able to take care of him when he needed it. That was all she had ever done, Haden realized. Taken care of him, though he hadn't seen it.

"You carried the Sword," he said. "Like my mother did."

"Power can be shared if it is given and received willingly, Huntsman. That of itself is a strength far greater than anything the Dark can conceive of. And that is how you will win the battle."

Haden stepped closer to Daela and looked into her eyes. She smiled shyly back at him and took his hand. Pieces began to fall into place, each piece becoming a brick in a wall of strength and resolve. The sorceress was right. As he could command even Kings if he chose, Haden was bidden by a higher power than himself, but it wasn't that he had no choice; he had already chosen. He had chosen before he had drawn his first breath free of his mother's womb.

"Where do I go from here?" he asked.

"Two paths are open to you. The first is Underland, the caverns the First Men were born into, and where the Dark is kept at bay by one of your own, though he does not call himself Huntsman. The second is by the Skyroad and into the realm of the Cloud King. Both are allies of the Light and will do as you bid."

"Which one should I choose?" Haden asked. "Which will bring me to the Wolf the swiftest?"

"I do not know, but no matter what you choose Huntsman, your path will lead you to the Light. This I do know."

"You can see the future?" Haden asked, only half in jest.

"I see many futures, great and small," the sorceress agreed. "But of the One Future we all must meet? Alas, that is beyond me. I have not that many eyes or that vast a mind. I can tell you this much, Huntsman. The Future you speak of is not for one person alone to see or to make. If we put all our eyes together, then we will see what lies ahead. If we put all our minds together, our strengths and our wills, we may yet make that Future. And it will be as great as only Men can make it."

Daela's hand was warm in Haden's and it held him grounded as his thoughts returned to the vision of the worlds. He realized he had known even before the sorceress had told him, and that gave him a measure of comfort.

They would face the Darkness, and Light would prevail.

About Nicole DragonBeck

Nicole was born in California one snowy summer long ago, the illegitimate offspring of an elf and a troll. At a young age her powers exploded and she was banished to the wilderness of South Africa because her spells kept going inexplicably awry. There she was raised by a tribe of pygmy Dragons and had tremendous adventures, including defeating a terrible Fire-Demon that had been tormenting a sect of Dwarf priests. In gratitude they taught her the arcane magic of writing and the rest is horribly misinterpreted history. She reads as much as she writes, is obsessed with dragons and Italians, enjoys cooking, listening to music and can often be heard fiddling on a keyboard or guitar. She currently lives in Clearwater, Florida, is a member of The Ink Slingers Guild and is working on several novels, all of which have at least one mention of a dragon. She lists friends, music and life among her greatest influences.

Connect with Nicole online:
www.nicoledragonbeck.com
facebook.com/nicolebeckauthor
twitter.com/DragonBeck

Other books by Nicole DragonBeck
Beyond the Threshold (Anthology)
Into the Abyss (Anthology)
The Death of Jimmy (Anthology)
Behind the Veil (Anthology)

Charlie

By Erika Lance

The alarm was sounding when Savannah became aware of the door opening.

Security in that portion of the building was tremendous. To start, one had to navigate a labyrinth of bio driven security panels and then slow entry through each of the pressurized doors. Because each door was pressurized, they made a sucking sound when the seals popped.

Savannah knew that the confined ventilation in her portion of the building was designed to protect employees from any possibility of a leak contaminating any of the "non-secure sections" of the facility. That made her smile a little. She had thought on several occasions how silly it was that the people working with the dangerous chemicals were not protected from their own mistakes.

She was lying on her side with her back against the farthest wall from the door. She had originally tried to sit up, but as she grew weaker, she slid down from her original position, unable to maintain the strength to hold herself up.

The floor felt cold against her skin, so cold it felt as if it was burning. She stared at the flower lying before her, the light reflected in its glass petals. As her vision blurred, it looked almost like a kaleidoscope.

Remembering the door, she slowly tilted her head up to get a glimpse of her visitor. Her eyes had a hard time focusing and she could only see a shadowy figure in the doorway. She let her head drop down again; it was too much to keep holding it up. It didn't matter who it was, it was too late for any of them. She had made sure of it.

"Van?" she heard a familiar voice say.

She hoped that she had imagined it. Out of habit she took a deep breath to steady her nerves. She knew she was almost done. Instead of bringing her needed calm, the breath caused her to begin coughing and gagging. When she couldn't catch her breath, she began panic. She felt hands grip her shoulders and prop her up to a sitting position.

Her eyes closed, she focused and then took a smaller breath, not too deep; she did it again and calmed herself. She knew she could do it. She had to.

The hands holding her shoulders began to try to pull her into an embrace. She held her hand out and wheezed, "Stop."

The arms didn't stop until she was being held. She mustered enough strength to raise her head and looked into familiar caramel colored eyes looking back at her from the mask of a biohazard suit.

His eyes were home to her. They were safe and warm and at that very moment portrayed a franticness she had never seen; one she had never hoped to see.

"Charlie... Please..." Her voice was a harsh whisper, unrecognizable even to her.

Charlie was speechless as he looked down at her, as if he couldn't comprehend what he was seeing. Savannah knew how she must look now if the experiments had been any indication of the results. The whites of her eyes would be a sickening orange color, along with her lips, gums and nasal passages. Her skin would appear ashen and almost scaly. That always happened before it began to fall off in little chunks. She wasn't sure if that had happened yet, but she knew it would.

She closed her eyes, unable to look at his distraught visage any longer. "Charlie... You shouldn't be here; you need to go before..." Her voice broke as a coughing fit erupted again.

He held on to her a little tighter to comfort her. Then he began to move and she felt relief. *He wasn't always the best at doing what she asked, but in this case he had to,* she thought.

As quickly as the relief came, it passed as she heard the crinkling of the suit and realized that he was adjusting to get a better hold on her and lift her up into his arms. With all the force she could muster, she pushed herself out of his grasp and fell to the floor.

When he reached for her again she held her hand up and said "No!" as forcefully as she could.

Her eyes closed again. *Focus on your breath*, she thought as she felt another coughing fit coming on. "Please," her voice was barely a whisper. "Please Charlie... Go." With a slow breath in and out, she continued, "Even if you...It's too late... I will die... soon."

"But Van..." he began. She looked up at him through the

protection that would save his life. There were tears streaming down his face.

"Please..." She said, lifting her hand towards his face, wanting to wipe the tears away before they fell. Her fingertips touched the plastic of the suit hood and slid off as she began coughing again uncontrollably. She felt her entire body begin to spasm and then just as suddenly stop.

Unable to draw another breath she again felt the cool burn of the tiles against her face.

Then...blackness.

TWO YEARS EARLIER:

Fountains lined both sides of the cement walkway that led up to the glass doors with the WVL logo in large frosted letters. Savannah thought, *This is going to be the best year of my life.*

Savannah, a graduate student from University of New Mexico, had a dual master's degrees in biology and chemistry. Always at the top of her class, even with all of her academic achievements and knowing she was in the top list of candidates for the program; she was still thrilled when she received the notification of her acceptance to the World Vision Laboratories fall internship program.

WVL headquarters was just outside of Boston, MA. Although she had travelled in her life, Savannah had never lived this far from her family. She had been nervous and excited for the months leading up to this moment. Renting a small studio apartment just a little over a mile from her work on the 128 loop that runs around Boston, she knew the internship would require many late nights and she didn't want to risk traveling too far on the little sleep she was predicting she'd be getting.

She looked up to the mostly cloudless blue sky and thought there couldn't be a better day. Of course, just then she was bumped from behind and felt the chill of cold liquid going down her shoulder.

"Oh my god, I am so sorry," she heard from behind her as she involuntarily shook her arm from the chill.

She turned to look at her assailant.

He stood just a couple of inches taller than her 5'10". With sandy brown hair cut short and looking as if he had just rolled out of bed, he had caramel brown eyes framed by black, horn-rimmed glasses and a cute dimple on his left cheek.

He began spouting, "I am such a klutz, I know it. I am sorry. My name is Charlie and this is my first day, and I guess I'm nervous, and I wasn't paying attention. I'll pay for it, your shirt, to get cleaned. Oh god, I am so, so sorry."

Savannah had to finally raise her hand to stop the flood of words coming from the very embarrassed... *he had said his name... Charlie.* That was it.

Charlie stopped speaking at the introduction of her hand. She lowered it, took a breath, smiled and said "It's ok, really. Accidents happen."

He smiled at her again and said, "Thanks. My name is..."

"Charlie," she finished for him. "Yes, I remember from the apology. I'm Savannah." She reached out her hand.

Shifting the white Styrofoam cup to his other hand he reached out to shake and began to speak again. "Nice to meet you, Savannah. I hope to run into you again sometime." He let go of her hand as the last words slipped from his lips and grimaced. "Bad choice of words. Well, this has been weird. I am going to go... because as much as I hate to say it, this can get much worse." With that, he smiled and gave a quick wave before he headed off toward the front doors.

Savannah assessed the damage to her clothes. Luckily, the iced coffee was only on her shoulder and the back part of her sleeve. She pulled a cardigan out of her bag, put it on and headed for her future.

When she reached the front desk, she was still in awe of actually being at WVL. The security guard behind the desk took her ID and after a couple of moments and a quick picture, he handed her a lanyard with an employee badge that had her name on it. When she placed it around her neck she was beaming. It said INTERN in green letters at the bottom, but it meant it was official and she was a part of the team that led the way in bio-technological advances.

The security guard then handed her a packet with a small map. He pointed out a room marked with a small star where she needed to report for orientation. She smiled and thanked him as she headed up the small flight of stairs.

She found the room easily enough. It had a placard on front of the double doors that said:

WELCOME INTERNS – TOGETHER WE WILL CHANGE THE FUTURE

Savannah knew that this was her chance to do just that, change the future, for her and she hoped, many countless others.

Savannah was on cloud nine when she walked through the doors into what looked like a slightly larger than normal conference room. An oval table that spanned the length of the room had futuristic looking clear plastic chairs pushed up to each place. On the table in front of each chair was a nametag with a symbol, a chilled bottle of water on a silver coaster and a silver pen.

Out of habit she counted the number of tags and found that there were 32. This surprised her, because all of the information she had gathered to this point told her that WVL only accepted four interns each year and usually only one in every twelve interns was eventually awarded a full time position with the company.

She found her chair about midway down the table and pulled it out so she could sit. She took out a notebook and reached for the pen just in front of her nametag. It felt heavy in her hand and she saw that it was engraved, "What Is *Your* Future?" She turned the pen over in her hands as she heard other voices and several more people came into the room.

She looked around the room as people arrived and found their places. The only decorations in the room were a series of oil paintings depicting a vineyard. As she continued to scan the room her gaze fell on Charlie; he was seated near the head of the table. She realized she might have been staring when he met her gaze, smiled, and waved.

She waved back then looked down quickly. She didn't want to have another awkward encounter for the day and pretended to ready herself for the meeting when a hush fell over the room. Looking around to see what had caused that quiet, she was suddenly in awe. Standing at the head of the table was Dr. Leadly M. Sidelinger.

Dr. Sidelinger was the head of Research and Development at WVL. He was known as one, if not the brightest, mind in the field of Biochemistry. Savannah had followed his work and it was what had inspired her to go into that field of study.

She told herself to calm down. She took a deep breath and closed her eyes. Savannah had mentally prepared herself for today. She was very confident in clinical situations and when prepared, social ones and when she applied for this internship she had hoped, after achieving the position, she may one day meet him. She had no idea that day would be today.

"Welcome to World Vision Laboratories Fall Internship program," he began and then paused as there was a loud round of applause. "I am Dr. Sidelinger," another round of applause, but this time he held up his hand to quiet the group.

"I know that many of you may be looking around and wondering why you are seated with 31 other interns," there were several nodding heads as he continued, "This year I decided to try a different methodology in finding our star candidates." He waited a beat and then said, "This year's internship program will progress differently than it has in the past. You will be divided up into teams. Each team will have four people for a total of eight teams. In each stage of the program, one person will be asked to step down from the internship group. When the groups are reduced to only two, they will be re-teamed to a group of four again. This process will continue until there is a solitary team of four. From this final group, two candidates will be chosen to join the team at World Vision Laboratories." Dr. Sidelinger took a moment to let this sink in for the room.

"Each stage of the program should take six months and in three years you will know if you have earned your position." There were some murmurs, but they were silenced when he concluded by saying, "I understand if this is more than you bargained for when you arrived here. Mr. Handleson will go over all of the details that have been provided in your orientation packet, including compensation. Thank you all." With a final round of applause, he exited the room.

The gentleman who took the Doctor's place at the head of the table was dressed in a WVL polo and khakis. "Hello. I am Mr. Josh Handleson. I am the head of the internship program this year. If you would, please open up the folders you were given at the start of the day. I will give you some time to review and sign the forms. I will be directly outside this room, with your Mentors for this program. Once you locate your mentor and all your team members have completed their forms, you will begin your first day of orientation." With that, he left the room.

Savannah reviewed and signed her forms, then headed out the door to find her mentor. She found him right away as he was holding up a sign with four names listed on it. He was quite tall, standing at about 6'5, with dark black hair, cut short. As she approached he greeted her, "You must be Savannah Curtis." He reached out his hand. "I am Marcus Huntinger and I will be your mentor for at least the first stage on the internship."

As she reached out her hand to shake his she met his deep blue eyes and his very playful smirk. "Yes, it is nice to meet you," she said sounding a little more surprised and confused than she intended.

"Don't worry. I make it a point to know the candidates I will be working with. You're prettier than your graduation photos," he said without a hint of sarcasm and the smirk never leaving his face.

She was thankful that at that moment the other members of her team walked up and introduced themselves. There was Michelle Travis, a petite girl with wavy dark hair and tanned skin that Savannah guessed was of Latin heritage. Maliek Davis was a tall African American. He his hair was close shaven and he had a bright smile. Last was Artemus Doukas, who was of Greek decent with olive skin and curly dark hair that fell just past his ears. Artemus was painfully shy in greeting his team and Savannah could tell that he had a severe acne condition in his teenage years. He was shorter than she was, standing at about 5'7" and was slightly overweight.

That first day Marcus started with a detailed tour of the facility. There had been a map included with the welcome packet and he encouraged everyone on the team to take it out and mark a few key places. They learned that in addition to the floors above ground, there were three underground levels as well. The bottom most level was restricted access and Marcus would not discuss any aspect of what happened there.

When the tour ended, he showed everyone to the cafeteria for lunch. Savannah decided to sit outside at one of the tables that overlooked the manicured lawns and tree line that surrounded the property. It had warmed up, so she took off her sweater and placed it on the back of her chair. She had made a simple lunch of a peanut butter sandwich with cherry jam, a bottle of water and an apple.

While she ate, she ran over everything she had learned. She was finishing the last bite of her apple when she heard a voice behind her say, "What happened to your shirt?" It was Marcus.

She had forgotten about her morning encounter and the condition of her sleeve. She smiled and said, "A inconcinnus hominis."

Marcus squinted at her and then said, "A clumsy man, huh?" Savannah was stunned. She had no reason to use Latin to explain what had happened and wasn't even quite sure why she had, but Marcus had known exactly what she had said.

"Well Savannah Curtis, I am impressed with your vernacular, and you do look better as a ginger then a blonde," he smirked. He tilted his head towards the door. "See you in five" and with that he disappeared inside. A little flustered, she threw her trash away, quickly put her sweater back on and headed toward her group.

On the first basement level there was a communal locker room that all the interns would share. Everyone already had a locker already assigned, and found inside a lab coat in his or her correct size, all with the WVL logo. After they were "suited up" Marcus showed them to the lab. Once all security measures were discussed, Marcus passed out tablets to each member of the team. There was a 55- inch monitor on one wall and as Marcus hit certain buttons on his tablet, it brought up information on the screen.

Savannah looked down on her tablet and it had a square green box with a fingerprint symbol. She placed her finger on it and it displayed "Identity Confirmed: Savannah Marie Curtis." The screen opened to reflect what was being displayed on the monitor.

Each team was assigned a specific project. Their team, Team 12, was to work on a cream that would assist in the treatment of eczema. Eczema was a condition that generally presented itself in early childhood, with chronic itchy, weeping, oozing skin. It tended to be on the hands and forearms of most patients.

A treatment cream had already been developed by WVL and it was their task to make it better. They went over the project and the basics of what the current version of the cream did and discussed what type of improvements they should be looking for.

In the early afternoon Artemus asked Marcus what they as interns were being judged on exactly. When he had asked the question, it occurred to Savannah that she had been wondering the same exact thing. From the looks on everyone's faces, she wasn't alone.

Marcus looked around the room and then said, "You are going to be measured on several things, some I can tell you, and some I cannot. You are going to be judged on both your individual ability and the ability to work with a team to start. Every step of this program is monitored and it is not recommended that you withhold any information from your team, "thinking" that will get you ahead. It will reflect poorly should you decide to go rogue and do things on your own. There is a balance between personal goals and the group dynamic and it is expected you will find it."

As the days, and then weeks, began to pass, it seemed to Savannah that her team found its stride. Where she was very scientific in her approach, similar to Artemus, Maliek and Michelle had more of an experimentation type of approach. Finding a good balance was interesting between the two methods.

Although Marcus remained flirty with her, she quickly came to the realization that that was simply his personality. His being the mentor of her group there was no chance of any romantic involvement.

Savannah was pleased that she had seen Charlie a couple times since the internship began. Each time, his amazing smile made her breath catch just a little and her cheeks to flush. The third time they "bumped" into each other, of course not as dramatically as the first time, he handed her a white envelope with a little smiley face drawn on it. It said "I'm still sorry." When she opened it at home that night, she found a $100 gift card to her favorite clothing store, which she had never mentioned to him. There was a note as well that read, "I hope this in some small part makes up for the terrible first impression. I would love to take you out for a drink sometime. I promise not spill it on you. Charlie."

It took Savannah a little while to decide what to do about the invitation. She was not very good at relationships, having only had two brief ones in her life, one in high school and one in college. Both had lasted under a month, and both had ended by her saying the exact wrong thing and not realizing it until the other person was no longer interested in talking to her. It hadn't done much for her self-esteem, so she immersed herself in what she knew and could control - school and work.

She had two more encounters with Charlie. She could tell by how awkward those brief moments were that he was looking for his answer, and she managed to stumble through each conversation without giving him one.

Savannah finally decided to get him her own card. She thought about how she would deliver it for over a week. She wanted it to be a cute, romantic gesture. She had even left on earlier than normal each night for a week to watch romantic comedies on Netflix with the hope of getting the right inspiration.

One Friday afternoon she waited in the café for over an hour around the normal lunchtime hoping to run into him. When he didn't show up, she gave up and started to head back down to the labs. She pressed the button for the elevator, but it seemed to be delayed. Frustrated, she swiped her card and pulled open the door to the stairwell. As the door swung open, faster than she was expecting, she realized someone was pushing from the other side. Too late, the momentum caused them to land in a heap on the floor. When she got a look at the person now lying on top of her, she found it was Charlie.

She shook her head as she stood up, thinking that this was possibly the worst thing that could happen. Charlie was apologizing and explaining that he had not really been looking where he was headed and hadn't been prepared for the door to open so "violently". Savannah simply held up her hand, similar to the first meeting they had and said, "It's ok Charlie. I am the one who should be sorry. Are you ok?"

"Yeah, of course, I am fine," he replied. His mussed up hair and smile dazzled her and she felt her cheeks begin to flush.

"I was just heading back to the lab," she said and gestured towards the stairs behind her.

"Oh, well then..." he said, swiping his card and opening the door for her. "I hope you have an *inventful* day."

God he was charming, she thought to herself. "You too," she replied and walked through the now opened door. Just as she began to descend the steps she heard his voice behind her. "Wait, I think you dropped this." She turned around and he was holding up the card. *His card.*

"Did you drop it?" he asked when she didn't reply.

"No actually...," her voice was a little shaky, "that's not mine,

well it was mine, but now it isn't, it's...well...it's yours...so yeah."
Charlie looked at the envelope and Savannah turned on her heels and
ran down the stairs without looking back.

I am a total idiot she thought as she opened the door to the
lab.

"Where have you been?" Maliek asked. Savannah didn't tend
to take very many breaks and when she did they were usually only
about fifteen or so minutes. "I was, reading, and thinking," she said,
sounding more confident than she did with Charlie just moments
before.

The team had been working on a theory that if instead of
trying to either dry out the sores or irritated skin, maybe they could
create a thin coating that would act as a barrier. It would protect the
surface of the skin, allowing the skin to heal itself on the thermal
level.

They had dug up everything on the subject of eczema and
how treatments had worked or failed in the past. Savannah had also
gathered quite a bit of information from several support group
websites that had more than just clinical or medical views of the
affliction. They had the human voice that most clinical research
would never contain.

Maliek had programmed a clock into everyone's tablet that
counted down the days until the first elimination date. He had taken
computer programming as part of his masters and the clock said that
they had 98 days remaining. It was almost 11pm when Savannah
finished uploading her research for the night onto everyone's USB.
She had purchased one for each team member to make transferring
and sharing their research easier. Their tablets were all set-up for
bio-recognition. Although Maliek had said that it was easy enough to
get around, Savannah knew it wouldn't score her or her team any
points if they broke the labs security routines.

She walked to her locker and found an envelope taped to it
with her name on it. She pulled it off the locker and read the note
inside:

> *Dear Van,*
> *Thank you for your note and your very cute way of*
> *presenting it to me.*
> *I would love to meet your for that drink. Since you are*

probably reading this sometime after 10pm, you should go home and get some sleep. But, I want you to meet me at O'Neil's Pub at 5th and Central tomorrow night at 7pm.
I will be waiting with that drink.

~Charlie

Savannah smiled and put the note back in its envelope and tucked it into her bag. She couldn't help but think that the note was the most romantic gesture of her life.

The next day was her day off and it was nerve wracking. Savannah realized she had no idea how to dress for the date. She didn't know if it was casual or fancy, and she didn't want to make a mistake in either direction. She went through her entire closet and couldn't find anything suitable. As she stood and looked in the mirror, she could only think that she desperately needed a haircut. Savannah had blue eyes, where the rest of her family's had been brown, green or somewhere in-between. The one thing they did all have in common was carrot top red hair, and hers fell in spiral curls down between her shoulder blades.

Savannah left her apartment and found a cute salon located in the older part of town. She was able to get a manicure and pedicure, and get her hair trimmed and styled in a cute ponytail with tendrils that framed her face. She also found a clothing shop two doors down from the salon and bought a blue dress with spaghetti straps that matched her eyes and a pair of strappy sandals. The outfit was casual but nice, and after a little makeup application at her apartment she looked ready, even if her insides were doing flip flops.

O'Neils Pub had been a staple in this community for years and when she entered, it had a comfortable feel. Round, dark wood tables were scattered throughout with a long bar along one wall. At the very back of the restaurant, near the hallway labeled "Privies", was a small stage with a banner that read "Trivia Night Tonight 8pm".

The hostess approached as she was scanning the tables for any sign of Charlie. Before the hostess was able to ask her anything, Savannah nearly jumped out of her skin when she heard a voice next to her say, "Who are you looking for so intently?" She turned to see Charlie, his hair in its normal muss, smiling at her. "Sorry didn't mean to startle you." He turned to the hostess and asked, "Table for two please." Savannah didn't think she could be more nervous, but when the hostess asked if they intended to play trivia tonight, Charlie said, "Yes".

Seated at a table near the middle of the restaurant, they were each handed a menu and she held hers up, blocking her face and pretended to read it. "Nervous?" Charlie asked after a time.

She partially lowered her menu to see that his was up, also covering his face. "A little," she replied sheepishly.

He lowered his menu and looked directly into her eyes. "Me too."

She righted the menu again, looked it over and decided on lamb stew, then put it down. Charlie put his down as well and looked as if he was going to say something when the waiter stepped up to the table and asked what they would like to drink. Charlie ordered ale from their in house selection; Savannah ordered water with lemon. The waiter asked if they wanted an appetizer. Charlie looked over to her for guidance, which she wasn't ready to give. "I'm good" she replied.

"We're good," Charlie confirmed. The waiter left after their drinks and Savannah's gaze wandered to the road signs all over the walls. She could tell they were from Europe, most likely Ireland. "I am glad you came," Charlie said.

She met his gaze and said, "Me too".

After a few minutes of silence she asked, "So, Trivia? Are you any good?" with the best smirk she could muster. That caused him to chuckle a bit, and not sure if he was chuckling at her or his own trivia prowess she added, "I do play a mean trivial pursuit game, I hope you're ready." She sounded much more confident then she expected.

Being overly intelligent was a huge turn off for most guys. She hoped that Charlie wasn't one of them. As she looked at his dimple and caramel eyes smiling at her she decided then that she was going to be herself with him, even if it meant this was the only time he would ask her out. She was working on her life now, her destiny, and she wasn't going to pretend to be anything other than who she was.

"I look forward to the challenge, Ms. Curtis," he replied formally. It made her laugh.

While the drinks arrived and the food was ordered, Charlie

asked her all sorts of questions about her life and helped her by answering the same questions about his own. He was originally born in Montana, but his parents had moved to Florida when he was very young. He was an only child. He had been a science nerd in school, which she could relate too. He told her stories of failed experiments in his garage, that he had set the garage on fire three times, and only one of them was more than a small one. He was also proud of the never ending patience of his parents in his pursuit of knowledge.

She told him all about growing up in the desert, learning everything she could get her hands on, that she loved the research part of science and the feeling there was always a stone to uncover. Savannah told him about her sister and how different they were. That being the youngest she was often compared to her sister, who was more into athletics than academics. She explained that this was her first big move from home, and that sometimes she missed her sister ribbing her about being such a nerd. Charlie listened to everything she said with rapt attention. He seemed interested in what she had to say, even when she rambled.

When the trivia started up, she was surprised at how comfortable Charlie made her feel in their short time together. He moved his chair close to hers so that he could face the stage when the first round began. There were four rounds to the first game with five questions in each round. Charlie handed the pad that had been provided to her, along with a pen from his pocket. When she twirled it around in her hand, she saw the engraving "What Is Your Future?"

She looked up at Charlie and thought that she had been right. This *was* going to be the best year of her life.

The trivia was easy for her except the sports questions. Charlie simply put his arm on the back of her chair and looked over her shoulder at her answers. If there were any she didn't know or seemed to be struggling with, he told her the answer for her to write in. They won every round. At the end of the first game they were called up on stage to collect their prize, two O'Neils t-shirts that said, "Yes, I am the smartest person in the room!", and a $25 bar tab. Savannah didn't like to be in front of crowds and Charlie seemed to sense it. He put his hand on her back to reassure her that he was right there with her.

After they left the stage, Charlie picked up the tab. She didn't even try to ask to split it. She knew he would just scoff at the idea.

"Thank you Van, for an amazing evening," he said as she hailed a cab.

Nodding she replied, "My sister calls me Van."

"Oh, sorry, I just thought... It suits you," he said. "You don't mind, do you?" He looked a little worried.

"No, it's cute – Chuck," she said and smiled. He gave her a dramatically offended look, which caused her to burst out laughing. He stood there and just looked "pretend mad" as her dad called it when she had pouted as a child.

When she finally stopped giggling, her eyes were watering a little. She wiped them and when she looked up Charlie stood very close. He opened the door to the cab, and as she was about to step in his hand came up, moved a tendril of hair and tucked it behind her ear. Then his hand held her chin up and he leaned down to kiss her. Savannah froze briefly, then, as his lips met hers she melted. He kissed her gently and then pulled back.

He smiled and said, "I think you have my pen Ms. Curtis. Might you use it to give me your number?" He used the same formal voice he had earlier. She nodded and looked through her purse. She could only find the gift certificate from the pub to write on. She pulled out his pen, wrote her number down and handled him both her number and the pen.

"Goodnight Van," he said and lightly kissed her cheek before closing the door to the cab.

It had been a perfect evening!

She replayed the night on the ride back to her apartment, even touching her lips where he had kissed her. It had been so simple and fun. She had never imagined it could be like that. As she lay in her bed that night, thinking about every moment, she felt a nagging thought began to creep across her mind. Charlie was a competitor to her in this challenge. They both could make it to the end, but statistically she knew that would be difficult. As she fell asleep, she wondered if she was setting herself up for another love life failure.

The next morning she woke up, made herself some toast with cherry jam and a cup of tea. She turned on her laptop to continue her research when her phone went off. It was a text.

Good morning, did you know that the word Trivia meant the joining of three roads in ancient Rome? Although she didn't have the number in her phone, she knew it was Charlie.

She replied. *Good Morning! Did you know that sometimes gladiator blood was recommended by Roman physicians as an aid to fertility?*

LOL was the reply she got back. *I want to take you out again soon, you choose the place. Just let me know when and where.*

She read the text a couple of times and then replied *Ok, deal!* and knew there was no pressure.

They kept up their busy work schedules, adjusting slightly to make time for each other. The sacrifice of the time, she always thought, was worth it for Charlie. He was fun and it gave her a part of life she hadn't experienced before. The first few weeks she thought she would screw it up at any moment, but he seemed to really "get" her, and never seemed put off or annoyed.

They fell into a routine. They would have a late dinner and watch a movie on Wednesday nights and they would have a date night on Friday nights. Sunday mornings were reserved for relaxing and doing something outdoors. Savannah was amazed how it just worked and they just fit. They never spoke about work except to ask how each other's day was. There was an unspoken understanding that discussing work was off limits.

It was nearing the end of the first six months when Savannah made an interesting discovery. There was a fruit from the jungles of South America called the Jambu. The red fruit was sweet and edible, but the white fruit possessed an acidic quality that natives thought was poisonous. The leaves from this fruit bearing plant possessed leather like quality and it was this combination that the team was looking for. Savannah ordered samples to test her theory before she presented it to the team. She didn't want to send them on a wild goose chase when they were so close to the end of round one and two of the team would be leaving. She knew the pressure weighed heavily on all of them.

The plants arrived the week before the first elimination round. Savannah stayed later than normal almost every night that week. She didn't miss her time with Charlie; some small part of her wasn't sure what would happen if either one of them didn't make the first round.

On Thursday night, she was on the last step with the plant samples. She mixed it with most of the parts of the refined formula for the cream the team had been working on. The change was astounding. It caused the cream to form a barrier that was almost impenetrable. She documented her findings and each step, including pictures.

She hadn't been sure if it was the breakthrough they were looking for, it would need further testing. The team could work on it the next day. She did one final test on batch of mice with eczema, placing some of the new cream on the affected areas, separated them to a different cage and secured the container. She loaded up everyone's USB and closed up the lab for the night.

The next morning when she arrived at the lab, there was a security guard standing outside the door. When she tried to enter he stopped her and informed her that no one was allowed to enter. She and her team were to report to conference room four. She went back to her locker, hung up her lab coat and grabbed her bag. She felt a lump in the pit of her stomach.

She made her way to conference room four and found Artemus pacing at the back of the room. He looked over when she walked in. "Savannah, what happened last night?" he asked, his voice nearing panic.

"Nothing," she replied. "I was working a bit with a plant sample, but everything was fine when I left," she said. Her heart sank. *The mice,* she thought.

She sat down, her elbows on the table and her head in her hands. *What had she done?* Her other teammates finally arrived, as bewildered as she had been. They all speculated on what was happening and Savannah didn't know if or what she should say. She was about to explain about the plant when Marcus walked through the doors, followed by Mr. Handleson, the head of the internship program. The room fell silent.

"Ms. Curtis, please come with me," Mr. Handleson said.

Savannah got up and grabbing her bag, she started walking towards the door with her head hanging. She was done, she knew it. Mr. Handleson opened the door for her and immediately followed her out. He led her down a series of hallways, but she wasn't focusing on where she was being taken. All she could think was that she had just blown her life apart. Her chest got tight when he finally stopped before a door, swiped his card and gestured for her to enter.

They entered an office that overlooked the courtyard and fountains. "Please have a seat," he gestured to chairs in front of the desk. "Can I get you some coffee, water or a soda?" he asked politely, motioning to the mini-bar located on the back corner of the room. She shook her head.

"Ms. Curtis, may I call you Savannah?" he asked, she nodded. She was starting to feel lightheaded. "As you may have surmised, we had a problem in the lab, last night." He was looking at her now.

"I am so sorry..." she began to say. He held up his hand to silence her.

"Ms. Curtis, as I am sure you are aware, all activity in the labs is monitored," he continued. "What you did last night was extraordinary."

"Wait... what?" she said. She didn't think she could possibly have heard him correctly.

"What you did last night was extraordinary," he repeated. "Oh, Savannah, I apologize for how this must look. You're not in any trouble, quite the opposite in fact."

It took her a moment to take in what he was saying. He went on to explain that each team had, in fact, been given the same project and that two of the teams had actually made progress and had changed properties of the cream. It occurred to her that she didn't know what team Charlie was on. She hoped he was on one of those teams.

Mr. Handleson continued, explaining that when she had ordered the plant samples they had been somewhat stumped until they looked at the experiments she was conducting. The formula had the effect, in a manner, which she had intended it to. It caused a barrier that made the skin impervious to the absorption of any foreign substances; however, it was still allowing air through.

It was an exciting breakthrough and they wanted her to continue her line of research. "Does that mean I am moving on to the next phase of the program?" she asked.

He chuckled. "Not exactly. We would like to offer you a position at WVL. It is entry level, but here," he handed her a folder similar to the one she had received on her first day, "look this over and let us know what you think."

She sat and looked down at the envelope. She was being offered a position after only six months. It was unheard of. She closed her eyes and shook her head a little as if that would clear away the unreal feeling. When she opened her eyes the silver WVL logo was shining back up at her from the folder she held. She moved her chair closer to the desk and opened the packet. It was a similar contract to the one she signed when she had started the internship program. However this one was offering her a three year contract, a great starting salary and a small profit sharing incentive. It was her dream.

She grabbed a pen from the holder on the desk. It was silver, the same pen given to them on their first day and the same pen she used to give Charlie her number. With the pen poised above the paper, she had hesitated. *What if Charlie doesn't make it?*

"Is there a problem Savannah?" Mr. Handleson asked.

"No. Actually, I do have a question, will the program continue?" she asked.

Mr. Handleson nodded, "Yes it will. There are still two positions to fill, your role at WVL is in a different area than was intended for those completing the Internship."

She felt a sense of relief wash over her. "Am I able to discuss my being offered a position with my close friends and family?" she asked.

Mr. Handleson nodded again. "Yes, of course, as long as you use your discretion. The teams are being culled today and those that remain will discover soon enough that you have taken on a new role."

She signed a copy of the contract, handed it over to him and replaced the pen in the holder. He told her it would be best if she took the rest of the day off, to ready herself for her new position on Monday. He walked her to Personnel and helped her get her new employee badge, parking space assignment and to fill out the remaining paperwork.

It was a little after 1pm when she finally left. She called her parents first, and then her sister. They were all thrilled for her. Her parents didn't ask about Charlie, they knew how the program worked and that there was a chance he wouldn't get accepted. Her sister asked however, and Savannah had to tell her that she didn't know yet. Charlie had insisted that they have a movie in the park date that night to celebrate their advancement. Only then would she know what happened to Charlie, when she met him under their favorite tree at eight that night.

She got home and found she couldn't concentrate. She wanted to call or text him but they had agreed that life was to go on as normal. She found herself cleaning her entire apartment from top to bottom. She was almost late getting ready when she finally looked at the time again.

She wore jeans and the O'Neils shirt they had won on their first trivia night. They had won again a few times, but that shirt was special to her. She needed it close as she walked up to the tree, blanket in hand. Charlie was already there with a cooler of treats. She looked at him, taking him all in. She knew that no matter what happened, she had something truly amazing with him. He was wearing the same O'Neils shirt she had on. In that moment, she knew she loved him.

She moved towards him, dropping the blanket and throwing her arms around his neck, kissing him deeply. She needed to feel him close to her. He wrapped his arms around her waist. They stood, frozen in time. She pulled back when she realized she had tears streaming down her face and rested her forehead against his chest, their arms still around each other.

"Tell me, please...," she whispered.

"I made it," he said and kissed her forehead.

She smiled and kissed him again. After letting him hold her close for a moment, she wiped the tears from her cheeks and went to grab the blanket. They sat, under their tree, and had another perfect night together. She had landed her dream job and her dream man.

When she arrived for work on Monday, nothing could dampen her elation.

She took the map from her pocket and reconfirmed the location of her new office. It was located on the 3rd basement floor, the restricted area.

She entered the elevator and pushed the button for the 3rd level. When she did, a red light shot out from the sensor and moved across the room. A pad slid from the wall with a finger print scanner. She placed her finger on the reader and it flashed green, withdrew into the wall and the elevator began moving. She found out later that if anyone was on the elevator without level three clearance, the elevator would not descend.

She arrived to her assigned lab and saw it had a similar set-up to the one she had been working in for the last six months. She had the same tablet with all of her previous research, and in addition, she had a large monitor that was a touch screen. She could use her tablet or touch screen directly. *Fancy* she thought to herself, *Maliek would be in heaven.*

She opened her tablet to find a file with a video. It was Dr. Burness, someone she recognized from a video shown at orientation, one of the Directors of the Research and Development team.

The video explained that they were expecting her to continue with the research she was doing and to report back when she stabilized the formula. He indicated that she should see three new icons on her tablet. Two were internal/external research pathways now at her disposal. The third was reporting software for her to log the progress of her project. All three had a tutorial and would be fairly easy for her to navigate he explained. At the end of the video, he let her know if there was anything she needed she was to let him know. He wished her good luck and the video ended.

Savannah continued to keep the same schedule as Charlie, and cherished every moment. As she was riding into work one morning, she couldn't help think that she had done it. She was one of the lucky ones. In the blink of an eye, it seemed another six months passed.

The days that led up to the next decision day brought with them a heavy rock that sat in Savannah's stomach. As per usual, Charlie wouldn't discuss it.

On Friday, the day of the eliminations, she heard a tapping at her lab door. Standing outside was one of the guards. He was holding a glass vase with several glass flowers and as he handed it over he pulled a card from his pocket. "Someone must like you," he said and went back to his post.

She set the vase down. There was a metal plate that was engraved with "TOGETHER WE WILL CHANGE THE FUTURE", the company motto on the welcome sign. She opened the card. "*You can stop worrying now – Charlie*". She let go of a breath she hadn't even know she had been holding as a huge smile crept across her face. She looked more closely at the glass flowers. He had gotten her something she could always look at - they could be sterilized.

A few weeks later, she was asked to present the current state of her research and her findings to date.

She was surprised to find over ten people seated around the conference table when she arrived. She had assumed it was just going to be Dr. Burness and maybe a couple others. Ten was almost overwhelming.

"Ms. Curtis, I assume you are ready?" Dr. Burness said.

She moved to the front of the room and using the large touch-screen monitor, logged in. She walked through her entire presentation. There were a few questions but most of the audience just listened. When she concluded, she stood waiting.

Dr. Burness was having a whispered conversation with someone to his left. With a start Savannah recognized him. It was Dr. Sidelinger. Her heart began to race. Her hands began to sweat and she looked down, shifting the tablet so she didn't drop it.

"Very impressive, Ms. Curtis," said Dr. Sidelinger. "Please come by my office this afternoon at three to discuss the next phase of your research." She nodded as he stood and left, the rest of the room following suit.

She was early for the meeting, but Dr. Sidelinger beckoned her to come in and to take a seat. She attempted to portray an air of calm, despite her rapidly beating heart.

"Ms. Curtis, I want to say again how impressed I am with what you have accomplished in such a short amount of time," he began. "I would like you to know that your research, from all appearances, has an application that we would like you to look into further. We have a project of a very sensitive nature. We would like you to make certain modifications. You will be enlightened on the specifics you need as the project progresses. Are you interested?"

It took her a moment to notice he was waiting on her to respond. Nodding again she said, "Yes, yes absolutely."

"Good. I am glad to hear that. You will receive your instructions starting tomorrow; this project is of the highest confidentiality. You may discuss it only with Dr. Burness and myself, is that understood?" his voice took on a more serious tone.

"Yes, perfectly understood, sir," she replied.

"I look forward to your results then," he said as he walked her to the door.

She didn't discover for two days what the next phase of her research meant. First, she was moved to a deeper part of the building; unbeknownst to her there was a fourth floor to the basement. It was really floor 3.5 as it wasn't entirely under the third floor. There was a larger lab that had a doorway that lead down a short flight of stairs to the more secure area. A person had to have two bio scans, eye and fingerprint, and voice recognition to enter. There were pressurized doors at every point of entry.

As she became acclimated to her new environment, she discovered that this area was entirely independent from the rest of the building. The ventilation and environmental controls were completely self-contained. When Dr. Burness gave her the tour, she saw that each of the labs had glass that darkened when the lab was occupied.

Savannah was surprised to see the high level of security in this type of facility. She assumed that this type of set-up would be reserved for military facilities. Dr. Burness chuckled a little when she asked during the tour. Each project was classified, he said, and only those on the project were to discuss it.

When she was shown to her new office, she saw that everything from her lab, including Charlie's flowers, had been transported to her new location.

The next day she was given her first task. The cream she had designed created a barrier that protected the skin from outside elements; water and air notwithstanding. Her task was to make it so that the cream could be translated into gas form.

It wasn't an easy undertaking; however, she was given no deadlines and no apparent pressure. She worked tirelessly, sending in her reports daily. Occasionally she would receive a note that gave her an idea to try to assist her. After sixty-four days, she had her third successful trial.

The next day Dr. Burness asked her to bring one of her specimens to test in his lab. She readied one of the rats she had been given for this purpose and when she entered, he took the specimen and placed it into a container that had three levels of seals. Once it was inside, he pressed a control on his tablet and she heard the sound of air being moved. A light mist began to fall within the container.

At first, the rat seemed fine but after a several minutes she saw that it was having some difficulty. Its skin began to turn color and it started to have seizures. The seizures did not last long before all movement ceased.

Savannah covered her mouth; she had never seen anything like that before.

"Ms. Curtis, I need you to make your formula stronger and less susceptible to airborne intrusion," Dr. Burness said without looking away from the specimen.

"What was *that*?" she heard herself ask.

"Classified," was all he said.

She went back to her lab, slightly dazed, and when she got there she searched for anything related to what she saw that day. There was nothing in the research files.

When she got home that night she started her search again. She couldn't find anything specific as it related to WVL, but she found pictures that resembled what she had seen in the lab. They were pictures of victims of bio-weapons. She shook her head. *That couldn't be right.*

At lunch the next day she sought out Marcus. He had a very standard schedule for lunch and she knew she was likely to find him. When she approached the table, he smiled up at her. "Well if it isn't the ginger genius," he said and gestured for her to take a seat. "What can I do you for Savannah?" he asked.

"How are you?" she asked. "How is the team?"

He shook his head. "When you were...transferred, the team was disbanded at the first round of the program. Michelle didn't t make it to round two; Artemus didn't make it to round three. That left Maliek and he is on the team with your friend Charlie," he said using his fingers to make quotes when he said "friend".

Since she and Charlie never discussed work, she wasn't that surprised she didn't know who his teammates were. "You don't happen to have Maliek's number do you?" she asked.

He narrowed his eyes for a moment then said, "No, but since he is right over there, why don't you ask him yourself?" He pointed to the window where Maliek was sitting.

"Thanks," she said.

Maliek jumped a little when she tapped him on the shoulder. When he saw her, he smiled. "Well, if it isn't the smartest girl in the room."

"Hi, how are you?" she asked and pointed to the seat next to him with a questioning look.

He nodded and replied, "I have been good, a little worried

about that last round, but good. What do they have you doing? he asked. "Wait, never mind, I know, you can't tell me. So, what brings you topside with us interns?"

Savannah looked around and then leaned in and whispered, "I need your help actually. When we were working together, you mentioned that you saw some of the icons that were... hidden... during the internship."

"Yes" he said, looking puzzled.

She sighed and continued, "I was just curious how you were able to see them, because I somehow hid two of mine and well, I feel a little silly. Since the person I would have to ask is Dr. Burness... I was hoping you could help me so... "

"So you don't look dumb in front of your new boss?" he finished for her.

She felt herself flush, because she was lying and she hated it. But since he thought she was embarrassed, she played on it. "Yes. Can you...will you help me please?" she asked.

He wrapped his arm around her shoulders and said, "Only if you remember us little people when you are a big deal around here."

She smiled up at him and nodded. "How could I ever forget?"

Maliek was able to explain how to find the hidden icons in a few minutes. It wasn't that it was a simple process; it was his ease explaining it. She walked through it with him twice to ensure she had it exactly and thanked him.

When she got back to the lab, she went through her normal steps while she thought about what she should do.

After a week or so of debating, she convinced herself that she was over reacting. She continued her work and made progress on Dr. Burness's request.

A month later, she was ready for the next test. She brought, as requested, two specimens. One that had been treated right before the test, and one treated the night before.

When she brought them into Dr. Burness's lab, she began to feel uneasy. Seeing the same set-up and before, the nagging voice in her head was shouting that she had buried what she didn't want to see instead of looking at it.

The test was run on both rats. The rat that had been treated right before the test last about ten minutes longer then the last one, but the rat treated the night before fared much better, lasting an additional forty-five minutes before it started to show symptoms.

She cleared her throat as Dr. Burness made some notes. "Excuse me, Dr. Burness? Perhaps if I understood exactly what it was I was trying to make the project resistant to, I could make more progress in the direction needed," she said as diplomatically as possible.

"It is CLASSIFIED Ms. Curtis, please do not ask again," he said sternly. She left his lab without another word.

When she returned to her lab she went right back into her research and continued to look for the longevity they were after in her "project". When the labs were empty and she had turned in her report for the night she sat and looked at the vase of glass flowers for a long time. She was supposed to meet Charlie that night, but she wasn't sure she could face him. She wanted nothing more than to hide in his arms, but she knew she had to discover what her research was being used for.

She grabbed her tablet and followed Maliek's instructions exactly. Surprisingly, she was able to access the confidential files. She started with Dr. Burness's project. Reading through the reports, she began to feel physically ill. The more she read, project after project, the more sickened she was by what she saw.

Later, as she sat on the floor and hugged a plastic container that contained all of the contents of her stomach, she began to weep. She felt lost for the first time in a very long time. She was alone, and scared. She sat there for some time and simply stared at nothing. Eventually she tried to will herself to become numb. She assumed that was what the others around her must have done.

Knowledge is power, she thought. But she didn't know what to do with this knowledge. After hours of considering every option, she could only think of one. She got up, cleaned up her lab, closed down her tablet and left for the night.

She took a cab to his apartment. She and Charlie had never spoken about work and as she walked up the steps, she realized she wasn't sure how to explain. She hesitated on the landing, his door looming in front of her.

What if he would be fine with it? What if to him it didn't matter? He wasn't supposed to know. Telling him anything put him in danger of losing everything. She would be taking his dream.

She had turned to leave when the door behind her opened. "Van?" Charlie said from the doorframe. She quickly wiped the tears from her face and turned around. "Oh, baby, are you ok?" he moved toward her.

"Yeah. I'm good, just a hard day" She said, her voice a little shaky. "I was coming to say I was sorry for, I mean... about tonight. I missed our date...." she said with a small forced smile. He pulled her into his arms, and the moment her head hit his shoulder she felt the tears begin.

He pulled back to give her a soft kiss on her forehead and walked her inside. He guided her to the couch and sat with her as she cried, not saying a word, just brushing the strands of hair from her face and planting soft kisses on her head with his arms wrapped around her.

The next morning, Savannah woke up to Charlie gently shaking her awake. As her eyes focused she saw the sun was streaming in through the sliding glass doors in the living room.

"I made you some coffee and a bagel," Charlie said. He gestured to a plate and mug on the coffee table in front of her.

She sat up and asked, "What happened?"

"You cried for a while and then you were out. You seemed really tired so I didn't want to wake you. But since it is Friday, I figured we both needed to get up. After all today is the day!" He said the last with a little smirk.

She brushed her hands against her face and pulled the hair back from her eyes. Today was the day. The end of round three. She looked at the food in front of her and felt sick all over again. She got up and went to the bathroom.

As she stared in the mirror she knew she wasn't going to say anything to Charlie. She wasn't going to say anything at all. The perfection of her life with him would not be ruined by this.

She splashed water on her face, brushed her teeth and headed back to the living room. Charlie had put her coffee in a travel cup and had her bagel all wrapped. "I know, you have to run," he said with a smile.

She threw her arms around his neck. "You're kinda perfect Mr. Miller," she said and kissed him deeply. "I will see you tonight to celebrate." Grabbing the coffee and bagel, she headed out the door.

Savannah slowed her pace as she walked up to the glass double doors of WVL. She remembered the first time seeing them and the feeling she had. She smiled when she remembered Charlie and how they met. Walking into her lab she looked around at the place she once saw as her future. Now, only the glass flowers held any value.

She took her time constructing her last words to Charlie. She wanted him to know that what he had given her meant the world, and that what she was doing was because she wanted a world where he wouldn't have to be a part of her choices or why she was making them. When she finished she hit send. She knew he wouldn't check his email until after he was done for the day. By then it would be too late.

She walked to the room that housed the containers carrying what she needed. Carefully, she removed what she was looking for. It was early in the afternoon and she knew the labs were fully staffed.

She walked to the entry room at the top of the stairs. She sealed the doors and set down the vase of glass flowers. She read the inscription one more time. "TOGETHER WE WILL CHANGE THE FUTURE". She was doing just that, changing the future she thought, and smiled. With a deep breath, she opened the first container and let the gas seep into the air.

AFTER THE BLACKNESS

When Savannah's body began to spasm, Charlie pulled off the hood and gloves of his suit and pulled her onto his lap. He continued to hold her, cradling her now lifeless form against him. After reading her email there had been a small part of him that had held out hope that this hadn't been her plan. He knew, as he looked at her now, her expression no longer pained, that this was exactly what she wanted.

He held her as close as possible, refusing to let go; he knew if he did he would have to admit she was gone. He started to feel the effects of what Savannah had unleashed begin to take hold. Charlie laid Savannah down gently as fresh tears streamed down his face. He began to cough and his body began to spasm but he managed to pull a small box from his pocket and remove the ring. He slid it on her finger, then lay down behind her. He closed his eyes and again pulled her into his embrace.

He wrapped his hand in hers and watched the light glint off the ring and the engraved letters that read *You are my Future.*

About Erika Lance

I would say I was fortunate, some would say otherwise, to have a chance to live across the US. Originally from Minneapolis, MN I spent most of my formative years in Hollywood, CA, then NM, CO, GA, WI and FL. Moving around a lot meant I got to see so many interesting parts of our country and the cultures that are all around us. All through my life I was lucky to have many artists; writers, actors, painters, poets and musicians. It made for a very wild upbringing. I grew up as an elusive female nerd. My head was either buried in a book or playing RPGs (if your cool you know what that means), it made for an imaginative existence. My love of writing started at a young age and although I wrote a lot for myself, it took hitting that certain moment in my life to decide I wanted to share my universe with the world. With that said, it will most likely be an amazing ride so old on tight.

Connect with Erika:
www.erikalance.com
Email: erikalance@gmail.com
Facebook.com/Erika-Lance
Twitter.com/AuthorELance
Instagram.com/AuthorELance

Other books by Erika Lance
Into the Abyss (Anthology)
The Death of Jimmy (Anthology)
Behind the Veil (Anthology)

Always and Forever

By Rhiannon Matlock

CHAPTER 1

Agony. That - aside from horrible, soul sucking, blame - was all that was inside of me. I wasn't really aware of the people that were in my grandmother's living room other than the fact that they were there and they were speaking. For all I knew they were uttering platitudes in Chinese.

I wanted to cry. The tears were there, stuck in my throat, but they just would not come. I was frozen inside, unable to think or speak or feel, or even move. Only one thing caused me to do anything. Across the room, in between the scattering of bodies, was a portrait. Hung up on an easel, I avoided looking at what was inside and focused instead on the frame. Dark mahogany carved with delicate swirls danced across the wood like vines in a vineyard. My eyes drifted towards the center of the picture, but I forced them away again before I could recognize what I was looking at.

I let my gaze drift along the edges of the photo. A pale blue up against the rich wood, it was a perfect color for a summer's sky, its clarity hinting at whimsical fun. The lump in my throat grew, scratching and clawing at me. I swallowed it back down.

With dazed vagueness, my eyes roamed over the picture and caught hints of other colors before they fell to the corner and saw the face of a little girl, cracked wide with a smile and laughter in her eyes. My fists clenched. The face belonged to me. I remembered that day, but it wasn't that memory which rose to the surface. There was another, far more vivid and far more important that banged mercilessly against my consciousness.

It was when I became consciously aware of how much my mother loved me. With my dad it had been effortless, the surety of his love stretched as far back as I could recall. From my first memory of him twirling me, eyes effervescent with joy and smile as wide as his face as he rubbed his ginger scruff over my cheek, I knew he was my best friend. With my mom, the conviction, and the depth of it, occurred one random night when I was about five or six years old. Though I tried, I never forgot that moment. Images flooded. I tried to fight them, to weave around them like a mouse in a labyrinth, but they just wouldn't stop. Finally, I closed my eyes and let the memory wash over me.

~~~

About 14 years earlier...

"Honey?" my dad called out from the kitchen. "I have dinner ready and it's time to go."

I bounded up from my bed at the notion of food and zipped to the kitchen. The counter top was far out of my reach but still I extended my hands up in anxious desire for what lay atop it. My dad chuckled as he scooped me up and plopped me on the cool porcelain tiles. Immediately, I reached for the peanut butter and jelly sandwich on the plate nearby.

"Always hungry, aren't you little bear?" he chided playfully, snatching one quarter of the sandwich he'd made and handing it to me before moving to the sink.

I was busy scooping out the jelly from between the bread when I heard him laugh again.

"You never can just eat it straight, can you?" he asked as he gave me a little kiss on the check. "Come on, let's go before the boss kills me."

He opened up his arms and I quickly crawled onto his chest.

"And speaking of your mom," he said as he wrapped the remains of the sandwich up in a napkin and put it into my backpack, "If she asks, you had steak and vegetables for dinner. She'll have my butt if she finds out you had PB&J."

I giggled at the word 'butt' but eagerly nodded at the idea of keeping something from mom. It always failed, but it was fun watching her make faces at dad. We walked into the garage and I continued to eat as he put me in the front seat of his police cruiser. Though I could barely see over the dashboard, it was exciting to ride in the front seat with him, even if mom didn't approve. It was just one of our many secrets.

By the time we reached the hospital, darkness had already started to descend. After giving dad a kiss, I grabbed my backpack and headed to the front desk. When I got there, I was greeted by a familiar face.

"Hi Uncle Kent," I said. I looked up his tall frame and found him smiling down at me with his kind, gray eyes.

Technically, he wasn't really my uncle but he'd delivered me and was always around - birthdays, holidays, barbecues or sometimes just because. He'd taken me on my first roller coaster ride and often watched me when my parents went out. He was family.

"Hey you," he said, his deep voice welcoming as he held out his hand. "Want a lift?"

I couldn't help the smile from forming on my face as I nodded. With a simple swoop, I was carted up into his arms and cradled in his warmth and safety. I turned in his embrace, waved at my dad who waved back, and then turned back to Kent.

"Wanna go see your mom kiddo?" he asked.

I nodded, eager to see her for the first time that day. Kent moved over to the desk behind the front counter and placed his hand firmly along the obsidian top. The plastic lit up in recognition of his handprint and welcomed him back.

"Find Rose Davenport," Kent instructed the machine. A few seconds later it beeped: "She's on the fifth level, room 5112B."

We found her pretty quickly and she gave me a kiss when she saw me. Then she scowled.

"What did you eat for dinner?" she asked, her brows furrowed.

"Steak and vegat, uh, vegetables," I said with wide-eyed innocence.

Uh-huh," she replied and brushed my cheek. "You know your father should wipe away the evidence before he tries to get you to lie for him."

I didn't know what she meant by that so I gave her a big smile. She sighed.

"You know, it's damn lucky you're cuter than him because otherwise I'd have to give you the talk, too," she mumbled and then looked at Kent.

Kent smiled. "Want me to get her some food?"

She looked grateful. "Would you please? Then later when my husband comes in through the emergency room just tell him it was all his fault."

Kent chuckled and mom walked off briskly. I frowned as I watched her go and was upset. I wanted to run after her, or rather, I wanted her to stay with me. She was always leaving and each time she did, I hoped she would choose differently.

"So how was school today?" Kent asked, distracting me.

"Same old, same old," I said with a dramatic sigh.

"Really?" he said, his voice dripping with sarcasm.

"Yup, justa 'nother day and a 'nother dollar."

"Oh boy. We have to start cutting down your viewing time around here. I don't think your mom would appreciate the amount of soaps you ingest."

I gave him an impish smile but he didn't have time to say anything else.

"Well, well, well, if it isn't the little rascal herself."

The voice belonged to Sammy, one of the nurses. She pushed out a chair and Kent set me down on it. I hauled up my backpack on the table and pointed at the wall where an episode of 'True Hospital' was playing on the TV.

"So what's going on now?" I asked, pulling out my sandwich from my backpack.

Kent sighed, but Sammy laughed. I was thoroughly occupied as Sammy and several of the other nurses started our daily debate about the show. Before I knew it, mom came to get me.

"See ya later kid," Sammy called out to us.

"Not if I see you first," I shot back with a wink.

Mom raised her brows at that but didn't comment as she adjusted me in her arms and brushed aside the hair in my face.

"Did you do any school work?" she asked.

"Uh huh," I replied quickly.

She sighed. "Yeah, we've got to do something about the lying to mom thing. I know your dad finds it funny but-"

"Doctor Davenport," someone called out urgently and mom immediately turned around.

My heart sank. The young nurse who yelled came running up to us. He was panting and trying to speak but he was having a hard time of it.

"Catch your breath Tim," she said gently. "I won't run out on you."

He gave her a smile and his cheeks reddened. After a

moment he spoke.

"I know you're off shift, but there is a patient that I need your help with."

Mom said nothing, but I felt her stiffen up and my small little world imploded. She looked at me with her beautiful green eyes, waiting for me. My first thought was to shake my head and throw a fit, but I knew that would upset her. I gulped and nodded, though I couldn't quite look at her.

"I'm sorry honey," she said. She gave me a kiss on the side of the head and then set me down. "What's the room?"

"3221," Tim said.

"Take my daughter to Sammy at the front desk and then meet me there," she said, transferring my hand into his before she took off.

A lump of disgruntlement settled inside me and I pulled my hand out from Tim's and ran straight to Sammy.

"Tim?" Sammy asked, clearly surprised. "Whatcha doing?"

He gulped some air and pointed down to where I was standing in front of the desk.

"Dr. Davenport said to get her little girl to you."

"OK, thanks. I have her," Sammy replied. After Tim was gone she peeked her head over the counter top at me. "You okay honey?"

I crossed my arms in front of me and refused to speak.

"Yeah, okay it sucks, but she'll be right back. I promise," Sammy said.

It was a promise ill kept according to my experience. Five minutes felt like a year and I quickly grew bored. I grabbed my ball from my backpack and headed out front. Finding a nearby wall, I kept in sight of the front desk and started to play. I wasn't very well coordinated and the ball jammed into my fingers and quickly bounced away. Without a thought, I ran after it. Just as I was grabbing for it, a pair of bright lights sprung up on me. In the second that it took me to register how close they were, I knew I couldn't outrun them.

Seconds before I was crushed under rubber and metal, two hands snaked around my middle and yanked me hard. Knees hit pavement, taking a couple of layers of skin, and my head hit hard into some kind of bone as the car came to a screeching halt.

There were voices, but I was shaking and so scared I couldn't make out what was being said. I heard a heartbeat under my ear and it calmed me. Two arms, strong and sure, enveloped me. I looked up to discover my mom's face. She was crushing me but I didn't care. I was alive and she was holding me. Her warmth permeated me and I sank into it.

"It's okay, it's okay," she said, crooning, her voice tremulous. I discovered much to my surprise that she was just as wobbly as I was.

A splash of wet hit my cheek. She was crying. Why was she crying?

"Are you upset mommy?" I asked with a shaky voice.

She half laughed and half cried, and tightened her grip on me just a little before releasing me.

"I'm not upset baby girl," she said but there were still tears running down her face. "I was just so scared. Oh god, please don't ever do that to me again. I couldn't...I just couldn't live with that, okay?"

There was something about her voice and the look in her eye that made me believe she really couldn't live without me. My heart swelled so much inside my chest I almost felt I couldn't contain it.

"I love you mom," I said, my own tears starting to fall.

"I love you too, my love. So very, very, very much."

"Always and forever?" I asked, almost scared of the answer.

It was something my dad always said to my mom but I'd never heard her repeat it. She smiled at me and kissed my forehead.

"Always and forever, baby girl, always and forever."

CHAPTER 2

I stood in the living room of my grandmother's apartment with a cup of water in my hand and I contemplated life. I didn't want to. I wanted my mind to be blank. I wanted my soul to be blank. It would mean the end of the pain that was threatening to tear me in two. If I could empty myself, I might've filled a lake but I hadn't shed a single tear. I wouldn't allow it. I squeezed the cup in my hand and looked away from the picture.

Around me were a hundred voices, but they were all muted

and faded, like gnats that hovered. If they all just went home, I'd be relieved.

A hand slid onto my shoulder, warm and caring. I didn't dare look up to see who it was. After a few moments, they left me to myself. I felt a rage start to build up inside of me. It was like lava, hot, thick and spiteful. I squeezed the cup harder.

There was a cracking sound and the next second the cup shattered. Colorless liquid and glass sprayed out. I looked at the now separated droplets of water as they slipped effortlessly through the air and couldn't help the grief that started to well from deep within.

There was a heavy silence that followed the noise. Oddly, the quiet was so much louder than the din. I looked down. Red coated my hand and started to drip down to the carpet. *Splat. Splat. Splat.* It took a second to register that it was blood and that it was mine.

A warm pain, minor in comparison to that which resided in my heart, spread up from my lacerated extremity. It started to throb and I could only stare at it.

Blood was weird. So vital and yet so slippery. There one second and gone the next. Sort of like life. I was pulled from my fixation by a pair of rough hands. I looked up and saw the handsome but haggard face of my father. He shook me once and then twice and I knew he was trying to say something to me, but it was too hard to absorb. He pulled me in for a hug and I felt the grief ride up a little further in my belly. I slammed it down hard.

Someone else grabbed my bleeding hand and started to wrap it. I couldn't see them. All I could see was the front of my father's cotton shirt as he held me close, and then I was lost again to memory.

~~~

10 years earlier....

I was ten years old when my world changed irrevocably. The sun was out and there was nary a cloud in the sky. California summer at its finest. My best friend Destiny and I were walking home from the beach, towels wrapped tightly around us to ward off the breeze that chilled the droplets along our skin. We were at the edge of my property before I noticed my mom's car in the driveway. She was never home on the weekends and I felt a surge of excitement. I turned to Destiny. "Your mom's home?" she asked, just as confused as I was.

I shrugged. "I guess so. Wanna come in?"

Destiny hesitated. I think she knew that I was only asking out of politeness because any moment I could get with my mom, I treasured. She shook her head.

"Naw, that's okay. I'll catch up with you tomorrow," she said.

I nodded vigorously. "Absolutely. Bye."

I ran to the front door and burst inside. What greeted me wasn't what I was expecting. Loud, severe voices carried out from the middle of the house and smacked right into me. I was shocked. I'd never heard either of my parents raise their voice, let alone say something harsh to one another, ever.

"Just when in the hell were you going to tell me about this little proposal?"

"Will, for god's sake just listen to me, for once."

"For once? It seems like that's all I've been doing for the last twenty minutes."

"I've been telling you about Atlanta for nearly six months."

"You've told me what they do there; you didn't say that you'd applied."

"Will-"

"Is Kent going too?" my dad asked sharply. He sounded jealous.

That confused me. I remember telling dad once that I thought Kent had a crush on mom. He'd laughed and waved it off. Most men had a crush on mom he'd said. She was beautiful inside and out, and she had a quality that made you want to be around her. While Dad and I argued about a lot of things, one thing we agreed on was how much we adored mom. He said he trusted no man more than he trusted Kent, and I whole-heartedly agreed. Now it seemed Dad wasn't so convinced.

"You're not serious," my mom said, clearly upset by that.

"Just tell me," dad insisted.

"Of course he is. He's a pathologist. One of the best, and you know better."

My dad was quiet when he responded but I was close enough to hear.

"I don't think anything is going on with him it's just-" dad said but mom held up a hand to quiet him.

I looked up to find her staring straight at me. I didn't know what was happening, but I knew it wasn't good.

"Mom?" I said, uncertain and worried.

"Oh honey, did you hear all of that?" she asked.

I didn't say anything. Dad started to step towards me but mom held out an arm, stopping him.

"No," she said sternly, looking at my father with determinism. "You don't get to tell her about this. I'm going to take her on a walk."

Without waiting for either us to speak, mom took me gently by the hand and led me outside. We walked and she talked, but I didn't hear much of what she said. The only thing that did register was that she was moving to Atlanta for a new job. That was where I stopped listening. Of course, it was for a job. It was always about the job. Anger swelled up in me and I ripped my hand from hers and took off before I could hear anything else. Her voice trailed after me to come back, but I kept running.

How could she? was all I could think as I wandered the streets for hours, feeling more like a rogue agent who was trying to prove a point, rather than a petulant child. When I started to get hungry, I knew I had to return home.

When I walked in the front door my dad's body immediately went limp. I refused to look at my mom. Without so much as a word, I was ushered to the table where I promptly ate some cold spaghetti. Nothing was said about my running away. Nothing was said about anything. In the space of a single afternoon my happy home life had been shattered and I had no idea what to do about it. My dad came to tuck me into bed.

"Dad?" I said, stopping him just before he left.

"What sweetheart?"

"I don't want to go with mom. I want to stay here with you."

How I knew that dad wasn't going to Atlanta escaped me, but I knew. There was a brief pause and then my dad spoke, his voice rough.

"Don't worry about it," he said. "I'll handle it."

Hours later, I woke from a horrible nightmare. My mother was drowning and I couldn't get to her in time. It was so real that I sprang up in bed, shaking and crying. The images were very vivid in my mind and drove me from my bed. I stumbled to my parents' bedroom door and only hesitated for a second before I opened it.

In the moonlight, I clearly saw my dad but my mother wasn't present. It made the horror of the dream come back. I really needed my mom. I carefully shut the door and headed toward the spare bedroom. This time I more than hesitated with the door handle. I'd run away from her earlier and I didn't know how she felt about me. After a few seconds, I eased the door ajar. Immediately my mom sat up and I felt her eyes on me.

"Rachel, honey, is that you?" she called out into the dark.

I nodded and walked up to her bed. Her cheeks were glimmering with tears in the faint light and instantly I felt guilty. I tried to back away, but she grabbed me and pulled me up into bed with her, wrapping her arms around me and hugging me tight.

I started crying too and quickly buried my face in her chest. She uttered no words of reassurance but she ran her hands lightly up and down my back, letting me know she still loved me. As always, she knew, without having to ask, what I needed. This brought a whole new wave of tears when I realized I'd be losing her soon. She leaned back and looked down at me. She brushed aside my bangs and invited me, without words, to speak.

"Mom?" I finally croaked out.

"Yes honey?"

"Why are you leaving me?"

Mom gulped and shook her head. "I'm not leaving you sweetie. I want you to come with me. I want both of you to come with me."

That was a little bit of a shock and deflated some of my anger.

"But daddy doesn't want to go?" I asked.

Mom shook her head again.

"Why can't you just stay here then?"

"Do you know what job I'm taking?"

I shook my head.

"Do you remember what happened during the Oil Crisis?" Mom asked. "All of those people that died from Vurlan and Foxtail, and the others?"

I thought back and shivered. It was a horrible moment in history that involved millions of deaths. Sadly, I nodded.

"Well, I'm going to work in a section that is called Preventative Medicine. We look for ways to stop diseases like that before they spread."

"Why can't you do that here?"

"I wish I could, but the labs are all in Atlanta."

"Why can't you just be a doctor?" I asked, almost pleaded.

She stroked my cheek.

"So much like your father," she murmured and then let out a little sigh. "I can't only because I know that I can do more. If I'm able, then it is my responsibility to do it. Does that make any sense?"

It did. Down deep, it really did, and a part of me admired the hell out of my mom, but the other part was still wrestling with loss. Softly my mom reached through that dark place.

"Do you feel like I'm betraying you?" she asked, somehow piercing through all of my thoughts and grabbing me right in the center.

My heart kicked up a little as I considered that maybe she could hear my thoughts and maybe she knew all of the bad things I'd been thinking about her over the past few hours.

"It's okay," she said gently, "you can always tell me what you're thinking and I'll never judge you, okay?"

She was so sincere. Her eyes were still red but she looked quite earnest. Still, admitting what was in my head was not easy. I looked down, my heart positively hammering away inside my chest.

"Am I not good enough for you?" I asked in the smallest of voices.

"Oh honey," I heard my mom say, the sound of tears evident in her voice, "How can you even ask me that?"

I couldn't look at her but she grabbed me again and hugged me tight.

"Baby, I love you more than life itself and if this world were a perfect place, I'd love nothing more than to just stay here with you and your dad forever. Do you understand?"

I nodded against her chest, the tears flowing freely.

"Do you believe me?" she asked.

I nodded again.

"I love you mom," I whispered hoarsely.

"Well that's good, because I love you too."

"Always?" I asked.

She gave a strangled laugh, "Always and forever, baby girl. Always and forever."

CHAPTER 3

I didn't know exactly what happened over the last two hours. It was a blank. What I did know was that my hand was throbbing with pain and that everyone was gone, except for my grandma and my father. They were in the kitchen, talking occasionally, but mostly they were just cooking. The smells were potent but I couldn't get into them.

It was weird seeing them together. I'd heard stories about how Grandma hadn't been happy with dad when her little girl married him. She never really took to him, but she'd come out to California between theater jobs and visit, charming us all, save for dad. They'd barely spoken then so to see them now, acting as if they were family, was incongruent with my memories.

I couldn't help what my mind snagged next. It was like going fishing in an overstocked lake. The memories were slow at first, like an old-fashioned movie reel, and then they sped up, whirring so fast that I couldn't keep up. Her face kept appearing over and over again, blending together like a kaleidoscope. My eyes burned and my cheeks started to tingle. It was an overload and I couldn't stop the scream that tore from my throat.

~~~

Five years earlier....

The days that followed my mother's announcement of her departure were horrible. There was a stiffness in my family that had never been present before, like we suddenly didn't know each other and were strangers. Being alone with either parent was marginally better, but I think we all wanted to talk about it and no one was willing to broach the subject. Mom left two weeks later and the tension in the house slowly started to ease, though my dad's mood didn't respond as quickly.

At first, I tried to cheer him up. There were plenty of good days but there were plenty of bad ones, too. He didn't turn to alcohol, he just shut me out more and more. The worse it got, the more I blamed my mother. It didn't help that whenever I went to see her, she had little time for me.

By the time I was fifteen, I'd grown fed up with my mom. I wanted her to notice me. I wanted to matter. Finally, during one visit, I took off. I was all the way to the checkpoint at the edge of the city when I was caught by a local police officer. I was brought down to the county jail and they called my mom. She was angry and worried when she finally got around to picking me up. I was both glad to elicit a reaction and ashamed of my antics.

A week later, nothing had improved. So, I did it again and again until one time I got smart. I obtained a fake ID, went down to the bus station, swiped my wrist over the checkout scanner and booked myself to the most random destination I could find. Turns out I was headed for New Orleans. It took almost three days before I was stopped. Local PD were waiting for me at one of the stops and they hauled me off without so much as a hello. They called mom but of course, she wasn't able to come and get me right away.

My Grandma arrived instead, much to my surprise, and she swept me up in her charm and wit, flying me off to New York for a mini vacation. She claimed it was all her idea, but I was sure my mom just wanted to get rid of me.

I lost myself in the City. We did everything: plays on Broadway, shopping at Barney's and Ferris Wheels on Coney Island. The lights, the sights, they captivated me. They took me in as a mistress and wooed me from the imagined slights of my mother. It was a wonderful balm, but it worked too well.

We arrived back at my grandmother's loft in Manhattan one day and were just stepping out of the elevator when a familiar scent hit my nose. Mom's perfume. I was stiff and reserved when I came face to face with the one who'd given me life. Her eyes were circled in black and her face was tired. I didn't think I'd ever seen her look more wiped out. My first impulse was to go to her but I checked myself very firmly.

"What are you doing here?" I asked prissily.

"I've come to take you home ba-"

"Don't call me that," I stated harshly. "It's not like it means anything."

"You know that's not true," she said quietly, her eyes entreating me to understand.

I shook my head. "It is true."

My mom flinched as if I'd slapped her and looked away for a second before she forced her gaze back to me. I saw the sheen of tears in her eyes and I felt a solid lump form in my throat. My heart shoved at me to stop my behavior, but my head refused to listen. She had to learn.

"Rachel," she tried again, "I know that you're mad at me right now but maybe we can just talk about it. Over an ice cream maybe. Rocky road, right?"

"Rocky road?" I said with a scoff. "Just goes to show you how much you don't know about me. I wonder if you ever did at all."

A couple of tears fell from her eyes and I knew I was going straight to hell when I died. Problem was, I was too stubborn to back down. Mom started toward me and I backed up. Grandma stepped in then. She took me roughly by the arm and put me inside her apartment. She didn't say anything to me, but I pressed against the door to find out what she had to say.

"Oh god mom, I just don't know what to do with her," my mom said.

"Well honey, being there for her would be a good start," grandma replied.

I almost pumped my fist in the air in victory.

"Don't you start on me too," mom said, more viciously than I'd ever heard her.

I could hear my mom cry then and any moral high ground I may have achieved was lost. Peering through the looking hole, I saw grandma holding my mom and rocking her gently.

"Look, no one doubts that you love her and that you want to be with her," grandma said, "but she's all messed up right now. Doesn't know up from down, if you ask me."

I frowned.

"All the more reason I should take her," mom said and pulled out of the embrace.

Grandma shook her head. "She won't listen to you right now. She's not listening to anyone. Got a hard head like her father and there's not a damn thing you can do about it."

Mom scowled as she wiped her eyes.

"Now is not the time to bag on Will, you know," mom said.

"Well, I certainly don't see him here right now, do you?"

"It's not his time to have her," mom replied weakly.

"And that's why he couldn't get away to pick her up?" Grandma queried and then held her hands up to ward off any protests. "Look, it's not really the point right now."

"Then what is?"

"Just leave her here for a little bit. Let her calm down and then, when she's ready to talk, come and get her."

Mom looked uncertain and in a moment of tenderness, Grandma stroked mom's cheeks and gave her a kiss on the forehead.

"It'll be okay sweetheart," Grandma said. "Promise."

Mom didn't look convinced as she stared for a good long while at the door. Finally, she sighed and gave her mom's hand a squeeze.

"Can you just tell her that I love her?" mom asked. When Grandma nodded, she added, "And tell her that I love her, always and forever."

"Okay," Grandma said, but even I could tell she looked a little confused.

"Just make sure to tell her that last part okay?"

"I will honey, I promise."

CHAPTER 4

Nothing registered for a while after my Dad hugged me. I knew I was shuffled about, but I was more conscious of the change of colors than I was of anything else. Eventually I found myself touching something warm and wet. I managed to push back my tears long enough to see what was in front of me. Clay. The red brown stuff that potters used to make things.

Looking at it, I could tell the mixture had been poured and stirred. I wondered when that had happened. The material was so soft and smooth that for just a moment I felt my mind take a break while I studied it. Without thinking about it, I picked up a pound of the clay and dropped it on the wheel next to the sink.

The room used to be a spare room. When Grandma discovered we had a shared love for pottery, my dear old patron converted the space almost overnight. We had a lot of fun in this room. The memories of those times wouldn't come though. Instead, my mind could only focus on the one thing that I would regret for the rest of my life, the moment where I had a chance to change things and I didn't.

I dropped some additional water on the clay, let my fingers move on their own and before long, I was lost to the memory.

~~~

Two weeks earlier...

A buzz hummed through the air. It stabbed into the droning of the teacher in front of the class, as well as the throbbing in my head. The night before had been wild and I was still mostly hung over. By the time that I realized it was my comm band going off, the caller had hung up. I didn't bother checking to see who it was. If it were important, they'd call back. Someone nudged me and I looked up to see half the class looking at me. I guess I was noisier than I thought but it was hard to tell over the trombone going off in my head.

I waved and they quickly went back to their regularly scheduled programming. I tried to make like I was studying, but mostly I was just doodling until the bell rang and I was released from the small prison that some people like to call college. A clutter of noise followed the bell and the students all hurried to put away their screens and get off to the next class. I wasn't so quick and it earned me a special talk from the teacher.

"Ms. Davenport, may I have a word?"

It was Professor Eggert. A crotchety old man who thought the world began and ended with education. I groaned internally but put on a smile and bound up to his desk like a good little girl. Grandma's theater training came in handy in times like these.

"Yes Professor," I said in my sweetest voice. I layered on a little of the Georgian drawl that had seen me out of many jambs. "Can I help you with something?"

Eggert frowned and took off his glasses as if that would help his frustration. He looked at me with something akin to disappointment.

"Ms. Davenport, I realize that you may not have much use for my class, but I would appreciate it if you didn't fall asleep."

"Professor Eggert, I value your class. I wouldn't be getting an A in it if I didn't find it useful."

His frowned deepened. "Acting skills aside Ms. Davenport, I know that you're an intuitive, yet disgustingly lazy, student who has either studied these materials before or read through the books in advance so that you wouldn't have to actually do any work later."

"If I read them before starting class, wouldn't that make me industrious rather than lazy?" I questioned in my sugared twang.

He opened his mouth to retort but my comm band buzzed again. He glanced at it.

"It's your mother. Maybe she can talk some sense into you."

My mother, I almost snorted. That ship had sailed a long time ago I wanted to say, but wisely held back. I was a bit ruffled as to why she was calling. It wasn't my birthday, which was the only time that I was forced and obliged to talk to her any more. Since that day five years before, we'd been distant. Mainly on account of me. I leaned back and dropped the twang.

"I'll make sure I don't fall asleep in your class again Professor," I said.

That earned me little more than a humph and a dismissive wave of his hand. I smiled at him but it was lost on the geezer. Collecting my purse, I exited the classroom. Students tramped through the Trinity College hallways like cattle. I was not excited to get to my next class. Over the din of voices, I heard a vroom and a smile split my face. Abruptly, I turned around and headed toward the front of the campus. I spotted the black motorcycle as well as its rider, Danny Boyd.

Damn, he looked good. Dressed in all black leather from shoulders to feet, his helmet covered his dark shaggy hair and perpetual five o'clock shadow, but I could feel his dark brown eyes through the visor. As if hearing me, he revved his engine again and then cocked his head to the side in invitation. My heart thumped inside my chest and a rebellious grin etched into my features. I hardly needed more of an excuse.

"Hey there sexy," I said when I stepped up to him.

He revved the bike again and I laughed.

"Are you coming or are you just going to stand there and stare at me all day?" he asked, his Irish lilt barely discernible over the engine.

"It's tempting," I said with a little shrug. "You know how much I like to look at you."

He shook his head, but stood up and handed me a helmet. He took my purse and tucked it into a compartment under his seat while I fitted the brain bucket on tightly. Though I was ignoring my mom's calls, I couldn't completely avoid her voice in my head or my experiences in her ER many years ago. To this day, motorcycles are one of the most lethal ways to travel. Too bad it was so much damn fun. As if somehow accessing me from across the Atlantic, my comm band buzzed again.

"Aren't you going to get that?" Danny asked me as he settled himself back down into the seat.

"Nope."

"It's your mom," he said as if that should change my mind.

"My mom would tell me that boys like you are bad and that I should wise up and get back in school. Should I answer and tell her what I'm planning on doing this afternoon?" I replied.

"Depends," he said. "What do you plan on doing?"

"Nothing good," I said.

Danny looked me up and down in an exaggerated fashion and then shook his head vigorously. I laughed and caught my skirt as Danny held out a hand to help me negotiate getting onto the back of his bike. Once I was situated, I tucked my arms possessively around his waist.

"You good to go?" he asked me.

"Always," I replied suggestively and he shook his head.

"You'll be the death of me."

Revving the engine again, he drowned out anything I could say and took off, threading through the traffic like only a local can. Soon, we passed the checkpoint to get out of the city and were free to roam the countryside. At length Danny pulled over and I hoped off first. My body was still vibrating when he grabbed my hand and took me into an ice cream shop. Rocky road for me and vanilla for him. If ever there was something to describe our personalities it was that damn ice cream. He led me back to the bike and we sat and ate for a bit. To my dismay, my comm band lit up again. The face of the band was pointed at Danny so I couldn't see who it was but by the flicker of curiosity on his face, I gathered it was my long absent mother again. Please don't talk about her, I mentally prayed. There was an awkward silence.

"You look like her you know," he said suddenly, breaking the gentle quiet.

I groaned inside. Did he not know that this was a bad subject? No, he wouldn't. I looked at the face on my screen briefly. Long dark hair that cascaded into wide curls at the apex of her tresses, a gregarious smile that beckoned you to find out its cause, and green eyes alight with that spark of life few have. It was one of my favorite pictures of her and though it filled me with a deep sense of anger to see her laughing and happy, it somehow also soothed me. Yeah, we may look alike, but I was nothing like her.

Casting a glance about, I saw the ruins of an old castle at the top of a nearby hill. I looked back at him. An evil grin stole across my features.

"What are you doing?" he asked me, wariness in his voice.

I backed away a few steps, threw the rest of my ice cream at the ground and pointed at the castle.

"If you catch me before I reach that, there may or may not be a reward in it for you," I said and before the words could fully register with him, I took off.

After maybe ten steps, I risked a glance behind me and found he'd nearly caught up with me. I squealed and ran harder, reaching the broken down structure a mere thirty seconds before he did. Slipping behind a fallen pillar, I evaded his outstretched hand.

"Too bad Danny boy," I teased and took off again.

This time he wasn't to be outdone and he darted out quicker than a bullet to snake an arm around my waist.

"Ah," I squawked with a peel of laughter as he hauled me up and slung me over his shoulder like a sack of potatoes. "Cave man put me down."

He thumped his chest in response and walked off with me beating on his back lightly.

"You Jane, me Tarzan. No put down," he said but he loosed his grip on me.

I slid down his chest and the humor quickly evaporated.

"So you mentioned something about a reward," he said, his voice huskier and his eyes darker.

"I said if you caught me," I replied, my own voice gravelly.

"I did."

"Not before I reached the top."

"I see," he said and took a step back from me.

I grabbed him before he could get far and pulled him back to me. He kissed me, hard. My toes curled under his ministrations and it quickly went from edible kisses to groping. I pushed Danny back before we got arrested. He went for my neck.

"You're killing me," he said between open mouth kisses.

I shivered. "You're not the only one."

"We could go somewhere."

"Where?" I asked breathlessly.

"Church, down the road."

I chuckled gruffly. "You're not serious."

He shrugged and gave me another kiss, which started towards something more in a hurry and I knew he wasn't kidding. It was tempting, so very tempting, but I was sure to go to hell for that one. At that moment, another call came in and we both suspected it was my mom again. Why she was being so persistent I didn't know, but it broke the moment. I pushed against his chest again. He groaned but stopped and bent his forehead to mine as he pulled me into his embrace.

I snuggled in against his chest and looked down at the valley below. The sun was quickly dipping behind a distant peak. Orange, pink, yellow and red burst up into the sky and lent a fiery glow to the vast expanse. I laced my fingers through his and leaned my head against his shoulder. Neither of us spoke as we watched the day fade away to dusk. Finally, Danny broke up the tranquility.

"So what's deal with you and your mom?" he asked softly.

Seriously, again? It really wasn't a subject I was interested in so I turned my head up to find his mouth and sunk my lips onto his warm, responsive ones. The kiss was softer this time and I could tell he had figured out I was escaping his question. After a few seconds, he pulled away and kissed the top of my nose.

"Nice try," he whispered.

I chuckled but turned back to the horizon. The words were there, hell they were always there, but I wasn't much of a talker. At least, not in regards to her.

"Can we not talk about this right now?" I asked seriously.

He was quiet for a second but then kissed the top of my head.

"Of course, we have time," he said and held me tighter.

CHAPTER 5

I came out of the memory with a jolt. I wasn't sure what brought me about, but I guessed it had something to do with the fact that I was done making whatever I'd been in the middle of. How I was aware of it, I wasn't sure. The object was flat and oddly shaped. I realized it was upside down. It was a mask. Carefully I turned it right side up until the face was staring at me. The delicate features were clear and done so perfectly it could almost have been a picture. I touched the tip of the nose and gently ran a finger along the cool smoothness. It was an exact likeness of my mom. My hands started to tremble and that scorching heat ripped through my throat again as I screamed a second time.

Jumping up from my seat, I dropped the face on the wheel. It swiveled and then fell to the side, mashing it almost instantly. I leaned forward and turned off the wheel. I heard the door open behind me and caught a snippet of conversation. My dad wanted to come in and comfort me but Grandma wouldn't allow it. I needed to be allowed space. Dad argued that it'd been days, but she said at least now I was doing something. She pressed to give me a little more time. I was grateful when I heard the door close.

Taking the clay out from the side of the machine, I set it aside and put on a fresh batch, this one much smaller than the last. I didn't want to repeat my mistake. Reclaiming my seat, I lost myself again to the textures of the clay as I worked it. The memories quickly came again.

~~~

Two weeks ago....

It was nearly ten o'clock by the time Danny and I made it back to my apartment. I carefully got off the bike.

"Wanna come up?" I asked as I returned my helmet to him.

"Do you want me to?" he asked.

"Hell yeah. I'd like to actually get you into a real bed one of these fine days. Might be a little more fun like that."

"Might not be," he warned, half serious.

"Aw come on, it can't be that bad. Besides if you end up staying the whole night, I'll make you breakfast."

"Hmm, that's tempting but you don't even know if you can stand me for more than an hour."

"I'll take my chances," I said, taking his hand closest to me and giving him a gentle tug.

He smiled through his visor and called for his bike to shut down. It was going to be a long night. My wrist buzzed again. I'd almost bet it was my mom again but I still didn't answer it. Just because she had a crisis of conscience didn't mean that I had to deal with her. Maybe later. Maybe. He pulled me against him and tucked me under his arm. When we reached the gate, I was startled to find two men stationed like gargoyles outside my place. In the dark their faces were obscured, but I looked closer and frowned.

"Rory? Charlie? What the hell are you guys doing here?"

Danny tensed against me and I realized that he had no idea who they were. I didn't have time to fill him in, either. A second look at their guarded faces and my stomach plummeted. My father was a cop and my mother was a doctor. I knew that look well.

"What's wrong?" I asked, instantly on high alert. "Where is grandma?"

"She's waiting upstairs," Charlie said.

In my rising distress, I completely forgot about Danny. Shoving past them, I sprinted to the door and ripped it open. Not bothering to wait for the rickety old elevator, I took the steps two at a time until I reached the top floor of the building and my door. Holding out my wrist to the reader on the wall next to my room, I waited impatiently for it to beep. When it did, I rushed inside.

There, on the opposite side of my living room, was my grandmother. Her white hair was swept up into a classy bun, and there were wrinkles on her usually smooth skin, but what really kicked me in the gut was the look in her green eyes. Rimmed in red and full of sorrow, I knew whatever she was about to say was not good. I looked down at her hands and discovered my overnight bag.

"We need to go."

Without conversation, I followed her out and into her waiting car. Rory was driving and Charlie was next to Grandma. It wasn't until we were at the airport that I realized there was one person missing. I turned to Charlie.

"Where's Danny?" I asked him.

He shrugged. "Told him you had some family matters to take care of and you'd call him later."

Half an hour later, we shuffled out of the car and into grandma's jet. People normally travelled between continents by tube through the Atlantic Ocean. It was fast and safe, but also crowded and could take weeks to get a ticket. Few flew, and even fewer had a jet at their disposal. I'd never been overly impressed with either Grandma's wealth or fame, but I was eternally grateful for it then.

Within minutes, we lifted off the ground. I wasn't ecstatic

about the g-force shoving hard against me as we climbed rapidly in the sky, but it wasn't the height that was tying my stomach into knots. I looked over at Grandma. Her eyes were screwed shut and her face was taut with pain. She'd said nothing after revealing mom was in the hospital. I needed something to do or my mind would wander and I didn't think I could handle much of that.

I waited until we leveled off and then hit the small console on the armrest. A holographic screen appeared in front of me and I scrolled through the apps with light finger swipes until I found the one I wanted. I tapped it and the screen dissolved into something that I'd been told resembled a rolodex.

"Kent Oliver," I said softly. "And send it to my comm band."

I didn't want to disturb Grandma so I got up and headed to the back of the plane. I was taking a seat at the tail end when the small, metal ring at the top of my right ear buzzed. Tapping it once, Kent's voice filled my head right after.

"Rachel, honey, is that you?" he asked.

I felt an immediate sense of relief.

"Yeah it's me. Where are you?"

"Top floor," he said tersely.

Unfortunately, that explained everything to me.

"What happened?"

"She went in with a faulty suit."

"Wasn't someone there to check her out beforehand?" I asked. I heard the blame leak into my words.

It took a second for Kent to respond.

"No," he said, his voice cracking.

"What do you mean 'no'? Who the hell let her in there?"

"Rachel-"

"No, tell me. Now."

"Rachel-"

"Kent, you'd better stop saying my name like that and just tell me what happened."

There was nothing but empty silence between us. His refusal to speak illuminated the story better than words. She'd let herself in.

"No," I said sharply and then hung up the phone.

I returned to my seat, my anger in full force. I was going to friggin' kill her. How dare she... I didn't complete the thought. I didn't know fully what was going on and it was best not to speculate until I got all the facts.

The rest of the flight was a blur. All I remember were the endless stream of lights as they zipped by and the familiar smell of the city as it crowded my senses. Every city I'd ever been to had a different scent. New York was sort of dirty and stale, Newport, California was salty and Atlanta had a sweet sort of tang to it that never left until you did.

It was all so familiar, and yet so foreign to me. I hadn't left these streets in a happy frame of mind and traversing them again riled up a lot of lost memories. It wasn't until the car came to a complete stop that I came back to myself.

I looked out the window and saw the same drab, four story building that I'd left. Someone was shaking me, stirring me from my ill thoughts.

"Rachel, honey?" came my grandmother's voice.

"Yeah," I said but the voice barely sounded like me.

"We need to go," she said kindly.

I didn't acknowledge her but I did snap open the door and step out. It was a crisp spring day, and the wind brushed aside my bangs and cooled my heated cheeks. I didn't know when I'd gotten so hot but the breeze was like a cup of water on a hot day. Someone took my hand and I was led toward the glass and stone building that held my mother within its walls. The dread I'd been carefully keeping a lid on kicked its way past my barriers and started to rapidly take over my body.

When we got to the elevator, we were immediately rushed inside. I didn't bother to look at any of the faces of the people escorting us. They would only tell me a story that I didn't want to see. My breathing became more labored as we ascended and I felt the world start to spin. When the elevator doors shuddered open, there were scores of people about. They blurred in front of me until one came into sharp focus. Kent. His eyes were already red and tears streaked shamelessly down his face. My dad's face was buried in his chest and over the top of that bent head, my eyes made contact with Kent. It felt like I was literally punched in the gut. All air and all reason left me.

No, no, no, no.

The word rang loudly in my head as I sprinted across the slick linoleum and collided with a woman. Her hair was dark and her features were pulled in concern, but I'd never seen her before and didn't waste even a second on her. I shoved her away from me, the hammering of my heart reaching a fevered pitch, and I ran into the room she'd just exited. The walls were a stark white, as if that could conceal the horridness of what was inside. There were no monitors, no doctors, nothing but a plain bed and someone inside of it.

I stared at the still figure and couldn't see the face. It was not my mom. I knew it wasn't. It really couldn't be. She'd just been calling me a few hours before. She couldn't be dead, not without talking to me first. She wasn't dead. She wasn't dead, I repeated to myself.

I focused on the hand that lay across the blanket. It was so pale white, so weak. I went to the bed and grabbed it. It was still slightly warm. Whoever had passed away hadn't done so very long before. I heard a collection of voices behind me but I couldn't understand them. The only thing that I could see or hear or feel was that hand in mine.

So delicate, so loving. It wasn't mom. It just couldn't be. I touched the hand to my face and forced myself to look up beyond it. I was up to the neck when I just couldn't look any more. Instead, I laid myself down on the bed, tucked that arm around me and rolled over so my face was against a shoulder. Then I promptly went blank.

CHAPTER 6

I looked down at the thing that I'd made from the clay. It was a small figurine. The face was incomplete but the rest was of a woman, her arms bent as if she was cradling something. I felt a lump in my throat the size of Colorado. I didn't have time to analyze when there was a knock on the door. I looked up to see my grandmother.

"You have a visitor honey," she said kindly.

I made a face. Grandma frowned.

"I know that you're still hurting Rachel, but you should take this."

I was too tired and too beaten to put up much of a fight, so I deferred to her judgment and got up. When I got to the living room I saw my father off to the side, near one of the balcony windows. His face was guarded and his jaw locked. His brown eyes were so dark they looked like marble, but he wasn't looking at me. His fierce gaze was set on a woman in the center of the room.

She had long black hair, with deep green eyes set in a heart shaped face and she wore a nurse's outfit. Her nameplate said "Cady". She was vaguely familiar, but I couldn't place her and my mind was too exhausted to try. There was a pregnant pause filled entirely with taut strain. Finally, my grandmother cleared her throat.

"Would you like something to drink, coffee or tea maybe?" she asked.

The woman glanced at my grandma and gave her a heartfelt smile but shook her head.

"No, thank you. I can't stay long. As I said on the phone, I have a message to deliver and that's all."

"What message?" I said abruptly.

My words were scratchy and my throat raw. It made the noise that came out of me horse and foreign to my own ears. I wondered briefly how long it had been since I last spoke. The woman looked at me, her gaze penetrating in its frankness. It was as if she was assessing me, deciding if I was worthy to speak to or not.

"You're the one who came here, so either speak or leave," I said roughly.

Grandma stepped toward me and I could feel her disapproval. Before she could say anything Cady held up her hand.

"It's alright," she said, acknowledging Grandma's attempt to apologize for me. Then her attention focused squarely on me. "You've lost your mother. That is no small thing to get over."

Lost! The word rankled me. As if my mom had been misplaced somewhere and I might be able to find her again. She's de-. I stopped my thoughts there. I wasn't interested in hearing stupid platitudes from someone I didn't know and I started to turn back around when the woman held something out. It took me a second to register that it was a small slip of paper, curled into something akin to a tiny scroll.

"What is that?" I asked in a tiny voice, unable to keep my eyes off it.

"It's from your mother," Cady said softly.

Inexorably, I was drawn towards it. I reached out to take it from her but she didn't release it. I looked up at her, my anger licking up inside at once.

"Her death was not something you could've controlled,"

Cady said directly, "but what you do because of it, is entirely on you."

I held her gaze for what felt like an eternity, meeting her challenge and throwing down one of my own. I wanted a fight, but she merely gave me a little smile and released the message. Then, without a word, she left. The entire room fell into a deathly quiet as all eyes fell to the innocuous looking paper. Inside, my ears started to pound, my heart thumped erratically and my head started to ache. What did it say? Did she hate me? Was she yelling at me, even now, about how stupid I was not to take her call when she was dying? At how selfish I was?

I found it hard to breath. I knew grandma and dad wanted to know what it said as much as I did, but it was so difficult. I was ashamed of myself, and reading those words, somehow, would mean that it was true, that she was actually gone. That was something that had I staunchly refused to accept. I looked up, my eyes searching until I found my dad's face. His lips were pressed together tightly but his gaze was the softest look I'd ever seen from him. He nodded at me briefly, tacitly giving me the consent I sought.

I looked back to the slip and a terrible ache formed in the pit of my stomach as I slowly unfurled it. It read:

I'm so sorry baby girl. Can you ever forgive me? I love you more than life itself, always and forever, Mom.

My hands started to tremble as a single set of tears plopped from my eyes and sank down onto the paper. I ran a delicate finger over the badly scrawled lettering as if I could somehow connect with her through the indelible ink.

I could see her, lying frail and wrecked in bed, wanting desperately to reach me and when she couldn't, she wrote this. Can I ever forgive *her*? She died wondering if I still *hated* her.

Something ugly twisted inside of me, and all of the pain and rage that I had been holding in came tumbling out of me. I smashed the paper into my fist as tears started to cascade down my face with wild abandon. The ache in my belly swelled, and my throat constricted, fighting with the savagery of my crying. I was heaving and before long I sank to the ground and buried my head into the carpet. My hands beat against the ground and the sting of it felt good. She died thinking I hated her. *No, no, no! Mom, I never hated you. God, I love you, so very much. How could you leave me like this? How you could you leave before we had a chance to fix things?*

At that exact moment I hated her. With every ounce of my being, I despised her. But I hated myself more. Two rough hands grabbed me and pulled me into a strong embrace. I shoved against them, not deserving the comfort, but the grip only tightened and after a few moments I sank into the warmth provided.

Eventually I became aware of the strong woodsy scent that I always associated with my father and I realized he was holding me, rocking me back and forth and whispering in my ear.

"It's okay honey, it's okay," he repeated over and over again.

I wrenched free from him and sat back. I looked at him with all the accusation that I had in my heart. His face was covered in tears and he was just as much of a mess as I was, but I didn't care.

"It's not okay," I said through gritted teeth. "It's not friggin' okay at all."

"That's not what I meant," he said hoarsely.

"Were you there when she died?" I demanded but I was pretty sure I already knew the answer. We were too much alike.

He hesitated and then shook his head.

"So she died alone. All she ever did was love us and want us to be together, and we turned our back on her and made her out to be the villain," I said around the burning lump in my throat.

Fresh tears were wrenched from his eyes and it made me feel horrible all over again, but it was true.

"She was the best person I knew," I said, breaking down again, the tears hot as they washed over me. "She just wanted to take care of people."

Dad started toward me, stopped, and then grabbed me and hugged me again.

"I know that sweetheart, and if there was anything I could possibly do, I would," he said, his voice choked with emotion.

"She asked you to go with her," I said, more a statement than anything. My anger was fading.

Dad didn't say anything, but I didn't really expect him to. Grandma joined us on the floor and put a hand on both of us. I looked at her, but dad just looked to his lap.

"She loved you," Grandma said and gave a pointed look at Dad, "both of you."

Dad choked back a silent sob but gave a weak nod. He knew

it and that made him feel even worse. Neither of them had remarried and the only thing that had kept them apart was themselves. It was such a simple revelation. It had been sitting there the whole time but I had refused to look at. All the time lost, all the anger, and it hadn't been worth it. The only thing that it gained me was the loss of my mom.

She was gone. She was gone and I was never going to see her again. My heart hurt. The tears and grief threatened to consume me again, but something lurked in the dark that I latched onto.

Her death was not something you could've controlled, but what you do because of it, is entirely on you.

The words from that woman Cady. They sounded an awful like something my mom would've said. I think it was for that reason that they took root. I calmed as I slowly started to collect myself. I felt myself starting to steel up, resolved that I was going to make it worthwhile. I was going to make her death matter somehow. I looked up at my dad. My heart was like stone and my eyes burned, but I was committed. I knew what I was going to do. I was going to make it up to her every day for the rest of my life. I was going to make her proud.

"Dad," I said softly. "What do I need to do to become a cop?"

About Rhiannon Matlock

Born in 1981 before YouTube, Twitter or Twilight, Rhiannon Matlock remembers when you played your songs on Walkmans and actually had to tell your mother where you were going before you went out to play.

Now a well-seasoned traveler who still considers herself a child at heart Rhiannon enjoys such diverse activities as bungee jumping, white water rafting and volunteering in third world countries, but dislikes slow drivers and people who malign their friends.

Rhiannon doesn't like to talk about herself much, insisting that everyone else has a much more interesting story to tell. She especially likes to spin a good yarn, particularly ones where the white hat wins.

Connect with Rhiannon online:
rhiannonmatlock.wordpress.com/
facebook.com/rhiannonmatlock

Other books by Rhiannon Matlock
Beyond the Threshold (Anthology)
Into the Abyss (Anthology)
The Death of Jimmy (Anthology)
Behind the Veil (Anthology)

Blood Journal

By JM Paquette

"Why, Klauden, what are you staring at?" Hannah asked, trying to make the question light and flirty, but it fell flat between them, the words too contrived to be truthful. Her intended mate gave her a sardonic look as he sat half-turned in the elegant library chair, one hand perched on the polished wooden arm, the other still resting on the open page of the book he was no longer reading.

"I am looking at you, *chaivin*," the vampire told her. Her skin prickled at the nickname, the closeness of a childhood spent together echoing in her fingertips. Not for the first time, Hannah wished she had a private name for him, but he was always Klauden van Sherinak, First Son to the Second Family in her father's castle. She couldn't recall when he had started calling her "chaivin," the old word a reference to fire. She always wondered if it was because of her red hair, or what Kelvin Malbrek, their teacher, would call her fiery temperament. Perhaps he had started when she was a baby. Though twenty years separated them, he would have been a child himself then, and just learning to read the old tongues. She considered the eighty years of her life spent in this castle, some of it in this very library in the basement, and hoped that the years ahead included more looks like this from her betrothed. The old books did say that the first hundred was the most exciting century.

"Well," she said as the moment stretched out, "at least they finally found a dress that you noticed."

Klauden smiled, shaking his head at her, and she was reminded again how handsome he could be when he tried. "I always notice," he claimed. "Sometimes I choose not to comment because I know what that would do to your already ridiculous ego."

She glared at him and watched as the sudden heat that she had felt in his first look faded, until he was just Klauden again, her friend, her tutor, her confidant, her intended mate. She knew that he was about to dismiss her, turning his attention back to yet another book he was reading, so she moved quickly to stand directly next to his chair, making sure the dress swished as she did. Klauden paused, his head elegantly inclined in her direction, but his hands had already resumed their position on the book before him.

The red satin made a luscious sound as it fell gracefully around her small waist, the waves of fabric highlighting the slight curves Klauden had only recently begun to notice. The cut of the dress was simple enough, a big skirt topped by a corset that left her shoulders and arms bare. She had watched his reaction to the other women in the castle during the dances and noted how his eyes followed the necklines and bare skin. Most of her dresses revealed her arms in the latest fashion, but this was the first time he seemed to notice at all.

And it hadn't been her neckline that he had focused on at all. It had been the sound. She knew that Klauden's hearing was far better than his sight, so she had made a point of walking up behind him slowly when she entered the library. She had taken careful steps on the carpeted floor, letting the fabric of the dress sway subtly from side to side, his sensitive ears picking up the sultry sound as she approached. She had seen the change in him, the slight stiffening of his shoulders, his head cocked ever so slightly to the left, and she knew that if she could see his face, his eyes would be closed.

Oh, Klauden, she thought, a wave of appreciation and longing rushing through her, *how well I know you.* On the heels of that, *I am so very lucky.*

She had known her entire life that she would marry Klauden. Such a life was her destiny, a decision made by their parents long before she was born and she had always been glad. Klauden was handsome. He was fun, sometimes, and more importantly, he was here and familiar. She knew that other First Daughters had been sent to other castles to marry complete strangers. Hadn't her own mother come from Gerter van Lartner's castle in the north, sent to marry her father, the esteemed Magnus van Kreeosk, when she turned one hundred?

Thoughts of her mother distracted her for a moment, and she thought of the last time she had seen Alin, so weak with sickness that Kelvin Malbrek and her father had to practically carry her into the room where she died. Hannah shook her head and tried not to think about it. Her mother had been gone for years now. Hannah was determined not to suffer a similar fate.

No, her place was here, First Daughter, promised mate to

Klauden. Eventually, they would rule the castle as her father did. *Except*, Hannah thought bitterly, *when I take over, I will first force Kelvin Malbrek to lick my fashionable boots before I banish him from this castle entirely.* The magician may be her father's second-in-command, and her own teacher, but he was nothing to her, and she would be glad to see him gone.

Hannah never had been very good at school. Klauden had been her savior there, as in other things. He took the time to tutor her, helping her with the magic, explaining so simply the things that Malbrek never seemed to say in a way that made sense.

She looked down at him and his pale blue eyes met hers in a rare moment of honest intimacy. They had been friends. They had been playmates. But this was something new.

Hannah wanted him to keep looking at her like that for the rest of the day. Then she remembered his last comment and couldn't stop herself from saying, "I am not vain."

Klauden's eyes traveled down her face to her bare shoulders, her torso encased in the tight satin, and then back up again. "I would never have guessed such a thing, my Lady," he said, in the perfect tone of the Second Family.

She scoffed, knowing that tone for what it was, complete flattery without honesty, sarcasm disguised as civility. They had long grown out of such niceties when alone, though they often put on a good show around her father and their teacher. Klauden's parents had raised a proper vampire, and he always behaved as such when they were in public. When they were alone, though, as they were more and more often of late, their tone always changed.

"Don't call me that," Hannah snapped, not knowing why the title should bother her, and she reached out to playfully tap his shoulder.

Klauden stood up, pushed the chair back with a smooth motion, and looked down at her. "As you wish," he said quietly. "But you know that you are lovely," he added. "Come here." His height sometimes surprised her. At barely five feet, Hannah knew everyone was taller than she was, but Klauden didn't tower over her as some of the other men in the castle. He wasn't a small man, but slender built, and his chin rested comfortably on top of her head when he leaned toward her, enfolding her in a deep embrace. His arms were wiry but sure, and Hannah was glad that he wasn't muscle bound like some of the other men. An image of Vailen van Joosen, First Son of the Third Family, flashed into her mind, his broad chest and thick arms, that wide face just starting to sprout a thin ginger fuzz, and she shuddered against Klauden's chest. She was glad that Klauden was to be hers; Vailen would not have been so easy to live with.

She thought of the look on the big boy's face when she had first bested him with her daggers. He would not forget that humiliation, and she had known then that she had not earned only her teacher's approval, but her underling's enmity. She was her father's daughter, after all. Such hatred could be put to use someday. Hannah just hoped she found that purpose before Vailen's slow mind had the time to plot something against her. Such thoughts were common, and she dismissed them, sinking into Klauden's chest.

"*Chaivin*," he whispered into her hair, pulling her tighter.

Hannah returned the embrace with more enthusiasm than he expected, and pressed against him with the full length of her body. He tried awkwardly to compensate for the movement. He may be First Son, born with the vampire's dexterity, but he was no warrior, and he stumbled, feet tripping over each other as he stepped back into the chair. The chair tipped on to its side, and Klauden's arms tangled in Hannah's skirts as he tried to right them both. They went down in a heap, Hannah's forehead striking his nose with a crunch that echoed in her skull. The smell of warm blood filled the air, and Hannah struggled against her first impulse to lunge for it, instead focusing on righting her limbs and rearranging her skirts. The scent filled her, the temptation to find the source and satisfy the need as she tried to regain control. Then Klauden's hand found her bare leg, and his fingers brushed against the skin of her thigh. She froze, unable to fight the new desire that ran through her, one so closely linked to the rising bloodlust.

Don't be ridiculous! She snapped at her body. *You are no fledgling, subject to spells of uncontrollable bloodfever. You are a pureblood, and you should be able to control yourself by now!* It had been a long time since she had been at the mercy of her needs, and she closed her eyes, kneeling amid a tumble of skirts, taking a long slow breath to calm her galloping heart. She didn't need to breathe, but the ritual gave her something to focus on. She was aware of a brief chant, and she felt a small surge of power as Klauden used his magic to heal his bloodied nose. There was subtle movement in front of her, and then Klauden's hands pressed down hard on her thighs, the firm pressure a comfort against the raging need. There was nothing untoward in his touch. He didn't speak, only held himself there, comforting and soothing. She pictured the ever judgmental eyes of Kelvin Malbrek seeing her now, and the desire disappeared in a warm rush of embarrassed heat. Klauden sensed her discomfort and removed his hands, leaning back out of reach, his long legs folding beneath him.

"Forgive me," he muttered, and Hannah could hear the self-recrimination in his voice.

"It was my fault," she insisted, her voice strained as the effects of the bloodfever faded. "I knocked us off balance." Her fangs were huge in her mouth, but she could feel them starting to retract as her pulse slowed, the promise of blood no longer a temptation.

"It is I who has no balance," Klauden countered. They both laughed at the honesty in his words and the tense moment broke.

"Point taken," Hannah chuckled hollowly, finally getting her dress into enough order to stand up. She paused before standing to give her head a moment to settle into normalcy, and she snuck a look at his pensive face.

"You have not had an episode like that in quite some time," he said quietly. Hannah looked away.

"I know," she admitted, feeling the flush as her face reddened. *To lose control like a common fledgling*, she thought miserably, and on the heels of that -- *my father would be furious.* "I thought I was done with that."

She recalled a series of such episodes -- when Anna had split her forehead against the steps; when Klauden had shattered a glass with a cascade of books, slicing his arm to the bone - and each time, her betrothed was there, calling her back to the moment, calming the fury of her blood. She thought of Anna for a moment, at the curiosity in her stepsibling's face, at the questions that her dear friend would never ask.

Though they shared the same father, Anna hadn't been subject to such desperate episodes. Neither was Klauden. Hannah was not happy to be reminded of her shortcomings yet again. It was bad enough that she couldn't call her magic without the aid of words;

losing control was shameful. She had been a child the last time it happened in public, and Hannah knew that if anyone had seen what had just happened, she might have an unfortunate accident, sooner rather than later. Magnus van Kreeosk did not have daughters who suffered from bloodfever.

"I just wish I knew why it happened," she said finally, watching the explanations flitter across Klauden's face. In the end, he said nothing and only nodded. She stood up in a rush, skirts swishing, though she barely heard them. She wanted to go back to her rooms, take off this dress, curl up in a corner, and die of embarrassment.

Klauden was still sitting. One corner of the carpet had flipped up, dislodged by their tumble. Hannah was surprised that it was still in one piece. The things in the library were ancient. Sometimes she would touch a book and the corners would crumble. She was careful to never let Klauden see when that happened. He was so particular about the books.

He leaned over to flip the rug back into place, one leg stretched out beneath him, when she stopped him. "Wait, what is that?"

"What is what?" he asked, hand holding the faded red edge.

She pointed at the stone floor beneath the rug, taking a delicate step over his outstretched leg. She lifted the fallen chair and pushed it aside. "That!" she said, and knelt down to trace a faint line in the floor - a line that was too straight to be the result of the ancient castle settling. Klauden peered at it, slapping her hand away as he traced the air above the crack. At her frown, he said, "There is magic here, *chaivin*." His brow furrowed with concentration, eyes closed, and then his hand froze, seeming to hit some invisible barrier. "Right here."

"What is it?" she whispered, not wanting to break his focus. Klauden held his hand steady, tensing up a little, and Hannah felt the echo of the magic from where she knelt. Then his hand pressed forward, down to the floor. His fingers traced the line carefully, and he was rewarded with a low snick as something shifted beneath the floor. A small square of stone fell into the new opening, and then slid aside, revealing a cubby about four inches deep. There was a book inside.

Hannah scoffed, sitting back. She'd been so excited to find

something interesting. She sighed, "Great. Yet another book."

Klauden reached cautiously into the opening, and lifted the book gently into the air. Hannah watched with a bored expression. Maybe the book was old enough to disintegrate when the air hit it. That would be somewhat interesting to see. She waited while her eyes scanned for the dust trail that would signal the start of the process.

Unfortunately, the book held firm, and Klauden placed it on the rug next to the hole. He peered into the opening again, and pulled out a silver necklace. A crude rendering of the moon hung from a thin chain. He held it up, the pendant swinging in the silent library, and handed it out to her.

"And a shiny for you, my dear," he offered, and she swatted his hand away.

"I don't want it," she told him, getting to her feet. "It's like a child's trinket."

"People don't take such pains to hide children's toys," he said. "This is old magic."

"Of course it's old magic. Everything down here is ancient. This library is older than my father." She took a few steps away from him, and then turned back. He was still looking at the opening, head cocked in that scholar's inquiry that came of long hours spent buried in some kind of book. It was a welcome distraction though. She could use some time to herself. She walked over to the table where he had been sitting, pulling an oil lamp to the edge. She could see in the dark, of course, all purebloods could, but it would require her to call on her night vision, and with the memory of the bloodlust still tingling in her skin, she didn't think it wise to tempt her senses. The lantern would lend sufficient light to get up the stairs and back to the main level of the castle. From there, she could disappear into her rooms.

She heard the snick as the hidden panel closed and the thump of the carpet as Klauden replaced it. He stood up, and took a few awkward steps towards her, face pressed close to the book already open in his hands. The locket was dangling from between his fingers, jangling back and forth and bouncing against the red robes he always wore, his eyes already skimming the words. It had always boggled her mind to see how fast he could read.

"*Chaivin*," he whispered, and though she had expected the

distant dismissal of the fascinated scholar, something in his tone made her pause and give him her full attention. "You need to look at this," he added, eyes rising from the page to meet hers.

"Why?" she asked, trying to ignore the frisson of fear that zinged up her spine at that look. "You know I don't enjoy reading."

"You want to read this one, I think."

She sighed, shaking her head and holding out her hand. "Fine," she said, fully expecting him to hand her some tome about the history of mating rituals. "I imagine it will be a scintillating read."

"It might be," Klauden said, holding her gaze as he handed the book over. "It was written by your grandmother."

~~~

Hannah sat staring straight ahead, her blurred vision skewing the fading lantern light. It didn't matter if she kept her eyes open or closed. The words had burned themselves across her vision, her grandmother's loopy scrawl pressed hard against the pages of the journal as if forced down by the weight of her secrets.

> *I do not care anymore. I know what they would say if they knew and I know what I would say if it was someone else, but none of that matters. I care no more for the court of public opinion now than I did then, though I realize such cares would probably keep me alive longer. It's only a matter of time, now.*

Hannah shook her head. *Who would think such things?* Hannah scoffed, the sound somewhere between a cough and a sob. *And what moronic imbecile would commit such thoughts to paper?* Hannah was suddenly very glad for her father's good sense - he would never have been so foolish. As for her mother, well, the journal spoke to that very issue.

She had been sitting in the chair in the corner of her front room for the better part of two days now. The first day had been spent plowing through the handwritten diary, hands gripping the book with ever-increasing fury as she continued to read.

> *He is so much more than I ever thought*

possible. I have been so wrong for hundreds of years. If I have already been living my life so poorly, then perhaps what comes next is not such a crime after all. I never do what I want to do, anyway. The time has come to put my desires first for once. I will not be sorry for it.

Hannah snorted. As if Isla van Lartner had ever wanted for anything. As if the Lady of the First Family of Lartner castle could ever suffer as these words seemed to suggest. The woman should quit her pathetic whining and get on with the business of bringing pride to the family name. Hannah paused at the thought, hearing echoes of her father in it, and wondered if she would suddenly understand him so well if she hadn't just learned a mind-blowing secret.

Her mother, the late esteemed Lady Alin van Kreeosk, nee Lady Alin van Lartner, was a half-breed. Worse than that, even, because apparently her father, Hannah's grandfather, was a mere human, some wandering rogue with whom her grandmother had rutted with during one of her brief trips beyond the castle proper. Hannah shuddered anew at the thought. She winced as she looked down at her hands, an echo of her mother's small hands, and fought her revulsion at the knowledge that human blood tainted her history.

Hannah had never met her grandparents. Her father was older; his father had been dead for centuries when Hannah was born. There were some whispers that perhaps Magnus had hurried his father on to that end, but such talk was common in the castle. Everyone was always speculating. But, she still heard the occasional word about her maternal grandmother. According to the gossip, Isla van Lartner was the perfect mate to her husband Gerter; they ruled as First Family in their castle as Hannah's father did here. Hannah was certain that if anyone had even suspected that Alin was not Gerter's child, Isla would be long dead, either publicly executed or privately dealt with. She wasn't certain about the way Gerter van Lartner ran his castle, but she doubted that such a secret would have survived long among her people. Most of the purebloods could read surface thoughts, and some were gifted enough to see into the depths with some prying. Hannah had spent a good part of her life learning to put walls up in her mind, never thinking anything unless she was alone in her rooms, and even then, sometimes curbing her true feelings.

With Klauden, she could be more free - there was nothing that she could hide from him anyway.

The thought made her stomach lurch anew. What would he think, once he found out? Hannah could not keep the secret, certainly not from him. Hell, she would be lucky to keep it from the others in the castle. She enjoyed certain privileges as First Daughter, special treatment that she had always enjoyed until now, but she was also under constant scrutiny - not just the other First Families, but the Kargin as well.

Hannah closed her eyes, imagining the scandal when it was revealed that not only was she not a pureblood, but that even those second sons and daughters of the Kargin had better heritage than she did. Livenna already watched her constantly, and rumor had it that the girl's abilities to see hidden desires would only continue to grow. It was only a matter of time until her father's other daughter learned the truth. Hannah wanted to have faith in her own cleverness, but she was enough of a pragmatist to know her own limits. She could run circles around Livenna with her daggers, or even with her own version of magic, but Livenna could see into people, and Hannah knew it was just too risky.

What would happen to her then? She didn't think they would execute her, sacrificed to Cairn; it had been her grandmother's folly, not hers, but they would certainly take her position and title. Hannah wondered why that seemed worse, somehow. She assumed that word would travel either way to Gerter van Lartner, and Isla would face her own fate. She couldn't bring herself to care. The woman had brought shame to her entire family, a degradation that now shadowed Hannah as well.

Oh, Klauden, she thought miserably. She felt a sudden stab of hatred for her betrothed, unexpected and shocking. This was all his fault. If he could only learn to leave books alone. Some things were not meant to be read, or written down.

Hannah glared at the book on her lap, her hatred finding a new target. How had the book even come to be there? She knew, of course. Alin must have brought it with her when she came to this castle, to keep her mother's secret safe. How had Alin managed to hide among them for so long? Hannah wondered how a half-blood could have survived. She thought of the look on her mother's face when Malbrek led her into that room, haggard with sickness, and a memory that had always been poignantly sad was suddenly laced with rage. Her mother had known what she was, and had said nothing. Granted, Hannah had been a child when her mother died, but surely, forty years was enough time to share the secret with her only child, to warn her somehow.

She threw the book across the room, pages fluttering as it thumped to the ground. It was too much.

She needed to talk to Klauden. He would know what to do.

She couldn't bring herself to get up, to leave this chair, never mind this room. She contemplated a move into her bedroom where she could curl up on the bed, but she didn't want to lie down. It would be too easy to curl up into a ball and never move again.

It wasn't uncommon for her to spend days in her rooms, and no one would comment on it, but she had been careful to hide the book under her skirts whenever a servant or slave came in. She had skipped a meal the day before, not interested in the thin man who stood before her, his downcast eyes and skin pale. She had always enjoyed taking the blood, but not now. She didn't know if she could control herself in this emotional state. It was one thing to kill the slave - she wasn't in the habit of biting slaves and allowing them to turn - but she thought she might make a mess of things, and that would certainly get around. News that the normally meticulous Lady van Kreeosk had made sport of her meal would cause people to start paying attention.

For all that being First Daughter had its privileges, there were moments when she wished she could be invisible.

She wasn't sure how much time had passed when she heard the snick of the secret door open in her bedroom. It was Klauden, of course. They had been using the hidden passages to get to one another's rooms since they were children. She heard the panel slip back into place, and then the slow footsteps of her betrothed as he walked around her bed. Though the door was in her bedroom, Klauden was always careful to walk swiftly passed her bed, never looking at the canopy-draped place where she slept, not glancing to the side to the small alcove that held her wardrobe. He pushed aside the curtain that hung between her bedroom and the sitting room, and stepped inside. Hannah wondered if he already knew. She watched his face, and waited for the telltale sign of revulsion that showed he knew everything. She knew what her father would say when he found out, the disgust that would curl his lip. She waited to see that expression now on Klauden's face. It would be new. Sometimes she had done things that annoyed him or disappointed him, but she had never seen disgust. She wondered what it would feel like.

Instead, he merely walked across the room, knelt before where she perched on the chair, and took her hands. She could feel the fine tremble running through him. Underneath that, she sensed something else, a small sense of satisfaction, as if a long-standing mystery had suddenly been solved, the final puzzle piece slipped into place. She could almost hear him filing the name away for future research - the rogue named Kerrin who was her maternal grandfather.

"It does not matter," he said finally.

She sighed, a sad smile curving her lips as she squeezed his hands. "You know better than that, Klauden."

He nodded. He seemed to consider for a moment, thoughts racing through his mind. Hannah couldn't get a sense of their nature, but she could sense the tension in him in the carefully controlled way he was considering and discarding solutions to this new situation.

"No one else needs to know," he suggested.

She gave him a pointed look. "You may be able to keep this a secret," she told him, "but not me." She sighed. "I never was very good at building walls." She could see the objection starting to form, he could help her, he could teach her, and she interrupted him, "And if I started building them now, it would only rouse suspicion."

He nodded again. There was another moment, and instead of rushing thoughts, she sensed hesitation instead. Finally, he spoke very carefully. "I could make it so no one would be able to see it in your mind."

She tilted her head. That was something she had not considered. "What do you mean?"

Klauden looked away for a second, then met her gaze full on, his hands perfectly still as he held hers. "I can take control of your mind, just enough to make sure this information stays hidden. No one would ever know."

Hannah jerked her hands out of his. "Klauden!" she accused, horrified. "You can do such things?"

He nodded, a hint of shame quickly eclipsed by pride, and then both emotions were quickly hidden. "It would not affect anything else, *chaivin*. I promise. I can be..." he paused, as if searching for the right word, "selective."

She gave him a scathing look. "You will not mess about inside my head, Klauden," she blurted, slipping into the vernacular in her outrage. Something in his face fell then, and Hannah wanted to reassure him. "It's not that I don't trust you," she said quickly. "I do trust you. I know you would do a good job." She paused, and tried to explain the outraged horror she felt at the idea of someone else controlling her thoughts, the most secret part of herself. "I just don't want anyone inside my head. I can't."

He sighed, eyes almost pleading with her. "It's the only way to stay," he told her.

She nodded, knowing what her refusal meant. "I can't do it, Klauden, not even if it means I have to leave this place." *And you*, she added silently. *I cannot do this thing even for you.* Shame flooded her then, the awful sense of guilt at failing this critical test of her loyalty. But it wasn't about Klauden at all, or even her life here at the castle. It was about her mind, her very self, and she could not, would not, submit that to the control of anyone else, not even her beloved confidante.

"Then you should go," he said quietly, standing up.

Hannah reached for his hands and tugged him back down. "I don't want to go," she insisted, "but I have to..." Now it was her turn to struggle for the right words, "I have to remain myself." She peered at him, willing him to understand. "Do you know what I mean?"

Klauden nodded, his face sad, his eyes resigned. "I do." He looked at her for a long moment, face close to hers, and she thought that he might kiss her, but instead he stood up abruptly, hands slipping from her grasp.

"If you are leaving, then we have some planning to do."

~~~

They stood in the tunnels deep beneath the castle, ancient passages worn by water and time as much as the passage of people. Hannah knelt on the stone floor, a small brazier placed carefully on the ground before her knees. She placed her grandmother's journal inside the metal container, and then leaned back. Klauden moved forward, hands moving above the book, and Hannah felt the small surge of power as he used his magic to light the book on fire. She could see the tension in him, and she knew that part of it was from this last task.

Klauden loved books. Burning the journal made his skin crawl. Even though he had read it every word and committed most of it to memory, it still pained him to lose such knowledge, to know that he was now the only one who contained the words and when he was gone, the information in those pages would go with him.

Hannah watched the journal burn with far more satisfaction. Words were dangerous, and even the knowledge of those words was dangerous. She wished she had never found the damn thing. The thought was fleeting. Hannah's pragmatism did not allow her to dwell too long on possibilities of what could have been. She could not undo the damage of what was already done.

They sat in silence until the book was ashes, and then Hannah moved her fingers above the remains, swirling the cinders until the brazier held nothing that even resembled a book. Klauden reached into the brazier and the red glow drained away as he waved his hand. Soon, nothing remained but grey soot. Klauden had always been good with fire.

"You are sure about this?" he asked.

She shrugged, and adjusted her shoulders in the newly acquired clothing she wore. It had been Klauden's idea to dress as a servant when she left the castle. No one would notice her at all. *How often do you actually look at any of the slaves or servants here?* he had asked her, and she had nodded. *But they all look at you, he had noted. They all know your face, and we don't want your father chasing after you before you even make it off the grounds.*

Will he chase me? The question echoed again in her mind, and she didn't know which answer she preferred. It had seemed like the right choice, leaving. She could get away before everyone found out, before everyone knew about her tainted blood, before everyone looked at her the way she knew they would, gloating and pitying. She would not endure that. No, it was better to leave now, before anyone knew that anything was amiss. Klauden would know, but he was strong-minded. No one would ever get any secrets from him.

She would never get any more secrets from him either, Hannah realized, and the thought made her heart sink even further in her chest. It wasn't really a choice, though. Once they knew about her bloodline, Hannah would not be permitted to mate with Klauden.

Hannah wondered what would happen to him, if someone from another House would be sent for him. She had a brief flash of Livenna, the tall dark-haired beauty standing at Klauden's side, and she clenched her fists in jealousy.

No, she assured herself. *My father would never allow such things. Just as I would not be allowed to be with him, neither would she. We are both tainted.* It was profoundly disturbing to suddenly have something in common with her father's other daughter.

"I am sure," she said finally, her voice more certain than she felt. "I have to go," she added firmly, hands tugging the simple brown sweater tighter across her chest. The layers of skirt and shirt were familiar, but the materials were not. The cloth was rough against her skin when she moved. The outfit was loose and nondescript, and she was nearly embarrassed to be seen so in front of the man who would have been her mate. He must think her so plain.

Klauden nodded, seeming not to notice her clothes as he reached into a pocket of his red robes and withdrew a small pouch. He reached for the now cool brazier and carefully poured the ashes into the leather bag. He called on his power again as he held the pouch and tied it shut, and then he handed it to Hannah carefully.

"If you ever need me," he said seriously, "use this." At Hannah's raised eyebrow, he continued. "Take it out, pour the ashes, and call for me. I will hear you, and I will come."

"Klauden," she admonished, taking the pouch reluctantly, "I am going south of the mountains. I will be too far away."

He smirked then, and the look transformed into a genuine smile, the first one she had seen since this whole debacle began. "You will never be too far away from me, *chaivin*."

She returned the smile, and the moment was bittersweet. She would miss him. Yes, she would miss this feeling, but then again, she could not deny the small flame inside her at the thought of leaving everything behind, exploring new places without any rules or expectations. She would not have chosen to leave, but given the circumstances, she was adaptable enough to be excited about the possibilities. Her future was no longer written; she could do anything she wanted.

The only price was leaving Klauden behind.

"Come with me," she said suddenly, the words out before she could stop herself.

She saw the eagerness in him, the desire to throw everything away and join her in exile, but then his face fell as he remembered his responsibilities at the castle. She knew he could not leave his family; it was unfair to ask.

"Never mind," she said quickly. "I know you cannot." The look of gratefulness drowned out everything else on his face, and she felt the sharp pull of regret. Klauden was a good son; he could not abandon his parents, not even for Hannah.

Hannah had a moment of jealousy. Of all the things she would miss about the castle, her father had not even crossed her mind. She was relieved to be free of him. But Klauden was close to his parents. She had seen him bent over a book with his father, the similarity between them striking. Though Klauden had the look of his father, he had his mother's eyes, a warm blue that spoke of the solid morals she had instilled in her only son. Klauden was a good vampire, kind to the slaves, pragmatic about his meals, and decorous in his behavior. Hannah could not see him living anywhere but this castle.

They sat in silence for a long time. When Hannah finally looked up again, it was near evens; he would be missed if they waited much longer. Hannah rarely attended the public dinner, preferring the privacy of her rooms to the blood-filled glasses of the high table. It would take some time for her absence to be noted, but Klauden often attended evens with his parents, reminiscing over the day. It would be suspicious if he was absent on the day that she went missing. It was important that no one suspect he knew about her flight. He had assured her that he could keep such secrets, and now knowing the extent of his mental abilities, she believed him.

"It's time," he said.

"I know," she replied, but she didn't move.

"Come, *chaivin*," he encouraged, and stood up. He held a hand to her, lifting her to her feet. He reached behind to grab her backpack on the floor, and spent a moment helping her into it. The bag was awkward against her shoulders. She wasn't accustomed to such weight, but it was a minor inconvenience. The bag held her belongings, everything that she now owned. Perhaps it would be a comfort as she set out into the unknown beyond the mountains. She had a vague sense of geography and history, things that Malbrek had drilled into them in Essentials, and she knew enough about the humans to fit in among them, but she knew she would learn much more as she went. She could adapt. She was her father's daughter, after all.

"So, this is it," she said, standing before Klauden in the stone hallway.

"Almost," he said, reaching into a pocket. He held out his hand, a small silver object resting on his palm.

"A ring?" she asked, unwilling to take the small object yet.

Klauden nodded. "It was made for you. You should have it." He took it and slid the ring onto the middle finger of her right hand. "I want you to have it." A wedding ring would have gone on her left hand.

"Klauden," she whispered, not knowing what else to say. "I..."

"Don't," he whispered, one hand caressing her face, tracing the line of her jaw. "Just take it."

She nodded, wanting to remember the feel of his fingers on her skin forever. The weight of the ring was new, a reminder of his hold on her that she would bring with her into her new life.

He pulled her close then, and enfolded her in a tight embrace, the line of his body hard against hers. She rested there as long as she thought possible, and then for another moment more.

"I will miss you," she said when they separated.

"And I you," he replied.

"I just wish..."

"I know."

Hannah took a deep breath then, knowing that her body didn't need the air, but enjoying the comfort of the motion anyway. "Ok," she said firmly. "Let's do this."

Klauden walked with her to the small wooden door that led to the labyrinth of canyons below the castle, and the small paths that wound out of the mountains into the foothills. He opened the door for her, and when she stepped through, he did not follow.

She turned around to face him, his tall frame silhouetted in the doorframe. "Goodbye Klauden."

"Fare thee well, Hannah," Klauden said, the formal blessing for a journey.

Hannah nodded, glad that he had used her name, something reserved for the most sober occasions. Then she turned around and began to walk away from the castle.

When she reached the first turn in the stone canyon, she looked back. The small wooden door into the castle was closed.

About JM Paquette

JM Paquette hails from upstate New York, so she misses the snow, but not the shoveling, and now lives in Florida, where she hates the heat, but not the beach. She has an embarrassingly large comic book collection that is only shamed by her ever growing horde of cheesy romance novels, and she openly admits to being both a fantasy enthusiast and a roleplaying aficionado--both of which have earned her solid stamps on her Geek Card. She lives in Clearwater with her husband, her daughter, her big-boned dog, and a cat who occasionally appears at mealtimes.

Connect with JM:
Facebook.com/AuthorJMPaquette
Email: authorjmpaquette@gmail.com

Other books by JM Paquette
Into the Abyss (Anthology)
The Death of Jimmy (Anthology)
Behind the Veil (Anthology)

Kitten's Play

By Lisa Barry

"I thought I saw you on the roster this evening," Nikki purred as she opened the door. She took in Simon's tall, trim physique openly. His hair color, a medium brown, reflected in the harsh fluorescent light; his true blond hair hidden. Even the blue eyes she stared at were not his own, the deep green hidden by a bit of plastic. His skin, having a pale, stone like quality, was the only thing besides his general size that he couldn't change. She grasped his muscled right arm with her left hand and squeezed. Her right arm opened the door further and she pulled him inside.

"Yep," Simon said and headed toward his locker. Nikki was a flash back to the 80's. Her bleach blond hair was cut short and styled a little bit messy. Her small eyes always had a thin line of dark blue eyeliner around them making her eyes look even smaller. Hot pink lipstick, a blue mini-skirt and tank top finished her ensemble.

Simon pulled a purple vest from the locker, indicating His Bouncerness, and put it on over his form fitting long sleeve black tee before turning back to Nikki. He knew she had watched his every move. She had placed herself on the greeting stool near the back door and sat with her legs open, inviting. Unfortunately for her, Simon was not even slightly interested. He flashed an appropriately melting smile. Nikki smiled back at him like the cat that got her cream. One thing Simon did not have a problem with was women, unless you counted too many choices a problem.

He started out the Employees Only door and heard her loud sigh before it snicked shut behind him. Right now Simon was bouncer extraordinaire at a posh club, named after its illustrious owner, Kitten Lanagan. Kitten's Play was your standard, upper-class meat market for the young, playful and often foolish. It was not Simon's first run as a bouncer and he found the human interaction in such an establishment fairly entertaining and surprisingly well paying.

It was half an hour before the doors opened for the rich, frivolous and well-connected New Orleans patrons. They would get an hour of mingling amongst themselves before the doors opened to the lucky public the door bouncers decided to let in.

Simon made his rounds to all the party rooms first and ensured they were in order before show time. He surveyed the main dance area and saw everything as it should be. The huge floor was open and waiting and the band, some group of pop wonders he had vaguely heard of, were doing their final sound checks on the stage. Three raised platforms, one on each side of the stage for dancing and one in front would soon be filled with writhing bodies. The other side of the dance floor was filled with empty tables and loveseats, clean and waiting to accommodate. No one talked to Simon. They let him alone while he did his silent inspection. The servers milled about waiting for the masses. The owner herself, Madame Kitten, would be in a hidden dressing room preparing to make her grand entrance.

For fifteen years, Simon had lived a normal life and loved every minute of it. Well, most of it. He never stayed in one place for very long, so he never had the opportunity to relax and fit in. Truth was it would be dangerous for anyone around him if he stayed too long. His instincts would come out sooner or later no matter how much he buried them.

An outcast of his own choosing, he made the best of it and enjoyed watching, and sometimes participating, in the petty games all the while keeping a sharp eye over his shoulder. He changed his last name each place he went, moved on when his gut told him to and kept an acceptable distance from everyone.

A moment before eight, Simon stuck his head out the front door. Behind him, the main lights of Kitten's Play had been dimmed, the strobe lights were pulsing and the band broke out with their first song of the evening. Ezra and Chuck glanced at him. Ezra was a medium height, small-boned wiry guy. Even his hair was wiry. His wide eyes stared at Simon for a moment, out of fear or admiration Simon wasn't sure, then he nodded. Chuck was Ezra's opposite. Short but big and beefy, biker-like with a shiny bald head and piercing blue eyes. He also nodded and Simon stepped back inside to watch the peacocks parade through the door.

It was generally interesting. He got to scrutinize them as they came in. Observe. His knowledge of them had grown tremendously by and this job was a perfect fit for learning. He still didn't understand them though. Humans were an emotionally volatile lot.

Shana, a regular, came through first with her boy toy of the week. She wasn't very pretty, but being the daughter of a very wealthy businessman had its advantages. She leered at him.

"Hey, Simon," she drew out slowly but loudly.

"Evening, Miss Shana," Simon answered, his baritone almost swallowed by the loud thumping of the music. She did her best to slink by while holding on to her toy's arm. He guessed their evening had started early. Simon knew they would head straight to the bar where Nikki would pour their first drinks heavy enough to keep them spending for a while.

The masses came through a few at a time and Simon settled in to his standard menacing posture and watched. An hour later he felt his replacements at his back. He turned and nodded at the Bobsy Twins, Joe and Guido. Yeah Guido. The two burly Italian, brothers stepped up to either side of the door which allowed Simon to start his rounds.

Three or four hours later Simon came to the startling realization that something was wrong.

Madame Kitten had come out in her blond and sparkling splendor hours ago, but he hadn't seen her since. He was slipping. He had just finished a pass through of the party rooms, broken up a fight between two guys over a very proud girl, stopped someone from being sick in a corner plant and sent one overly pushy big girl wearing almost nothing out the back door to sober up.

He leaned against the left end of the long bar and motioned to Nikki. She was happy to oblige.

"Have you seen the Madame?" he spoke loud enough to get through the mind numbing noise. Nikki smiled knowingly.

"She said she didn't feel well and was escorted to her room by a young little hottie."

Alarms went off in the back of Simon's head. In his four months at Kitten's Play the Madame had never done such a thing. He frowned as Nikki left him to serve the patrons.

Someone touched his elbow and he forced himself not to startle. No one snuck up on him, ever. His senses were turned up too high for it. He turned and had to look down to meet the eyes of the petite lady standing before him. Her eyes were a deep ginger color; each slanted like one half of a yin and yang. Her nose was a gentle curve on her face and her lips were shiny and full. Dark hair fell down the sides of her face and continued, making him want to turn her about for closer inspection. A small, lithe body was covered with black leather pants and a tube top, showing her tanned, muscled shoulders. The sultry lips were moving. The music that had momentarily vanished flooded into Simon's ears and he almost flinched from the pain of it.

Coming back to his senses he leaned down to hear her better. He froze for just a second when he caught her scent; a musky smell that could only mean one thing.

Werecat.

~~~

Simon's defenses kicked in hard and he became aware of her every move. Her scent, her exotic look and the gleam in her eye were almost a drug. It took almost everything he had to focus. And that bothered him. Only once before had a women screwed with him like this. He was the one that did the screwing.

As he brought his head down to hear her, he scanned the crowd on the dance floor. There were several males cruising the floor methodically, looking over each person and moving on. He counted five. The low seductive voice in his ear almost made his heart stop.

"Would you like to join me in one of the back rooms?" it said. Oh boy did he. Simon almost stomped his foot through the floor he was so annoyed at his lack of control.

"I don't know what you're up to, but I'm going to find out," he whispered to her. Her pouty face flashed with surprise and then became hard. He knew that look. She put one arm on his shoulder seductively and started to bring the other down fast and hard. A smart move. One hit in the right place and he would be down, nerves scrambled and she could carry on with whatever she was here for knowing he wouldn't be able to move for a while.

Except for one problem. He was faster. He grabbed the incoming straightedge hand and twisted it behind her back. She actually snarled at him. He smiled his best shiny smile and looked into her eyes.

"What do you think you're doing?" he asked softly, knowing her were ears would hear just fine.

"What the hell are you?" she spat, her pupils large and dark; attack mode.

"Possibly a friend. Tell me what you're looking for Kitty Cat, and maybe I can help you."

Her eyes narrowed to slits. He waited to see if she would pounce or try something sensible. There was always a risk with cats. After a long moment she stopped struggling. He took a moment to scan the floor. They hadn't found what they were looking for yet. He wondered if it was even there. He looked back at the bomb he held firmly in his grip. The puzzled look vanished from her face and determination set in. He almost laughed. If you can't beat 'em, join 'em. He was starting to enjoy this. It reminded him of the old days before he had gone rogue.

"A man, a dangerous man, is here and we need to find him," she finally said, "and we need to find him fast."

"What is he and what has he done?" Simon asked. He could almost see the fur bristling under her skin. She was about to answer when he spotted one of her sentries from the dance floor heading straight toward them with malice in his eyes. He was trying to be inconspicuous and failing miserably; his impressive size and anger pushed him through the crowds. She saw him too.

"Let me go and Kasuchi there won't turn you into a snack," she hissed. Simon smiled at her.

"Now what fun would that be?" He pulled her around in front of him, keeping her arm at almost a breaking point behind her back. Kasuchi walked right up to them and stopped a hair away from touching her.

"Let her go or we will have issues," he said arrogantly. Simon flashed a smile that made his new friend pull his head back.

"Come with me," Simon ordered. He stepped backwards and to the right, keeping the girl in front of him. He found the door he was looking for and backed through it, Kasuchi following close. When the door shut, Simon released the girl. She rubbed her arm and he noticed her claws sinking back into her hands. Flunk that he hadn't noticed them before. What was his problem?

"Cough it up. If you're doing something pack related, I can probably help," he said.

The two cats stared him down for long moments. He was getting annoyed.

"Oh, come on," sarcasm gone, he let his annoyance show, "you'll rarely run into the likes of me and I'm one of the good guys." Kasuchi glanced at the girl. She was frowning.

"Sheba?" he queried. Simon held his lips together tight so he wouldn't laugh. Someone actually named their daughter too appropriately. She caught it and glared at him. Despite the emotion boiling from her she acquiesced.

"We have a stray on the loose. He's eaten three people in the last two days and we finally tracked him here. We have to find him before..." she trailed off. No imagination needed there. Simon nodded.

"Handsome, young?" Simon asked. Sheba nodded and concern flickered across her face.

"I know where he is and I hope we're not too late." Simon went to another door in one fluid move. He heard Kasuchi hiss behind him and Sheba take a sharp breath. They had no idea what they were dealing with yet. It came back to him as easily as sucking through a straw.

Sheba stuck her head out the door they had just come through and waved to the four others in the crowd. They quickly made their way over. Simon went through the other door before they could regroup and they had to hurry to keep up.

Simon led them through a labyrinth of halls to a closet door. Brooms hung along one wall inside, with a shelf above loaded with cleaning supplies. Mops and buckets leaned against the other wall. The back wall had shelves of maintenance items; light bulbs, tools, etcetera. Simon pressed the screw beneath the light switch and waited as the shelved wall lurched back, leaving a three foot gap.

He went through first and quickly covered the short distance to Madame Kitten's hideaway room. He stopped and looked at Sheba. She was standing so near her scent made his skin flame up. He smiled and touched her cheek. She startled and pulled back for a moment. Their eyes met and she allowed a small smile to tell him what he wanted to know. He glanced at the others. They couldn't possibly know what he was, but they knew enough. He waved them in close leaving only enough room for him to kick the door. He brought his fist up.

One finger went up, then two. At three his leg shot out with blinding speed and the door flew off its hinges. A loud snarl from inside greeted them as they spun into the room like practiced dancers. A man stood on the other side of the bed. He was half changed and smiled at Simon as he licked blood from one of his sharp and deadly claws. Simon shook his head.

"Now, now," he said condescendingly, "it's not nice to play rough with kittens."

~~~

The werecat stopped licking his claw to hiss at them. Simon felt a pang of pity. This one was just a kitten himself. One of the Were's closed the door and the rest fanned out to his left and right. Simon knew there was no hope for this one. A flash and Sheba stood in front of them all.

"Leo," she said her voice almost a plea. Simon didn't have to fight hard not to chuckle. Another appropriately named cat, but obviously one that meant something to this girl. She moved forward slowly and held out a hand, "Come home."

The half-man dropped his hand and cocked his head. Sadness ran over his face. "It's too late," he said softly. Before Simon's very eyes Leo's pupils dilated and hate overtook his gentle features. It looked like the werecat version of rabies. Simon stepped up behind Sheba and put a hand on her shoulder. She didn't flinch.

"It's too late for him," he whispered for her ears only. He watched a tear roll down one beautiful check. She wiped it off angrily and crouched. Leo pounced at her and soared over the bed. Sheba growled and prepared to take the tackle, take the fight. Simon's long hidden emotions surfaced. His protection instincts, long buried, surfaced with a fine edge.

Before Leo could land on the crouching Sheba, Simon's left arm changed in one fluid motion. His pale arm exploded to thick gray leather and claws ripped through his fingers, the sleeve of his shirt turning to shreds as it went. He grabbed Leo out of the air and with a one handed twist broke his neck.

The thrill of being himself, even if just an arms worth, rushed through him. He knew they were staring at him. He would have to leave again, sooner then he wanted. He formed his arm back to normal and arranged the broken werecat in a dignified manner on the floor. He pointed at the back door. "Take him and vanish. I will take care of the rest."

Three of the men picked up the body and a fourth let them out. Kasuchi held the door for Sheba. She motioned for a minute and he stepped out.

Their eyes met, igniting things in him that were surprising and scary. She walked to him and touched the strips of shredded cloth that hung from his left shoulder. She took his arm and looked it over, turning it this way and that. Simon kept breathing in, breathing out. Still holding his hand, she looked up at him again and searched his guarded face.

"You're a..." he put his finger to her amazing lips, feeling a jolt through his fingers as he cut her off. She backed away, pulling his hand with her for a moment and then let it go. He slowly brought it back to his side. She backed to the door, never taking her eyes off his. And then she was gone.

Simon let out a long breath as he walked to the other side of the bed to see what had become of Madame Kitten. She lay on the floor face down, her back torn up and oozing with thick red blood. She was still breathing; tough broad. He went to the bedside table, picked up her phone, dialed 911 and left it off the hook.

He didn't glance back when he let himself out the back door into the alley. Head down, he headed away from the club.

Not ten feet down the alley he smelled her; the thick, rich musk and something that was just her greeted him. She was crouched, hidden behind an air conditioner, waiting. He approached slowly, reached down before she could react and pulled her to him. She started to struggle but then stopped, burying her face in his chest. She sobbed. He held her close and smelled her hair, explored her back gently.

Leo had been her kin. He knew it like he knew the sun would rise. The scents didn't lie. He turned, cradling her with his left arm and started moving down the alley, away from the club. Away from one life toward another. She pulled away and stood in front of him, blocking further progress.

"We must go," he said softly.

"Show me," she demanded. The tears were drying and her invincible cat face was back on. He touched her face, traced her lips. She caught his hand, gently licked his palm and then bit down without breaking skin and shoved it back at him. He smiled. There was something very intoxicating about the mating ritual of cats. He never would have thought his mate would end up being one. He started to pull off his vest. He would have to go back to his other life now. He couldn't stay with her *and* keep running from his destiny. She knew about his world, his worth. But stay with her he would. He pulled off his shirt and wished he was wearing sweats instead of jeans. They ripped a heck of a lot easier.

As they stood in the shadows of the alley, the sirens still in the distance, he started the change slowly, so she could see exactly what she was getting into. His body became a roiling mass of gray shadow, his muscles bulged and expanded and his skin smoothed into a tough leather. His hair pulled into his scalp as thick skin and horns sprouted. He reveled in the feeling; it had been so long since he had been himself. He pushed ridges from his back and whipped his spiked tail around behind him. His jeans hung in shreds so he pulled them off. Sheba watched in silence, her eyes wide.

Simon had held the best for last. He stretched out his arms, for looks of course, and sprouted his wings; almost double his height, leathered and veined. He gave them a quick flap and then folded them behind. Sheba stepped up and ran her hand down his chest, touched his protruding jaw, ran a finger down a three inch fang. She stepped back and took him all in, her eyes devouring him. He stood still as a statue as Sheba pressed her body against his and snaked her arms around his torso.

He put his arms around her protectively and jumped straight up, pushing his wings out and catching the air in one smooth motion. He swelled with a feeling that he had almost forgotten. Happiness.

About Lisa Barry

Growing up in Florida was not a good enough reason for author, Lisa Barry, to avoid wearing black. A daily color choice, Lisa constantly pines for cool enough weather to wear boots.

Living with her supportive (and hot) husband and amazingly awesome kidlets, Lisa counts it a blessing that they still love her despite the deafening sound of her music muse throughout the house.

Writing and reading every minute she can, Lisa counts on the cats to keep her keyboard warm and on the countless gargoyles who listen carefully when she reads to them aloud.

Connect with Lisa online:
www.lisa-barry.com
Email: authorlisabarry@gmail.com
twitter.com/authorlisabarry
facebook.com/authorlisabarry

Other books by Lisa Barry
The Guardians (Book One of the Gargoyles Den Series)
Beyond the Threshold (Anthology)
Into the Abyss (Anthology)
The Death of Jimmy (Anthology)
Behind the Veil (Anthology)

Game Change
Part three of the Foo Fighters Series

By Robert Broughton

Present day – 60 miles northeast of Las Vegas

Twin Eagles stood on the rocky outcrop; below him, he could see the isolated three room wooden shack. Inside were his friends Spider and Gaza; outside on the porch steps sat pilot First Lieutenant Paul Strong. He had thrown their lives into turmoil and now, they would most likely be killed.

His relationship with Paul was hard to define - they were friends, but hardly knew each other. Eagles cast his mind back to 1944 when the two had met on an English airfield. Eagles had been an investigator for the USAAC (United States Army Air Corps) specializing in UFO phenomena. Pilots in Paul's bomber squadron had reported sightings of unexplained balls of white light, nicknamed Foo Fighters, and Eagles had been sent to assess the threat to the Air Force.

The next day on a bombing mission over Germany, Paul's aircraft, the *Retribution,* had been badly damaged. Several Foo Fighters had hovered under the stricken aircraft and kept it airborne. While extracting Eagles and transporting him into the future, and then leaving him unconscious beside the main runway in Area 51, Paul too had been rescued and sent forward to assist Eagles on his quest.

Gaza and Spider were from the present - fanatics about government conspiracy theories and UFO cover-ups, Eagles had sought their help. Apparently, a weapon was being developed in Area 51, which could threaten the Foo Fighters and humanity.

That problem lay just a few miles away. All Eagles had to do was come up with a plan to infiltrate the secure base and eliminate the threat before the NSA arrived. Eagles reasoned that the Foo Fighters would help him get in undetected, but his efforts to contact them again had been thwarted. The heat was oppressive; still he lingered to finish his Lucky Strike, reluctant to tell his team that he

135

had failed them. Finally, he decided to face the music and made his way down to join Paul on the porch. Paul watched Eagles approach, the familiar cigarette in his hand. "They can't be good for you, those cigarettes. Why do you smoke them? "

Eagles turned to his friend. "Habit. I enjoy them, besides I never know what to do with my hands."

"In this time, it seems unfashionable," Paul said.

"You're right, it ties me to 1944. It's my anchor I guess. Tell me, do you ever wonder why?"

"What do you mean, why? Wait, don't answer that, I know I'm going to regret it."

"Why you? One minute we are over Germany in 1944. Then we are shot down, rescued by aliens and dropped in the future. All to stop an experiment which started in 1944. I know why I am involved - it's my destiny, but I wonder why the Foo Fighters picked you. As far as we know, we are the only two survivors from the *Retribution*, so I am asking - why you?" Eagles said.

"I just happened to be in the wrong place at the right time, that's all."

"Well, from what I have seen, the Foo Fighters are highly intelligent. They work to a plan, so it's no accident."

"Then it's obvious, they thought that you may drop the ball on this one, so they brought me in as back up."

Eagles smiled and drew on his cigarette. "So, you're not curious?"

"Of course I am, but since I have no answers it would seem pointless to speculate. That is, unless you know something that I don't?"

"No, just making it up as I go along, like you."

"It's better that way, if you ask me. I would much rather not know what will happen to us if we try to enter Area 51. One thing that I did learn on all those insane bombing missions, your number can come up any time. There is no sense to it. I've witnessed too many good men die far too young."

Inside they could hear footsteps on the old wooden floor. Paul fell silent as they approached.

"So what's the plan?" Gaza asked as he handed Paul and Eagles each a cold drink and then sat on the porch steps.

Spider followed him with a beer of her own. "Yeah, I can't wait to hear this. Just how do you infiltrate the most heavily guarded and secret base on the planet and live to tell the tale?"

Eagles removed the Lucky Strike from his mouth and gratefully took the soda. "Thank you. Basically, Paul and I are going to fly in to Area 51 and save the day."

"Don't worry. We do this sort of thing all the time. Cheers," Paul said and raised his beer in salute.

Gaza laughed. "Fortunately for you two, we have a much better plan. Tell them, Spider."

"What you don't know is that the NSA arrested our families and are holding them in custody. So we need to go public in a big way."

Paul shook his head. "This may seem like a dumb question, but I'm new to the 21st century. Why would they do that?"

"Because, the NSA needed leverage on Gaza and I."

Paul smiled. "Then you have no choice, you should turn us over."

Gaza jumped in. "No, that would be playing into their hands; listen to what Spider has come up with."

"Organizations like the NSA are deemed to be a necessary evil, they operate with impunity. Truth inevitably gets buried under expediency. We have investigated enough cover-ups to know that vested interests pull the strings behind these agencies. It's time we exposed the duplicity and the lies."

"Do you think it's wise with your families in custody?" Eagles asked.

Gaza could hardly contain his anger. "All the more reason to fry their asses, we lose more and more freedoms every day. America has changed and not for the better, we fight for the Constitution."

Spider guided the conversation back on course. "No one has ever infiltrated Area 51 from the outside. We have wanted to expose their secret weapons crap for years. If you two are naive enough to think that you can just fly in and out while saving the Foo Fighters without a lot of help, well that ain't gonna happen. You will just end up two dead bodies in the desert!"

Gaza supported her. "Spider's right; we have to make your entrance very public if you're ever going to have any chance of getting back out alive."

"So what's the new plan?" Paul asked.

"Spider has all the connections we could ever need. We're talking viral internet exposure, and we need satellite coverage from the second you enter restricted airspace. There are private companies now that fly over 51 and taking photographs and video all the time. It's not illegal. Mainly it's for geological surveys. Normally, there is nothing to see - everything is done undercover or underground now."

Eagles was doubtful. "Won't that cost a lot of money?"

Spider laughed. "Yes, but we have a plan for that too."

Gaza continued, "The government likes its secrets to be secret. We need to make Area 51 a media frenzy in as big a way as we can. If we can do that, the government agencies will be too busy covering their collective asses to bother us, and the pressure of exposing their operation may be enough to get our families back."

Eagles turned to Paul. "That's a lot of ifs and a big gamble. What do you think?"

"It would create a big diversion and the security forces would be less likely to kill us if they knew that everyone was watching. From what I have been told, Vegas is the place to gamble; besides, it's far better than our plan."

Gaza and Spider stood and gave each other a double high five. "Yes! Finally we get to work our brand of magic."

Spider laughed. "We have a lot to do, so let's get busy. Vegas here we come!" Gaza followed her inside. "When you said that about magic, I assumed you were talking about Magic Mike?"

"The one and only...we don't have the resources we need here, but he does. We had to destroy our cell phones and if we use our laptops, we will have the NSA down on us in a heartbeat. Mike has the people, contacts and equipment we need to create a video, post it on YouTube, and use Twitter to go viral."

Outside, Paul turned to Eagles. "What was our plan by the way?"

"Guess I hoped that the Foo Fighters would somehow provide that; after all, they brought us here."

Magic Mike's Las Vegas

Mike Mulholland had inherited the family business, which had been started by his grandfather Stuart in 1914, eleven years after Vegas had sprung up out of the barren desert, and taken over the shop when his father died. He shared his family's love of the business, and claimed to supply anyone who was anyone in the Magic Circle. When computers had been developed, Mike discovered his real passion and built his own computer in the basement of the shop. With the introduction of the internet, Mike began to practice his own brand of magic. When a friend came to him for help, Mike hacked into secure government systems and only narrowly escaped with the data he needed. Ever since, he was obsessed with uncovering the government's dirty secrets.

The facade of the Emporium reminded Spider of the old English movie, *David Copperfield*. There were two curved bay windows and an old-fashioned eight light glass door in the brick shop front. The bell attached to the top of the door jangled as Spider opened it. Inside was an eclectic mix of the strange and wonderful, from Egyptian sarcophagi to guillotines, crammed in with barely enough space to move. The shop had always been like that, tradition ruled in Mulholland's Magic Emporium, or Magic Mikes, as Spider called it.

Gaza looked around in amazement. "I have never seen anything like this. Are all these stage props?"

"Every one. Some of the most famous magicians that ever existed willed their props to my family." The voice came from everywhere.

Spider laughed. "Mike loves the dramatic and is a bit of a ham. Still, it's always so much fun to come here."

"Just security conscious. Good to see you Spider, you know the way back," the voice said.

Spider nodded and led Gaza past the oak counter parting the heavy curtains, which closed behind them. "Keep your arms by your side," she warned as the section of the floor they stood on started to slowly descend. When they stepped off the platform, Gaza found himself in a brightly lit room. Mike approached and offered Spider his hand. He was a diminutive man who reminded Spider of Mini Me of *Austin Powers* fame. His voice was loud and booming. "Long time Spider, who's this?"

"This is Gaza. He's cool, we're tight."

Gaza held out his hand and Mike ignored it.

"You know my rules, no one comes here that I don't vet beforehand."

"I know, but we didn't have time to go through that. This is serious," Spider said.

"It always is, come through to my office."

The main room resembled the control center of NASA, with one whole wall filled with multiple screens. The room was a hive of activity. Briefly, everyone stopped. Mike rarely allowed visitors into the control room. Then, curiosity satisfied, they resumed their appointed tasks.

"So Spider, what brings you to the gambling capital of the world?"

"Mike, you better sit down. I've got a story for you."

Mike told Gaza to close the door, lit a big fat cigar and proceeded to create a blue haze smokescreen.

When Spider finished her story, Mike stubbed out the cigar. "You know, people say I'm strange. Are you on some sort of psychiatric medication?"

Spider crossed her heart. "Swear to God, it's all true, every word."

Mike looked at Gaza, who nodded.

"Strangest thing I ever heard, and believe me, living in Vegas is about as strange as it gets. So you need me and my team to create some serious media hype for you?"

Spider pressed, "Mike, the NSA has our families in jail and two genuine heroes are going to die."

"No pressure right? It sounds like fun, tell me the plan."

Spider outlined her strategy with the occasional prompt from Gaza.

"That kind of operation will cost. Not for me, I would do it for free just to stick it to the government. But the satellite surveillance, that's expensive."

"We intend to hold an auction, contact all the major press. Whoever bids the most gets the exclusive story. I think we can add in a fee for you."

Mike rubbed his chin. "I see, story like this one should be worth a lot, in that case my fee is $30,000."

Spider held out her hand. "Sounds fair. We are going to need a couple of laptops and a video camera."

Mike, knowing that he had been outmaneuvered, grumbled that he should have asked for $50,000.

Spider laughed. "Don't worry Mike, we won't sell you short on this one, we need you. How good are your connections at the local radio stations?"

"Good. I have several that I have used over the years. You want to do a few interviews to get the ball rolling? Give me a sec," Mike produced a voice-activated cell and began talking. "All arranged for tonight - four stations, ten minutes on each should be enough."

Gaza had been listening to Mike. "They didn't feel the subject matter strange?"

"You're not paying attention. This is Vegas, I could tell them that I am the result of an alien experiment and they would air the story. The local stations won't get you much exposure you know."

Spider smiled. "I need Vegas buzzing, that way we can get people out on the front lines at Area 51. Seriously, we need your whole team on this one. Time is against us."

Mike led them back into the main control room. "Listen up everyone, Spider here has a new project for us - one you're going to love." Heads popped up from monitors and silent, intelligent faces scanned the room. Spider suppressed a laugh. They reminded her of meerkats.

"Thanks Mike. Everyone, this is my friend Gaza. Both our families are in the hands of the NSA. Not because they have done anything wrong, but because the NSA wants to control us. There is a top-secret weapons project in Area 51 tied into the whole story. We have two people going into Area 51 within the next 72 hours. Your job is to make it very public – to generate as much media and public attention as possible. Mike will receive a video on why they need to fly into Area 51 and I need you to get it on YouTube and make it go viral. Government, military, major media, contact everyone you know and get the word out. Their lives are in your hands. Thank you all. We can really make a difference on this one." The heads disappeared and Spider looked questioningly at Mike.

Mike waved his hand. "No need to worry about them. They are just very focused."

Spider handed over a piece of paper with two names and serial numbers on it. "One more thing, you have to dig into the military files. I need everything you can get on these two men. You will have to go back before 1944. I need that for the video that we will send to you as soon as it's done, say two hours."

On the way out, Gaza and Spider found the video equipment they requested sitting on the front counter.

Once outside Mike's Magic Emporium Gaza turned to Spider. "Well, that was very strange. I have to say you impressed the hell out of me. There's a whole side to you that I never knew existed."

"Why thank you. I have to say that you're no slouch either."

Radio Station WKTI

Both Eagles and Paul had been coached on the version of their story that would best serve their cause. Neither man was comfortable with lying. However, they could see the necessity of keeping the Foo Fighters out of the picture. They flipped a coin and Spider went in with Paul while Gaza accompanied Eagles - two radio shows each.

Eagles felt very uncomfortable sitting with a big microphone dangling in front of him. Opposite was the D.J., 'The Duke of the Desert' Dwight D. Duran, or as everyone called him, Deranged Dwight. Dwight spoke so fast that, at first, Eagles thought he was speaking another language. Dwight then pointed at Eagles, and a pregnant silence filled the studio. Dwight raised his hands and said, "Say what?"

Eagles caught on and began his story. Occasionally interrupted by Dwight, he ploughed on. When he had finished, Dwight shook his head. "Don't know 'bout you all, but that's the biggest load of hooey I dun ever heard. But you heard it first on WKTI. Time for some soul!"

Paul's experience was no less strange. He found himself on Catholic Radio, opposite Father Rodriguez, who put his own religious spin on everything Paul said. "So, you and your friend Eagles are victims of oppression, illegal immigrants in this great country of ours, seeking a path?"

"Well, er...not actually. We're from 1944, we were transported here by a secret government experiment called Project X."

"Many of God's sheep are lost. Some never find the true path to Salvation."

"Right...so basically we have to go in to Area 51 to confront the people who have done this to us," Paul said.

"Hell is no place for a righteous man, but the devil must be confronted and cast out along with his demons."

"Amen, to that Father."

Paul and Eagles were driven from station to station. Fortunately, the next two stations gave them the kind of exposure they were looking for.

Lake Arbor Washington

Late that night Rice Knightly drove north from the Pentagon to his retreat, a cabin in the woods on Lake Arbor. The darkness mirrored his inner turmoil. Rice reviewed the chain of events, starting when Eagles had been found unconscious in Area 51.

The USAF had brought the NSA into the picture while Eagles was in the hospital. Colonel Grant had wanted answers and had been prepared to torture Eagles. Rice persuaded him to implant Eagles with a tracking device instead. Following Eagles' escape from the hospital, he found allies in Gaza and Spider. Colonel Grant ordered the arrest of both their families, an unnecessary move that Rice had disagreed with, as the NSA and USAF had more than enough resources to handle the situation. Rice had to admit he didn't like Grant - the man's abrasive manner irked him. It wasn't about territory or who was top dog, Rice's instincts said that Grant was either insane or truly evil. That brought up the uncomfortable question he had been avoiding. *Just what was Grant's agenda and what should he, Rice, do about it?*

The road wound between the trees, headlights blazing a trail through the night. He had driven it so many times that he could drive on automatic; allowing his mind to analyze his dilemma and dissect it like a surgeon. As he rounded a bend, he switched to emergency mode and his reflexes took over. The Audi A5 screeched to a halt, leaving twin trails of rubber on the road.

Rice sat and stared out of the windshield in disbelief. Heart pounding as adrenalin filled his body, he removed his seatbelt and opened the door. Standing only yards away a stag gazed back at him, unperturbed that it had almost been killed. Rice admired its magnificent antlers, its curiosity and its calm. He had hunted deer before and they were usually skittish creatures, easily startled.

"Run, you stupid animal, I could have killed you." The deer refused to move. Rice became aware of the sky between the tree canopies and noticed one star brighter than the rest. *Must be Venus,* he thought. It seemed to grow brighter and larger. "Oh great, now I am seeing UFOs. Get a grip Rice, there is no such thing," he muttered. Even as he clung to this stable fact to keep himself from feeling foolish, his senses told him otherwise.

The ball of light slid through the night sky effortlessly and soundlessly. Rice became transfixed. "Foo Fighter! It's a god damn Foo Fighter, I don't believe it." As the sphere descended, he was able to gauge its true size, about ten feet in diameter, larger than he imagined from the reports. Twin Eagles was right, not only did they exist, but they almost defied imagination.

The adrenaline in his system heightened his senses and every detail stood out in sharp clarity. It was one thing to read reports of UFOs, but it was quite a different experience to actually see one. The light shimmered with an almost mystical glow, alien, yet at the same time strangely familiar. Rice had completely forgotten about the deer. As the Foo Fighter descended, it enveloped the deer within a glowing sphere, transported it across the road into the trees and lowered it to the ground again. Rice watched the deer wander off as if nothing untoward had happened. Its task complete, the Foo Fighter began to leave.

"Wait," Rice moved forward and held up his hand, "Please wait. What are you? Communicate with me." The sphere continued to rise and grow smaller and in the blink of an eye, it was gone.

His mind struggled to accept the impossible, yet he felt a sense of joy, of wonder -something he had not experienced since childhood. Was this how Eagles felt on his first contact with the Foo Fighters? If so, no wonder Eagles had dedicated his life to the study of them. If only they had communicated with him. Then an epiphany came as a blinding revelation - they had communicated! Their intention was peaceful and they were not the national threat that Grant painted them out to be. They weren't some secret weapon, but instead highly intelligent beings - compassionate, beautiful, and serene. They had wanted him to know, to understand. One important question had been answered, but many more tumbled through his mind. What were they? What was their purpose? The reports he had read stated these aliens normally just observed, but with Eagles they had chosen to interfere, and now again. Whatever the reason, it must be important.

Rice reflected on his life as he sat there in amazement. When had life become so serious? When had he lost the joy, the wonder? Realizing he had been stuck in the tragic loss of his father who had been gunned down before his very eyes, he felt a great release. Tears ran down his face as he allowed himself to grieve for the first time.

The man who climbed back into the Audi was not the same man who had stepped out a lifetime ago.

Project X

While Eagles and Paul laughed as they recounted their experiences at the radio stations, Spider orchestrated the next phase of her plan. She had received the information she requested from Magic Mike: two complete dossiers on First Lieutenant Paul Strong and Lieutenant David (Twin) Eagles and any known background on Project X. Going through the files with Paul and Eagles, they hammered out a plausible story.

Gaza aimed a video camera to record the interview for Mike's team to put on YouTube. Spider asked the questions off camera. "Could you please tell us who you are and how you came to be here?"

"My name is Lieutenant David Eagles, I was born in 1921 in the Dakotas." Eagles rattled off his army ID and specifics of how he had been recruited into Project Rainbow. "In August of 1943 I was approached and volunteered for duty on Project Rainbow, a secret government project designed to use electro-magnetic energy to render a navy ship, the USS *Eldridge,* undetectable to the enemy. The experiment was conducted in the Philadelphia Naval shipyard. I have since learned it was both a success and a failure – the ship was rendered invisible, but terrible things happened to the sailors on board. First Lieutenant Paul Strong and I happened to be closest to the device at the time it was activated. We were apparently transported through some dimensional rift that formed and brought us here to the 21st century. We have been here several weeks now, hunted by government security forces because of what we know and because we wish to return to our own time."

"My name is First Lieutenant Paul Strong, United States Army Air Core. I was born in Clearwater, Florida in 1922." Paul also gave his military ID and history. "I was seconded to Project Rainbow which was abandoned by the Navy after the *Eldridge* incident. Much later, the Air Force took over the project and moved the research to Area 51, and renamed it Project X. As Lieutenant Eagles has stated, we were the lucky ones who survived the experiment. We are stranded in time and we seek nothing more than to return to where we belong. The USAF alone has the technology to return us to 1944, but our requests to the government for assistance have been rejected. We have become wanted men, hunted by our own government; the NSA and the USAF have other plans for us. We have no choice but to go into Area 51 to find the answers we need. We are going public with our story because we need your help if we are not to be shot on sight for entering a secret military base. We need your support. Please, tell everyone you know our story, petition your Congressional representatives. If you live anywhere near Las Vegas, please go protest outside Area 51. From the second our aircraft enters restricted airspace, you can view us by satellite. Please help us in any way you can."

Spider played the Devil's advocate. "Forgive our skepticism, but how can people be sure that you two are who you say you are?"

Paul answered, "You have our files, and we are prepared for the media to print our complete story."

Spider clapped her hands. "That's a wrap! Awesome dudes, that should really get the ball rolling."

Gaza smiled. "Great spin on the story, takes the focus off the Foo Fighters and puts it on the government. Once this gets out it doesn't matter whether people believe it or not, it will give us the media exposure that we need, and maybe, just maybe save both your lives."

"Gaza, we still have a lot of work to do. We need to get this to Magic Mike and then record the main interview for sale to the highest bidder." Spider hoped to get offers above $250,000 for the interview, but had no idea how much the media would actually pay. The book rights she intended to reserve for herself and Gaza.

"Right, and pray that the media don't find us before we are ready, or the whole plan will fail."

Pentagon

The agent behind him coughed and Rice Knightly turned.

"Well, are you going to tell me the bad news or do you want to play charades?"

"Sorry sir, Eagles has gone public. It's everywhere."

"Show me!" Rice stared at the screen. Outwardly, he appeared upset, inwardly he smiled - this was just what he wanted. "Listen up everyone. We have to find the fugitives - top priority." Since his encounter with the Foo Fighters Rice had undergone a radical transformation. His inner demons had been purged and at last he could see the truth.

He could no longer play Grant's game, nor could he stand by and watch. Grant had been right about one thing - Eagles was a very intelligent man, he had somehow found the allies he needed. Rice now had to figure out how to help Eagles. He sighed. This new development would certainly escalate matters. There was nothing like the scent of blood to stir the primal instinct of the predators.

Vegas

Magic Mike had been true to his word - his team had posted the YouTube video and it had gone viral within 24 hours, generating a lot of media interest. The story eclipsed even Hollywood and the White House as the topic of the moment. Twitter followers worldwide fractured their fingers in a frantic foray to be the first to bring the news. Network TV stations picked it up and ran with the story, dispatching choppers crammed with salivating reporters and cameramen to Area 51. Winnebago's bristling with antenna and satellite dishes headed for Vegas in a mad cross-country scramble.

The story was tailor made for the nighttime talk show hosts with their skepticism and sarcasm in corny one-liner's that received canned laughter responses.

"Area 51, UFOs, gambling and now time travel...Vegas really has it all."

"Vegas has come up with a new way to avoid your gambling debts, if you lose you just go back in time and try again...or better yet, go forward and find out what the winning numbers are."

Vegas prided itself that nothing was too outlandish or extreme. If nothing else, its citizens could recognize a good opportunity to make a fast buck and so seized the opportunity early. Motel and hotel prices skyrocketed; restaurants raised their prices and announced time traveler specials. Churches prayed for the salvation of the two lost souls in their services. Naturally, Elvis impersonators were interviewed as to what were the implications of time travel. "Why, we can go back and see the King, of course." "Why doesn't the government bring back Elvis? That's what we want to know?"

The police were soon overwhelmed and had to call in the National Guard. The crime rate rose by the hour and airports were overwhelmed as private jets and helicopters ferried in and out. Traffic slowed to a gridlock on every road to and from Vegas. Truckers, biker gangs, retirees in mobile homes, red necks in muscle trucks, everyone wanted in on the spectacle.

The situation spiraled out of control as everyone tried to put their own particular spin on events.

UFO fans dressed as aliens in green jump suits and masks with big dark eyes, and walked down the streets beside characters from popular movies and TV shows. Everyone from religious groups to representatives of NASA headed for Vegas - no group wanted to be left out.

Everyone chose a side. The only question was who would win, the two time travelers, or the military? Placards, flags, buttons and banners, each side proclaimed their support, which frequently led to fighting. No one seemed to mind, it was all part of the entertainment.

Susan Sandecker, a stylish New York reporter known for her sharp mind and even sharper tongue took center stage. "I'm here in Vegas reporting for station NYD, the New York Daily, and interviewing average Americans to see what they think of a very unusual story. Two men, claiming to be part of a government experiment gone wrong, have been transported here from 1944. They say that the government is now hunting them down in yet another conspiracy cover up. Who is telling the truth? And who will win? You be the judge." She was surrounded by hundreds of noisy placard waving citizens eager to be part of the spectacle. "We have a group of cheerleaders here." Picking out one, she offered the microphone. "Where are you from? And why are you here?" When the screams died down the blond smiled and posed for the camera, obviously enjoying the attention, "We're from Ohio, we represent Hometown High, Go Bulls! And we support the time travelers!" More screams followed, and then the cheerleaders performed a routine. "Time travel, time travel, go, go, go, Government interference, no, no, no!"

Susan scanned the crowd and spotted someone wearing a t-shirt and camouflage fatigues. She beckoned the man forward. "Good morning sir, can you please tell our viewers who you support and why you're here?"

The man grabbed the microphone, held it close to his mouth and loudly proclaimed in a southern drawl, "I represent SPITT, the Society for the Prevention and Intervention of Time Travel." He twisted around so that the camera could see his black armband with the letters SPITT written in black capitals. "We are agin time travel; it will disrupt the continuum and cause devastating catastrophes, many of which cannot be predicted, and if we allow it to go on we will all suffer the dire consequences," the man said in measured tones. When it looked like he was going to continue, Susan pulled the microphone away. "Thank you for your insights sir; we have many other people to interview."

"Furthermore...!"

Susan walked away, smiled at the camera and cut to a commercial.

Late night TV

Comedian turned talk show host Denny Devine walked before the cameras and acknowledged the applause. Thanking his audience, he held up his hands.

"Tonight we have something very special, straight out of Vegas where of course the big story is the two time travelers. The whole world is talking about this amazing story - two men claiming to be from 1944, brought here in a secret government experiment, now saying that they just want to go home. The government, in yet another cover up, is trying to hunt them down. I don't understand why they want to leave. If I remember my history correctly, things were far worse in 1944 than they are now. Am I right or what?"

Equally divided, the audience was very vocal and turned on one another. Cameras panned between the main dissenters as security moved in to keep them apart, then panned back to Denny who carried on regardless, "As you can see, this topic has polarized the nation. We'll be right back after these messages from our sponsors."

Outside Vegas

Gaza, Spider, Paul and Eagles watched the late night TV show on the laptop.

Paul pointed at the screen. "What have we done? It's getting totally out of control. We have every imaginable group on the planet heading in our direction. God help us if they ever find us."

Eagles lit a Lucky Strike. "Whatever happens now is our responsibility. We have to stay focused. Paul is right, the genie is out of the bottle and there's no putting it back. We follow the plan no matter what. Have you heard back from the major media? Are there any bids yet? Once we have satellite surveillance, we can go."

Spider shook her head. "They are all busy verifying the information we gave them. Seems there is some fierce competition among the major players, so we should hear back soon."

"Very well. Paul, is the aircraft refueled and ready to go? Heaven help us if anyone discovers the plane, then we're really up the creek.

"Yes, I'm sure it's ready, but I'll go check on it anyway."

Spider voiced her concerns, "I hate the thought of sending the two of you in there without weapons or at least a cell phone that can capture the events when you land. It would potentially be very incriminating to the government, but we know that they will do a full body search and confiscate anything we give you."

"Don't worry, this can only go two ways and you guys have done all that you can. Once we take off, it's up to us. It always has been."

Paul walked away and Eagles waved to him. "Hang on Paul, I'll go with you." The two friends walked together in the late afternoon sun.

Paul laughed. "Who would have guessed when I first met you on that airfield in southern England that we would end up here?"

"Not me. The Great Spirit certainly moves in mysterious ways, but at least I have learned that he has a good of humor. I don't know about you, but I find that comforting."

"So tell me, what do you think of the 21st century?"

"Not much – there is too much science and technology, and it feels as if they have lost something important."

Paul nodded in agreement. "Their humanity. It hasn't happened overnight though. Perhaps it was a result of the two World Wars. That has to change a civilization. There was something more gentile about England before the War, people cared about one another. Maybe I'm just old fashioned or just out of my time, but this media circus we've created is frightening, out of control."

"My people found it hard to understand the white man and his motivations. In the end they could not assimilate, and passed into history."

"Just because one nation is technologically superior to another, doesn't make them better, or even stronger, just able to kill faster," Paul said.

Eagles stopped. "You are a good man and a good friend."

"Let's hope that the Great Spirit has a plan as well as a sense of humor. We have had quite an adventure, haven't we? You can fly with me anytime Twin Eagles."

"Did I ever tell you about the legends that were passed through my tribe for countless generations? The old men would sit around the campfire and tell of mysterious round lights that floated in the sky. The *Watchers,* that's what my people called them. It was said they would only interact with someone pure of spirit. As a child, I never really believed the stories until my spirit quest led me to a cave.

"Inside were very old drawings of animals and stick figure warriors and the *Watchers*, you know them as Foo Fighters. I realized that they have been around as long as mankind, perhaps even much longer. My people were not the only tribe to pass on legends of encounters with them. It raises many interesting questions...I wanted more than anything to see them, and they revealed themselves to me. It was a day I will never forget, perhaps the best day of my life."

Paul found himself deeply moved by Eagles' description of his first encounter with the Foo Fighters.

"Since then I have investigated many such sightings around the world. It has been a fascinating journey, from Micu Picu in the Andes to the Sahara desert, and often in war zones," Eagles laughed, "and I have still no idea what they are or what their purpose is. Yet my life has become a crusade to understand and protect them."

Paul understood why Eagles had shared his story. He wanted

him to know what he was fighting for, and why he would give up his life if need be. "Will they help us, do you think, your Foo Fighters?"

Eagles shrugged. "Honestly, I have no idea. It's certainly in their own interest, but who's to say what motivates them."

Paul studied the face of his friend and thought he personified the Eagle he was named after in so many ways: his eyes, dark, sharp and direct, never missed anything, his bearing was proud and he had a strong soul. The Great Spirit had chosen well. Twin Eagles held no malice in his heart. Paul on the other hand, could not let go of the past. His heart lay in the moist earth of the English countryside, buried with his beloved wife and daughter. Even though the accident had happened in 1944, Paul still carried the pain.

Eagles understood that he and Paul had to each fulfill their own destiny. Therein lay both the salvation and damnation of man - he must forever move forward; there could be no going back.

War Room below the White House

President Terrance Alcott was blessed with good political instincts and a considerable family fortune, all of which he had used both to make his way into office. His allies were some of the most influential men on Capitol Hill. The powers behind the White House felt they had chosen well - Terrance understood the game and its rules, and willingly complied.

His Intelligence Services were there to supply him with leverage, J. Edgar Hoover style, and in return he supported them. The Armed Services loved him, because he never allowed ethics to stand in his way. The President eyed the men sitting at the large circular table. To his right sat the Secretary of State, the Intelligence Services and the Armed Services. To his left sat his own advisors. They had all been watching the news on several large screens.

President Alcott glared as he spoke, "How in the hell did you allow this to get so out of control?" No one wanted to be the first to put his neck on the line. The President fixed his gaze on the Chief of the NSA, Lieutenant General Roger Rutledge, or Roger Ramjet as he was known to his enemies.

"Mr. President, while it's true that we have been running a joint operation with the USAF on this one, it is they who have really been calling the shots."

The Secretary of the Air Force, or SECAF, Arty Goldman, in turn glared at Roger. He had just been thrown to the wolves. "Mr. President that's not strictly true, there are other interests involved." This statement was political code and referred to the powerful commercial interests outside the political arena. With that statement, the blame had passed around the table back to the President. The President slammed his hand down on the table. "This is not some game of pass the buck! You will both take responsibility for your respective organizations and sort this mess out."

SECAF coughed. "Sir, there is a problem. Area 51 is on a Code Red high alert, it's locked down tight. No communication in or out."

"What? Who the hell authorized that?"

"Colonel Grant sir."

"And who authorized him?"

The SECAF sighed. "The other interests that I just mentioned sir."

The President became further frustrated. No matter how he tried to throw this problem away, it boomeranged back. "Arty, why did you not inform me of this situation sooner?"

SECAF knew how the game was played and he rolled out the most hackneyed phrase in Washington politics. "Plausible deniability Mr. President."

The President felt his blood pressure rise. "Very well, let me see if I have this right - the NSA and the USAF ran a joint top secret operation involving two time travelers that were inadvertently brought to the present. Now, these travelers want to go back to their own time and Colonel Grant is inviting them into Area 51 so he can kill them while the whole nation watches...oh, and everyone knows about the top secret operation. Do I have it right?"

The whole room erupted as everyone gave their own version of events. The President could take no more and exploded. "I can't listen to this anymore. I am surrounded by incompetence. I have plausible deniability, remember? You caused the problem! You can all sort it out." With that, he stormed from the room, praying this mess didn't come back again and bite him on the ass.

The Secretary of State got up and followed the President from the room. He had briefed the President on the time travelers' situation the week before. The President turned and interrogated him with a penetrating look, "I trust that there is no record of your having briefed me earlier?"

"You're in the clear sir, no record," the Secretary of State lied. He knew how the President operated, and he wanted some insurance.

Vegas

Ellis Studebaker III, or Rogue as he preferred to be called, sat high in his monster truck in the parking lot of Costsavers. With one hand he sipped his beer and with the other he adjusted his police scanner. Bored, his girlfriend Cherry Delight tried to entice his attention. "Rogue, do you love me? Stop messing with that thing and pay me some attention, or I'll go see Duke." Rogue paid her no mind; he knew that women responded better to indifference. He certainly was not going to get drawn into sentimental bull. He had heard it all before.

The two pickup trucks on either side of him were exactly the same as his - painted black, with a roll bar and two Confederate flags flying from the rear. Country music blasted as the drivers sat on their tailgates guzzling beer. Sharing the parking lot were two biker gangs- one from Texas, the other from California - and a horde of Americans looking for adventure.

Something caught Rogue's attention on the scanner and he waved for Cherry to be quiet. "*All units be advised. We have the location of the suspects. The Eagle has landed. Repeat, the Eagle has landed.*" Detailed instructions followed, but Rogue was confused. The message wasn't coming through on a normal police band frequency.

"Hot dog, I think I found them - the time travelers!"

Cherry let out a squeal of delight, which quickly turned into a pout when Rogue jumped out of his truck. Duke saw him coming. "Hey buddy, you been with Cherry?"

"I found them time travelers! I know where they are holed up."

"No way! Everyone's looking for them, how'd you do it?"

While he brought Duke up to speed, a heavily tattooed biker with a Hell Raiser's logo on the back of his denim jacket wandered over. Jackal overheard the conversation and asked, "You guys for or against the time travelers?"

Duke looked up. "For...and who the hell are you?"

"Jackal. Relax, I just came over to offer you a beer, couldn't help but overhear." Jackal held out the peace offering, which Duke gladly accepted.

"I'm Duke, that's Pete and this here is Rogue," Duke said.

Jackal nodded as he handed out two more beers. "Good work," he slapped Rogue on his shoulder. "So you found them?"

Rogue staggered and looked embarrassed. "We have to keep this quiet. No one else can know."

"Chill, Rogue. This is what we all came here for, right? We need to get going before someone else gets on a scanner. What's the location?"

NSA HQ

On Savage Road midway between Baltimore, Maryland and Washington D.C., stands the heavily guarded headquarters of the NSA. A massive car park surrounds the modern multi-story building with its tinted bulletproof glass windows. Lieutenant General Roger Rutledge stood in his office on the uppermost level. The General was a powerful man. Wearing full military uniform, his chest was heavily decorated with medals. He lived and breathed the defense of his country by strong military means and held no illusions about the state of the modern world - it was a dangerous place where bad things happened daily. If people could read the intel that passed across his desk... He stood staring out the window at a sea of parked cars, his hands clasped behind him. The General studied his reflection in the glass as he addressed the agent behind him. "Son, I just got back from the White House where I had my ass handed to me by that pussy President Alcott. God, I hate politicians. They are the most useless people on the planet, self-serving liars, every one."

Rice Knightly sat patiently and waited for his commander to bring his attention into the present.

The General turned and fixed his steel grey eyes like a bayonet on Rice. "I pulled you out of the Pentagon son, because we are no longer running a joint operation on this one. The SECAF Arty Goldman has dropped the ball badly and now he's ducking for cover while he tries to push us into the firing line. Well, I won't have the NSA become the target for everyone else's incompetence. I want you to work from here and report only to me. Bring me fully up to speed. I have read the reports, but I need your insight."

"Yes sir." Rice explained the predicament, but carefully omitted his own encounter with a Foo Fighter.

"No wonder Arty is passing the buck. This is a major debacle. I can see why the time travelers went public. They needed to get public support so they put a spin on the story. Clever, it paints us as the bad guys. There is no sending them back, I suppose?"

Rice shook his head. "We still have no idea how the Foo Fighters brought them here."

"Do you believe that the experiments started in the 1940's have continued at Area 51, and that this Project X poses some threat to the Foo Fighters?"

"Yes sir, I do."

"With 51 under lockdown and the time travelers missing, we have run out of options."

"Sir, if I may, we have no need to detain the families of the fugitives. It would send a message to Eagles if we released them."

General waved his hand. "I will leave that up to you, but find the fugitives first. We need to get back in the game somehow."

Rice returned to his office and had no sooner sat down than his phone rang. Agents of the NSA working round the clock, using a myriad of surveillance techniques, had finally struck pay dirt.

By backtracking the social media blitz, the source had been pinpointed as Mike's Magic Emporium in Vegas. Now they had a solid lead – it wouldn't be long before they had the actual location of the fugitives. Rice called a meeting and briefed his agents. He stressed that the fugitives were to be taken into custody alive. The might of the NSA moved into action.

Costsavers

The monster trucks lurched forward as one as the gang of bikers revved their engines.

The rival gangs, seeing them squeal out of the parking lot, quickly followed. The noise alerted everyone else. Tailgate parties came to an abrupt halt as cars and vans were hurriedly repacked, and within a short time, the car park at Costsavers was deserted. Word spread like a brush fire on a hot summer day and the exodus began. Vegas became a ghost town.

Desert cabin

Spider could hardly believe how well her plan had worked. A major newspaper conglomerate had agreed to pay $10,000,000 for exclusive rights to the story and the satellite surveillance was now in place. Spider, Gaza and Mike were sorting out the last details when Magic Mike warned on the video feed, "You have to go now, no more time, the NSA has broken through our defenses and they know where you are. Good luck my friends!" The screen went blank.

Spider galvanized into action. "Paul, Eagles, you have to get out now! If you make it to the plane, just take off. Don't wait for us, we will be right behind you, hurry!"

Eagles hesitated.

Spider shook her head. "No time for good bye, go please, just go!"

Eagles nodded and ran after Paul, but only made it as far as the porch when he discovered Paul face down in the dust. Ten NSA agents had him covered with automatic weapons. Spider and Gaza almost collided with Eagles and their hearts sank as they realized it had all been for naught.

"All of you – down on the ground now!" The agent in charge motioned with his gun.

Dixie music blared out as monster trucks and fifty motorcycles roared into view. Rogue slid his truck to a halt in a cloud of dust, let out a rebel yell and jumped down to lead the charge. Cherry stood on the roof of the truck clapping and urging him on. The bikers surrounded the agents and overwhelmed them five to one. Taken by surprise, the NSA agents were reluctant to shoot unarmed civilians.

Gaza turned to Spider and asked, "What on earth is going on?"

"No idea, but we need to get out of here. Follow me," she said as she barged the nearest agent out of the way and ran for their vehicle.

Eagles and Paul sprinted for the light plane, parked alongside the road on the other side of a nearby hill. They were panting hard as they started to remove the camouflage netting.

"Put your hands in the air and get down on your knees."

They froze and Paul turned to find two burly NSA agents in suits and shades.

Eagles was about to kneel down when he heard a thud,

followed by a groan. Wheeling around he discovered one agent down and the other cowering. Cherry stood defiant, a tire iron in her hand. She nodded, indicating the agent should watch his back. He fell for the ruse and she laid him out, too. Cherry stood and slapped the tool in her hand. "Well, watcha waiting for? My boyfriend ain't gonna be able to hold them government assholes all day."

Eagles pulled the camouflage out of the way as Paul started the prop. As the aircraft started to roll forward, Eagles jumped onboard. Paul taxied out on the same road they had landed on days before. "I don't believe it!" he said.

Eagles climbed into the front seat so that he could see out of the window. "What on earth?" On the road, as far as he could see, were bumper-to-bumper vehicles, stretched out like a giant snake. Paul pushed the throttle fully to its stops. "Hold on. This is going to be close," he yelled.

Eagles held his breath as the nearest cars rushed toward them. Slowly, but not fast enough, the aircraft began to rise. The lead driver slammed on his brakes as the aircraft speeding directly towards him filled his vision. The drivers close behind had no warning, and the convoy closed up like a concertina as each vehicle ran into the back of the one in front. The undercarriage of Paul's plane barely cleared the windscreen of the front car in line. Occupants of the nearest cars hung out of their windows and hurled a string of abuse at the departing aircraft.

Eagles looked down and watched vehicles ploughing into one another, as the effect rippled into the distance. "That has to be the world's longest car crash."

Area 51

The Nevada sun baked the forbidding wilderness known to the world simply as Area 51. A desolate place, it was ideally suited for covert weapons development and testing. Area 51 in reality is a very small section of Nellis Air Force range and the Nevada test site. The base itself sits in the Tonopah basin and runs about seven miles long with several runways, multiple hangers, and a radar tower. However, the bulk of the base is a maze of tunnels below ground, away from prying eyes. Groom Mountain range to the north skirts the massive white salt flat of Groom Lake.

The main concentration of the military installation lay south of the lake, with the longest runway running north to south, splitting the lake into two sections.

In 1955 the CIA set up shop at Area 51 and developed the Lockheed U-2 spy plane.

Ever since, the base had become a legend of conspiracies and mysteries. Airspace above the base is restricted. In these days of satellites however, few secrets stay secret for very long.

The situation that had developed within the last few days was far from normal. The eyes of the world had turned once more onto this desolate enigma and the military, in its usual paranoid response to public scrutiny, used its massive transport aircraft to ferry in thousands of extra troops, armored troop carriers, tanks and missile launchers. The whole base had been fortified with sandbagged missile launchers and bunkers. F15s flew tight formations above multiple choppers and drones.

The GeoEye-1 satellite, owned by Earth-View technologies, had been hired by a major newspaper conglomerate and re-tasked to a geosynchronous orbit above Area 51. Live images were now available on televisions and computer screens everywhere. Millions of viewers watched this new form of entertainment in great anticipation. The initial images were of an area roughly a hundred miles long, and then the powerful camera panned on the base and gradually smaller and smaller details revealed themselves. Viewers felt empowered - like gods they looked down on the puny humans from above. It became apparent that this was a very active military base. Thousands of troops were deployed around the hangers and runways, but the camera zeroed in on a group of men in the center.

Colonel Grant, surrounded by heavily armed soldiers, stood on the longest runway in the world. He pressed the communication device into his ear and nodded. "Affirmative. Listen up, we have a contact fifteen miles out, small plane. This is what we have been waiting for." He patiently watched the clear blue sky to the west through the simmering haze of heat. Ignoring the flies that sought the sweat on his skin, Grant raised his binoculars and felt the thrill of anticipation ran through him. As soon as Eagles landed, he would be captured and used as bait to lure in the Foo Fighters. Then, once he possessed the alien technology, he would be a hero, a legend. Grant always kept his plans simple.

Spider clung to the huge steering wheel of the petrol tanker, her knuckles white. She found the brake and clutch heavy as she crunched her way through the gears.

She sped past rows of parked cars in a blur, repeatedly blowing the truck's horn and scattering huge crowds of protestors. When they parted, Spider could see the armed guards and vehicles blocking the road. She reasoned that firing on a fully loaded tanker would not be logical. Changing down a gear, she put the pedal to the metal and blew the air horn continuously to signal her intent.

Soldiers raised their weapons. Spider held her breath, willing them to move aside. The crowd watched in awe, then cheered as the tanker roared past in a cloud of dust. She had called the guards' bluff and won, the road ahead was clear.

"Coming through, boys. That will teach you to mess with a modern woman!"

Miles away, Gaza drove his petrol tanker along a similar desert road that Spider was on; he too had charged through protesters and soldiers with the same result. In the wing mirrors, he watched to see if he was being pursued, but the soldiers appeared to have their hands full.

Warning signs flashed by: "*Government property, armed guards authorized to shoot on sight.*" Gaza pressed on and as the truck lurched beneath him, he kept his foot down and his hopes up. He thought of Spider. He had finally found someone to love and now he couldn't bear the thought of her in danger.

Paul flew the Cherokee light plane into the restricted airspace. No sooner had he crossed the border when an F15 fighter cut close by his prop. The turbulence rocked the lighter plane and they dropped with a sickening lurch. In his earphones, Eagles could hear the fighter pilot warning him to land immediately or be fired upon. Eagles watched two more F15s take up station on either side of him.

"So we were right, they want us to land. Is the runway long enough for you?"

Paul concentrated on his flying. "You know, ever since I started flying with you, it's just been one thing after another."

"There is a marked improvement in your sarcasm."

Paul lined up with the runway. Ahead were tanks and hundreds of troops that had been deployed. "Looks like they have been expecting us," Paul said.

The Cherokee lightly touched down and taxied toward the reception committee. The F15s overhead roared past on afterburners. Looking through the windscreen, Eagles recognized Colonel Grant front and center. Even before the Cherokee rolled to a halt guards surrounded them, their weapons pointed menacingly.

Ordered to step out of the aircraft and lie face down, their hands were tied and they were searched. Then they were brought before Colonel Grant.

"So the Eagle has finally landed. You two are in the wrong place at the wrong time," Grant said to them. Colonel Grants Bluetooth chirped an update that two petrol tankers had broken through the security checkpoints. He ordered the remote control Predators to destroy the tankers, and then ordered the Cherokee destroyed.

Within seconds the Cherokee exploded, the blast hot against their backs. Debris rained down as the colonel stood and stared through his sunglasses. In the distance, two more explosions rang out and thick black columns of smoke rose into the hot air. "That will be the two petrol tankers you sent as diversions."

Eagles and Paul were shocked. It could only have been Spider and Gaza.

Grant watched their reactions and realized they had not planned the diversions. This was icing on the cake. He gloated, "You saved me the trouble of rounding up your friends and executing them."

Paul glared at Grant. "You know Eagles, the Air Force isn't what it used to be."

Colonel Grant smashed him in the face, blooding his nose. "You two have caused me enough trouble."

Paul spit blood over the Colonel's uniform. "Your time is about to run out Mister."

Colonel Grant ignored Paul and ordered, "Take them for interrogation and find me a clean uniform."

Remote controlled Predators began to circle the tanker. They looked like model aircraft in the distance, but Gaza knew that they carried very real missiles. Surprisingly, he felt calm and resigned to his fate. Both he and Spider had known that they might never see each other again. The diversion had been his idea and Spider had readily agreed, though she had insisted they keep it secret. Eagles and Paul would never have sanctioned putting them at risk. Through the windscreen, he watched as the Predators launched their missiles. Time had run out and smiling, he watched death race towards him on fiery wings.

White House

The tension in the Oval Office was palpable. President Terrance Alcott along, with his joint chiefs, watched the events unfold.

Like the rest of the world, they could not drag their eyes from the screen. The satellite images showed the light plane land and then explode, two more explosions followed in quick succession. His desk shook as the President pounded it with his fists. He could see his term in office coming to a humiliating end. The powers behind the political machine would not tolerate this failure.

Area 51

Paul and Eagles were dragged into the back of an armored transport, hands tied behind them. Thick dark hoods had been pulled over their heads, and tasers had then been used until they passed out. Once inside the tunnels, the prisoners were transferred to electric cars and driven to the weapons testing area. Still unconscious, Eagles and Paul were taken from the cars and seated, tied back-to-back, in metal chairs that were bolted to the concrete floor.

Through the darkness, Paul heard his name being called. It seemed to echo everywhere.

"Paul, its Eagles. Can you hear me?"

"Yes. Where are we?"

"My guess is underground, the silence is unnatural."

"This was your plan. Now that we're inside Area 51, what do we do?" Paul asked.

"We wait."

Next door, Grant watched on a monitor from the control room. Finally, after all this time he would be able to bring the CEO of Allied Armaments, Anthony P. Hopwood, his prize – a captured Foo Fighter. What started as Project Rainbow years before, and later renamed Project X, had finally given Grant a devastating weapon: an innocent looking small black box that could immobilize or destroy a Foo Fighter. The scorch marks on the walls and the ceiling in the testing area, the result of countless experiments, were proof of its power. The demonstration he had witnessed only days before had been impressive. Colonel Grant had to succeed. If he failed, Hopwood would destroy both him and his family. There remained only one thing to do – push the button.

Eagles and Paul jackknifed out of their seats, in excruciating pain. Smoke rose as their flesh burned. In the darkness, Eagles tried unsuccessfully to breathe through the pain, while Paul fought his restraints. Colonel Grant increased the voltage and then pushed the button again.

This time their bodies thrashed around and their screams rebounded off the domed ceiling. When the torture finally stopped Eagles taunted Grant, "Ever since this all began you have made one blunder after another, and you will fail now."

Paul laughed and said, "Here I thought that the Nazis were despicable."

On Colonel Grant's command, several scientists wearing ear protectors, rubber gloves and welder's goggles, entered the room. Each held a small black box. They moved into predetermined positions around the prisoners, accompanied by dozens of armed guards.

The torture started again and the pain was unbearable. Blood trickled from the prisoners' mouths and ears and it seemed to last an eternity. Both men fought to stay conscious, but their minds started to shut down, a defense against the pain.

Striding into the room like a conquering hero, Colonel Grant watched in satisfaction as he circled the prisoners. Turning to the scientists, he made his instructions clear. "Check the settings on your weapons once more for immobilization and capture."

A transparent sphere began to form around the two prisoners, large enough to encompass both Paul and Eagles. It quickly turned opaque and then solidified. The prisoners disappeared from view.

Colonel Grant pointed at the Foo Fighter. "Fire!" he screamed.

The scientists switched on the black boxes and streams of blue electromagnetic energy streamed from the front aperture of each box, erratically forking their way towards the Foo Fighter. The air crackled with energy, and the acrid smell of ozone became incredibly strong. The Foo Fighter disappeared as quickly as it had appeared. Colonel Grant cursed as he fired his sidearm, empting the magazine into thin air where the Foo Fighter had been.

Coincident with the shots, the electromagnetic streams from the black boxes converged on the now empty chairs where the Foo Fighter had dematerialized. The energy began to build upon itself, forming a single source, which then polarized. Lightning bolts shot out toward the concrete dome and blew off large chunks. The scientists fought to hold the boxes steady, but when the energy looped back to the black boxes, they were thrown to the ground.

Huge slabs of concrete rained down on both the scientists and the guards, and several were killed before they could escape.

The energy continued to build as it looped around and around, totally out of control.

Colonel Grant stared in disbelief as the blue ball of unstable energy grew and grew. Too late, he realized the scientists had never tested more than one device at a time. Now the fools had abandoned their weapons without even trying to turn them off. Leveling his sidearm, he tried to kill them as they ran from the room but his magazine was empty. In fury, he threw away the gun. Now insane with rage, Grant picked up one of the abandoned black boxes and threw it towards the energy convergence. The resulting explosion soon engulfed him, vaporizing him instantly. Rapidly, the explosion spread into the tunnels, killing both guards and scientists.

Contained by the mountain above, the fireball followed the line of least resistance and expanded along the miles of intersecting tunnels, incinerating everything in its path. There was no escaping the carnage. Ventilation shafts to the surface became mini volcanoes as the inferno sought to expand. Large sections of tunnel caved in and formed craters on the surface into which buildings and hangers toppled.

Above ground the main battle raged as hundreds of Foo Fighters of various sizes appeared. Moving unpredictably at incredible speeds, they commanded the skies above Area 51. A platoon of soldiers trained in the use of the black boxes had been stationed all over the base. Their task was not to capture Foo Fighters, but to kill them. They were the first to be targeted, simply transported by the Foo Fighters and left stranded miles away in the desert, minus the black boxes. Those soldiers who remained on the base tried to lock their missiles on to the Foo Fighters, but the spheres were too fast. Automatic weapons also proved ineffectual, and one by one, soldiers began disappearing as they were relocated into the desert, scattered far and wide.

Munitions exploded underground and columns of smoke rose all over the base as more craters formed. Pilots of F15s, helicopters and Predators were no more successful than the soldiers had been. They were plucked from their aircraft and the pilotless craft crashed to earth. Incredibly, the battle lasted only a few minutes. Millions watched it all in total disbelief.

The Foo Fighters then disappeared - all but one, the largest of them all. The satellite zoomed in on this last Foo Fighter. As viewers watched the flash of brilliant light, their memories of the battle and everything for one week prior were erased.

The satellite moved on, no longer functioning.

NSA

Rice sat in his office watching the satellite feed in fascination. As events unfolded, he could see that Eagles had not needed his help after all. *Good for him*, Rice thought.

Rice walked away before the battle was finished, satisfied that Grant had underestimated his enemy and lost.

He had more important things to do. The families of both Gaza and Spider had to be released and taken home.

Gaza's home

Gaza and Spider found themselves outside of Gaza's house. They had been transported to safety, pulled out of the tankers an instant before they had blown up.

Spider trembled as Gaza held her near. "What happened, was it the Foo Fighters?" she asked.

"I don't remember, but it had to be them," Gaza said.

"I wonder if Paul and Eagles survived?"

Gaza shrugged. "We may never know, but I choose to believe that they did. No one is ever going to believe us."

"We could try writing a science fiction story."

Gaza's face lit up. "Good idea, how did you ever get so smart?"

"I was born that way, dummy," she said and kissed him.

Foo Fighters base

Paul and Eagles stood in a brilliant white, featureless environment. The silence seemed eternal. Even though they had not witnessed the battle first hand, they knew what had transpired. Paul scratched his head. "My injuries are healed, yours too. So that's it then, what happens now?"

Eagles smiled. "What do you want to happen?"

"I don't know really. I never thought beyond going to Area 51. I know that I don't belong here, in this time I mean."

Eagles received a mental picture from the Foo Fighters. Smiling, he nodded his approval. "You're right, Paul. This time is not for you. I can't thank you enough for your friendship. Good luck old chap. Fly high."

Paul looked down. His body had started to become transparent. Before he fully disappeared he asked, "What will you do now?"

"Fulfill my destiny, as always Paul."

September 12th 1944, Cornwall

First Lieutenant Paul Strong materialized outside of the stone walls of his cottage in Cornwall. He recognized the cottage, but felt confused. He had not been here since the funeral of his wife Penny and his ten-year-old daughter Constance, killed in an auto accident right outside their front gate. Opening the wooden door into the kitchen, he noticed the calendar on the wall. It read August 22nd 1944 - the day was circled, it was his birthday. How could he possibly be back in 1944...it was impossible.

All of his memories began to slide, tumbling over one another in an avalanche of gut wrenching emotion. Desperately, he ran outside, his breath ragged, his legs weak, and threw up over the roses. He could not organize his thoughts into a logical pattern. His mind seized up and he passed out.

Hours later, he awoke and looked around. He wondered where Penny and Constance were. Paul remembered that at breakfast he had pretended not to know they were going shopping for his birthday. "Well, I have time for a ride before they get back," he thought. Walking to the stable, a strong feeling of déjà vu overcame him. There was something very important which he had forgotten. The harder he tried to remember what it was, the more it slipped away. Paul saddled the mare and rode out toward the stone wall by the main road. He hoped glimpse Penny and Constance when they arrived home.

Things were strange, different somehow... He heard a car horn beeping and rode over to meet Penny and Constance parked by the side of the road in their red MG. Penny had a scarf wrapped around her head. "Paul you were miles away, penny for your thoughts?" she said.

Constance chimed in, "Yes daddy, you didn't see us pull up."

"I rode here so that I could see you come home. I was just thinking how lucky I am to have two such beautiful women in my life."

They all heard a long screech of tires, followed by the sound of a loud impact.

Penny looked to Paul. "Oh my, sounds like an accident outside our front gate."

Paul kicked his horse forward. "There may be someone injured, follow me."

At the accident, Paul could see that the front of a removal truck had smashed into their stone wall. The truck's radiator was leaking steam. Paul looked up and said to Penny, "The driver and his mate will be fine. They had a puncture and hit the wall, going too fast judging by the tire marks, a bit suicidal on these narrow roads. Better go make some tea and call the police."

Penny's face turned white. "Can you imagine Paul, if we hadn't stopped to talk to you, we could have been involved in the accident and possibly killed."

"Doesn't bear thinking about, I can't imagine my life without you two," Paul said firmly.

Penny reached down to kiss Paul on the head.

Foo Fighter base

Twin Eagles stood alone, his arms out-stretched above his upturned head. "Great Spirit, what happens now?"

A form began to materialize from the light that surrounded

him. Eagles recognized it from his spirit quest. The shape shifter appeared as a beautiful squaw and replied, "I see you Twin Eagles. You have come far indeed." Before he could reply the shape shifter morphed one more time, and Eagles could scarce believe his eyes. The materialization seemed to float on huge celestial wings. The androgynous face radiated affinity, a love of all creation.

"Is this your true form?"

Eagles heard the reply in his mind, "The Great Spirit takes many forms. Humans are not fully developed spiritually and by taking many forms we can guide them."

"Are you an angel?"

"We are what you will be, when your evolution is complete."

"What of Paul, Spider and Gaza?"

"Your friends are safe. They are where they should be for their own development."

"What about me, is this the end?"

"It is never the end. We simply start new adventures, you know that."

"I mean, do I stay with you?"

"If that is what you desire, all things are possible."

"When Paul and I were on board the *Retribution,* the Foo Fighter first transported me around the world to an aircraft carrier the *Enterprise*. Why?"

"Like humans, not all Foo Fighters are equally evolved. We were training a novice and he made a slight miscalculation. Like you, we are continually evolving. Are you ready?"

"There is one thing. It's obvious that your technology far exceeds ours, so why did you need me?"

"We had no wish to alienate humans by our direct action. You are a bridge between our two cultures, an ambassador for both sides."

Eagles nodded. "I wish to be of service, for the greater good, to make manifest the will of the Great Spirit."

The apparition folded its wings around Twin Eagles and they became one with the light.

About Robert Broughton

Robert was born in Yorkshire England, then immigrated to Australia in 1970 after living for one year in New Zealand. After marrying a New Yorker he moved to Florida. Robert's greatest pleasure is to create and as an artisan he specializes in making dreams reality. Working a wide variety of jobs in his life he has, to name a few: promoted Hovercraft, spent two years as an outback photographer and made wedding videos. Currently a member of the Ink Slingers Guild he writes for fun and is working on the third novel of his epic trilogy, MAGI.

Connect with Robert online:
Facebook.com/robertbroughton

Other books by Robert Broughton
Beyond the Threshold (Anthology)
Into the Abyss (Anthology)

Rogue

By Laura Price

Part One

Stepping into the dim jewelry store from the bright May afternoon, Devon winked, almost imperceptibly, at the waif behind the counter. His lady-friends half joked and half swooned over his roguish smile and devilishly good looks. Once, one had asked him what he would do without his looks or his charm, because deep down he was really just an asshole. She had been right, of course. He'd replied, "What would you do without yours?" She'd shut her mouth then and taught him what people meant when they said eyes like daggers.

This sales girl had those wide blank eyes that told him she was waiting for him to write a princess-fantasy destiny for her. She'd be so easy, he thought, that it actually took the fun out of the whole prospect. He sighed at her, under the guise of blowing his bangs off his brow. Women, really - he could just hold out his hand and they would wrap themselves around his finger!

He leaned over the display counter on one elbow and smiled at the waif-girl. Her boring gold-plated name badge had *Tabitha* stamped on it in black comic sans. Not the most swanky of jewelry shops in town, he knew, but *comic sans?* Lowering the natural tone and volume of his voice, Devon drew her closer. "Hello there," he said. He reached toward her breast and pointed at her badge, "Tabitha."

Seeing her cheeks immediately flush, he smiled a guilty smile. There wasn't a woman on earth, not even his mother, who didn't fall for that one. Women loved guilty boys. "I have a problem. Maybe you can help me?" He lilted his voice, quickly forming a question instead of the beginning of a narrated dilemma. Women liked to save the day as much as they liked to be told what to do. It was important to give them questions and options, make them feel as if they were seen as equals.

~~~

Smiling, Tabitha's face became less star-struck and more self-assured. Helping people was a role she played confidently. People were such lost, ridiculous creatures. Watching this man, she caught herself from laughing aloud at his over-acted heartthrob routine. *Let's see what he's up to*, she thought. In a demure voice she said, "I can try." She lowered her eyes to create a visual appearance of submission, but couldn't help bringing them back up for direct eye contact. She had never been good at being weak.

~~~

Devon took a mental step back. This one had a little spark. Perhaps she would pose a challenge after all. He drained his *confident liar* expression, dropped his gaze, and shuffled one foot back. Touching his face, he resumed eye contact with a smile that was a little more *boy-next-door*. "It's actually embarrassing, but what have I got to lose?" He gave an insecure smile. "You see, I want to look at the pendants over there, but I want to talk to you. I hope you don't think I'm too forward, or an axe murderer."

~~~

Tabitha laughed along with his axe murderer comment while turning to assess the counter across the store and the pendants displayed beneath the meaty elbows of her Aunt Gwynnie. This guy just wanted to talk with the pretty sales girl instead of the middle-aged woman. Mother's Day *was* coming up. She sighed and leaned back as she tried to think of a plan to show him the jewelry in the other woman's case. She appraised him again, and thought there had to be more to him than a pick up line to get a better view while buying trinkets for Mom. Why the bad-boy act for a Mother's Day gift? Humans, really - she could have an instruction manual and still not ever understand them. In this case, as in most, cocky or simple were both traits that inevitably landed all men in the same trap.

Aunt Gwynnie wouldn't raise an eyebrow if Tabitha were to simply walk over to the counter and show her new friend the jewelry herself. The moon, however, was on a schedule, and Tabitha desperately needed a man for the coming ritual. This one fit all of her specifications physically, and had walked his own self right into her web. Not to mention he was seemingly desperate for her attention. Letting him slip away unscathed would be a shame at best, and it would be her ruin if she didn't have a male to perform the act of Ritual Union with her at the new moon that night.

She looked at his chest and imagined his skin. Visualizing herself pregnant with the *Daemon Incarnate,* as promised, she easily conjured the image of this man's deceitful green-blue eyes in the child she would bear. She scrunched up her little nose and made a quiet sound of uncertainty. "Pendants are really her passion, and she'd want to interrogate you about your mother for an hour. If you really want my advice on the matter, I could come back tonight, after we're closed, and help you out myself?"

~~~

Devon actually stuttered. "Uh, yeah. That sounds good - great, perfect."

There is *a God,* he thought, caught off guard. She just put herself right into his hands and he could do nothing but stare at her like an idiot. No plotting to get her into the shop at night, seduce her into the back room - or flat out rob her - would be needed. They exchanged phone numbers and he would return at ten that night!

~~~

Tabitha smiled at Devon. "Okay, then, see you tonight." He was so visibly excited that she wondered if he'd ever even spoken to a woman before. The man that looked back at her as he left the shop was *not* the same man who'd walked in as if he were the only rooster in town.

Part Two

Aunt Gwynnie pulled the security gate shut, leaving it unlocked for the boy to enter later. She did lock the entrance doors, and turned the window sign to display *"Sorry, we're closed"* while Tabitha locked up the last of the pieces from the display windows. The shop's lights were on, although dimmed to just a level of lighting to permit the security cameras to see. Aunt Gwynnie had already used up all of her sarcastic comments about the boy and the ritual to come, leaving a very quiet but welcome silence. Nodding to each other soberly, the women walked to an unassuming door set into the back wall and entered through it.

Inside the dark back room, Tabitha blew a kiss into the general air in front her and candle fire sprang to life throughout the large storeroom. Removing their clothes at a coat rack just inside the door, they donned black velvet gowns. Tabitha silently moved past the shelves of jewelry boxes and clocks, and saw the large ritual circle already cleared, cleaned and chalked out. The altar was bare except for a large stone bowl of water to perform the ritual cleansing. She let her thoughts flow with Aunt Gwynnie as the old crone cast the circle and then came to stand opposite her. Tabitha saw the amulet of Lilith, so deeply red it barely shone, juxtaposed against the dry white skin of Aunt Gwynnie's neck. She felt its power surge through her as Aunt Gwynnie's fingers grazed her skin, untying the cloak, causing her robes to drop to the floor around her feet.

~~

Devon had never felt like this before. Everything was adding up in his favor, yet he felt a foreboding. Maybe; he wasn't exactly sure *foreboding* was a word. He was certain, however, that he felt not entirely confident. It doesn't matter, he told himself. What mattered was not letting Claudette pick up on it. If Devon was going to be afraid of a thing, that thing would be Claudette's unhappiness. He'd never caused it before, and he knew that was the case because he was still breathing.

Opening the front door as quietly as he was able to, Devon slunk into the living room like a nervous teenager past curfew. His eyes darted around the room assuring nothing was amiss, or that nothing odd was sitting on a shelf watching him. He heard her voice, singing, from behind the door to her library. He knew the song well. She sang only a handful of the old songs and their familiarity stretched back into his earliest memories.

Upon reaching a set of heavy double swinging doors, Devon systematically took off all of his clothes. He covered himself with a thin cotton garment, folded around his waist like a bath towel, and then slowly pushed open one of the doors to enter the dimly lit sacred space of his mother.

Devon could see every curve of her body, outlined by candlelight and shadow, through a thin gauze robe of unbleached cotton. She sat cross-legged on top of a great mahogany table. The last time he'd seen this table it had been covered in papers, books, and pressed flowers. Now it was practically breathing beneath a dozen wax candles, steaming bowls, and little gurgling cauldrons. The air was thick with steam and smoke from burning potions and herbs. The scent was musky, though not overpowering, and not at all unpleasant.

Devon took in the scene, Claudette watched him, as well. Moving her lips in her son while drinking in the vision of his angelic face, her voice never faltered in the slightest. The last note vanished thinly into the air and finally she heard him breathe as if he had stopped for that note. His eyes rose to meet hers. She then spoke, her voice also thick and musky, "Where is my amulet, darling?"

~~~

Claudette, a classic beauty with flawless olive skin and long thick tresses of rich dark hair, looked much younger than her age of forty, sometimes passing for a decade younger. No one ever thought Devon was her son and not her lover. She rose from the table, walked over to a plush chaise lounge in the corner - Devon's favorite reading chair - and patted the cushion for him to sit. He lay down diagonally across the foot of the chaise and propped himself up on his elbows. Telling her of his meeting and plan, he seemed very innocent or perhaps just not as cocky as usual. His strange behavior was intriguing, though Claudette wasn't sure what to make of it.

Petting his hair absently while he continued to talk, she began to consider a revision to her backup plan. Devon rarely failed to get what he went after, but his barely concealed insecurity unnerved her own confidence. It was imperative to get that amulet before her sister summoned a demon into the world.

"My love," she said and stood decisively, barely aware that she'd interrupted him, "I think I can give you an edge in the matter. I know the aunt, and I know that you'll have to play along with your little girlfriend, who sounds lovely, by the way." She continued thinking and talking as she grabbed little jars from here and there. "Dev, would you grab a kettle of water, please? I'm going to make you a little drink that will help you keep your thoughts straight. I want you to have fun with the girl. You know, eat, drink, and be merry, but I want you to be able to stay focused should they try anything tricksy on you."

Part Three

Wearing her clothes from that afternoon, Tabitha waited anxiously, pacing between door and window and peeking out every few seconds to try to spot him. She saw his silhouette come around the corner, heading toward the shop and stopped in her tracks. She slowed her breathing. Her consciousness automatically drifted into a broader state of awareness, one that moved the more intimate reality far away, disconnected from her. Inserting and turning the key in the lock, turning the handle and pushing open the door, seemed intense and surreal to her. The mundane actions balanced her mental state. Breathing a little easier, she smiled a cool greeting when he reached the bottom of the front steps. For the slightest moment, as he turned to slide the gate shut behind him, the reflection of the porch light twinkled in his eyes. He's beautiful, she thought, and if she weren't in such a calm state, she'd be incredibly nervous and excited.

Holding the door open with her body to let him slide past her had its own little thrill. She could feel the electricity between them as his arm grazed hers. She closed the door and slipped the key into her small breast pocket, aware that he was watching her every move.

"So," she said softly, "we place a lot of items in the back at night, so we'll probably have to go back there to look at the nicer pendants." Seeing him nod in understanding, she continued. "I'll turn up the lighting so you can see what's out here. Maybe you'll find something you like."

Stepping away toward the light switch, she felt his hand circle around her wrist. She stopped mid-stride and looked back at him with a smile. He explained, "I want to get her something really nice. I think what I'm looking for will definitely be in a safe."

"That's good. I mean, I'm glad that you'd get your mom something really nice," she said and smiled at him again. Making eye contact to imprint her judgment, she enjoyed his squinting eyes and blushing cheeks.

Feeling quite comfortable touching him, she led him by the hand to the innocuous grey door at the back of the room. "What do you have in mind so far? Have you got a little bit of time?"

~~~

Devon was actually enjoying himself. His mind was maintaining a healthy anxiety over getting the amulet to Claudette sooner rather than later, but this girl was enchanting and obviously hitting on him. *Since when has that been a big deal,* his more sarcastic self-chided. But that was exactly the point, it was rare to actually enjoy a woman. He watched her glossy pink lips as she spoke, her fluid movements as she walked in front of him, and felt her delicate fingers thread through his. Her eyes were big and beckoning, even when she kept them partially closed beneath shadowed and heavy lids. He couldn't help but smile and follow. "I can definitely spare a few minutes," he said.

Past the door, which the girl softly closed, the room was much brighter than Devon had expected. Flickering yellow lights danced behind the shelves, as if there were a large spread of... *candles?* Darting quickly to a break in the shelving to locate the source, he caught a glimpse of a woman, naked but for a necklace, surrounded by an enormous circle of thick black candles. He recognized the woman as the older woman in the shop that afternoon. The necklace could not be mistaken. Silver, steel and iron, wrapped like knotted tree roots around a thick, roughly cut stone of garnet, he had no doubt that was Claudette's prize.

"Oh." A small sound of wonder escaped his lips and his mind quickly mapped out the necessary maneuvers to get from where he was, through the shelves and the vast space, to where the necklace was. Taking a step to run for the amulet, he was halted mid-stride by the gentle sensation of Tabitha's hand sliding back into his.

"Oh, don't mind my crazy aunt. Let's not bother her," she said, bringing his attention fully back to her.

Devon was torn between dashing for the amulet and playing the role of lover in the hopes of snagging it later. He'd expected it to be in a case though, not chained to a naked witch in the middle of a circle of protection. Sighing and smiling at the girl, he accepted the drink she held out to him.

Claudette had used the word *tricksy*, he thought, a term she used to mean black magic. She had also made it clear that he should eat, drink and be merry, so he felt confident in playing along, believing his mother had foreseen all of this somehow. He raised the little cordial glass in salute and tipped it back to his lips. As the liquid warmed his throat and chest, settling finally in his belly, he smiled at Tabitha. "That necklace your aunt is wearing - that is beautiful. That is exactly what I want."

~~~

Good, thought Tabitha. Until then, she hadn't been exactly sure how she was going to get him into the circle. A chance to look at the amulet more closely would work perfectly. With the serum in the drink working on him, he'd be calm, and up for just about anything in a few minutes. "We can go see it, but we should look at the others first. I don't know if she'll part with that one. She's also not wearing any clothes right now, and doesn't know I've brought you back here."

Devon laughed, taking his volume down when Tabitha shushed him with a giggle of her own. No, the lady was not wearing any clothes. "She's a witch, that's why," he confided to Tabitha in a whisper.

Smiling and realizing the liqueur was beginning to affect him, she held up her glass to cheer another drink.

~~~

He was feeling a bit tipsy already, but didn't see any harm in one tiny sip. No sooner did he lower the glass from his lips then her lips were there, kissing him. Before he could even register surprise, he was consumed by her warmth. A small sound escaped him as her fingers caressed his jaw line to the back of his neck and up through his hair.

~~~

Tabitha pulled back from the embrace, engendering the most delightful of responses from her future mate as he leaned toward her, hardly opening his eyes. She swayed sideways and then further back, teasing, as he followed her with his soft, pliable lips. He certainly is gorgeous, she thought again. She touched his lips and wondered if her son would have them, too. Using her index finger, she lifted his chin to persuade him to rise from his seat on a stack of wooden pallets. "Come with me. I want to make love inside my aunt's witch-circle," she whispered to him mischievously.

~~~

Devon heard her as though she was farther away than she was, right there against his chest. Her voice was witchy, he thought, as if it sang out from a silver bell and through a layer of smoke. Her lip was hitched up on one side in a mischievous smile. He hadn't known she was capable of such a charming little guise. He whispered into her ear, "Me too."

He had enough mental capacity to recall that the aunt was near the circle, but he realized he couldn't calculate a plan, nor focus clearly on his surrounding environment. All he could see was Tabitha and all he could remember was the amulet. He took her outstretched hand and followed her little bare feet around the last row of shelves and into the candle-lit sacred space of the amulet-wearing aunt.

The old witch was standing at a small stone altar with her hands folded in front of her face, humming some tuneless song. Resting in the niche between the woman's clavicles, the stone in the amulet shone a deep dark red in the light of the candles. He felt Tabitha's hand on his jaw again, directing his attention back to her. A large bed, covered with white linen sheets and plush pillows, was set further back into the circle, about mid-way between them and the witch.

The alluring call of the bed was all the distraction his confused mind needed. In his half-drugged state, the necklace took a back burner to urges that were more primal. She undressed them both slowly, in turns, smiling and watching him. He couldn't take his eyes off her face, even though the other woman stood not three feet away, wearing nothing but the necklace.

Tabitha took his right hand in both of hers and directed it to her chest, using it to swipe the collar of her blouse over her shoulder. She then moved his hand up her neck, to her jaw line and ear, while rising onto her tiptoes to kiss him. His fingers instinctively traced down the spine of her back, effectively disrobing her of her blouse entirely. Now it was she who betrayed herself with an involuntary moan.

~~~

Devon found a moment of some mental clarity. His hands and mouth could do this in his sleep, he was sure, but he needed to catch both women off guard to snatch the amulet. The aunt was apparently not concerned that they'd walked right into her circle, or that her niece was about to have sex with a stranger three feet away from her. He thought he could probably get the girl to the bed and then rush the aunt, grabbing the chain on a path out the door. He was glad he was still wearing pants, and even his shirt was only unbuttoned. Before he could fully flesh out his plan, there was a change in the room.

The air shifted and a cold draft blew in from the shop door as it swung open and slammed into the wall. Devon heard it, rather than saw it, though he did see the crazy dance of the candles as they suffered the blow. Along the ceiling and walls, he saw fleeting shadows and hints of a woman moving into the room, maneuvering lithely through the labyrinth of shelves and boxes. A woman's voice screeched out from behind him. It was the girl's aunt, her voice loud and gravelly, as if she'd chain-smoked since she was four years old. Keeping his wits about him, Devon seized the opportunity to catch Tabitha off guard and swung her bodily away from him while spinning on his heel and lunging for the amulet around the old hag's neck.

~~~

Tabitha, drunk in the thralls of passion, lost her sense of direction and had no idea what happened. Failing to coordinate her feet beneath her, she missed the bed, grazing her shoulder on the very edge. Only that slowed her descent and kept her from landing on her face. Her head smacked against the concrete with a loud *thunk*. There was no pain when her head hit the floor. "Odd," she mumbled. Feeling dazed and trying to focus, she realized her eyes were open though her vision was pitch-black. She lifted herself up to her hands and knees weakly and groped for the safety of the bed.

~~~

Meanwhile, Devon's long, thick fingers wrapped around the amulet. He paid no heed to the old woman swiping at his hand, instead clenching his fist to rip the chain right off her, when he heard the distinct clicking of a handgun being cocked behind him. He loosened his grip in fear and confusion, which allowed the crone to back up and jerk free of his hold altogether. When he heard the voice of the gunman, Devon discovered the error of his hesitation. His stomach churned as the thick, sweet voice of his mother sang past his ears. "Don't move a muscle, Gwynn. Give my boy the amulet and we all walk away."

Aware that he was directly in the line of fire, Devon tried to will his body to look to Claudette for reassurance, but found that he could not. The witch, Gwynn, snarled back at Claudette. "You will not interfere with this, Claudette!"

The old woman swiped at the altar with lightning speed and raised her hand up, holding a revolver of her own - aimed at him. "Two can play at this game," she said and laughed triumphantly. The crone's cackling assaulted Devon's ears.

No noise came from behind Devon, but he watched the crone's eyes follow some movement slightly to his right and widen in alarm. He assumed Claudette changed her target from the old witch to Tabitha. The crone's brows furrowed angrily as she returned her focus to Claudette.

Claudette's smooth voice remained calm. "Yes, two can. Now hand over the amulet; there will be no unions this night."

Devon thought that he would appreciate the ability to move out of the way, or at least see Claudette for some hint of what to do, rather than stand there with a gun pointed at him. He heard Tabitha moan somewhere off to his right. The girl's movement appeared to alarm Gwynn.

Gwynn had no idea what her enemy might do, so she pulled back the hammer of the gun and prepared to pull the trigger. Cradling the gun tightly and tensing to squeeze, her trigger-finger slowed to a pause when Claudette spoke again.

"Tabitha, stay calm and don't move," Claudette advised the confused girl.

Tabitha froze at the sound of her name being spoken by the voice of a stranger.

~~~

Gwynn was no idiot; she could do the math and see there would be no ritual that night unless Claudette was removed. The women were at a stalemate, their progeny on the line. Needing both kids alive, Gwynn knew she had the short end of the stick. Claudette adored Devon, but she didn't need him. Gwynn could lose from every angle and likely not live long enough to find another girl suitable to incubate a demon spawn. The thought occurred to her that she could swing her aim just a few inches to fire at Claudette, but the boy looked ready to run. If she hit him on accident, it was all over.

Gwynn squeezed the trigger as she shifted her aim to the right of the boy. Where the bullet would hit she couldn't predict with any precision, but it would be about head-height of her little sister.

~~~

Claudette saw her sister's finger flex in the same instant she saw the spark at the tip of the barrel. The deafening whistle of the bullet whizzed past her ear, the shot flying wide. Responding immediately, she swung her arms to the left, hard and fast. The very moment the sight of her gun was aimed at Gwynn, she squeezed the trigger with deft surety, not even blinking when the recoil jarred her arms back.

Gwynn's torso jerked back from the impact, the woman's eyes widening in wonder as she looked down to the growing stream of red that flowed from the black and smoking hole in her chest. Claudette took one large step forward and snatched at the unbuttoned collar of her boy, pulling him backwards toward her. Knowing her sister would pursue revenge for her own imminent death as soon as her thoughts cleared, Claudette pushed the boy down and toward the door, into the cover of the boxes and their shadows. She dove into a tumbling escape into the darkness herself, vaguely in the same direction.

With her back to the circle as she scrambled to the shelving, Claudette heard Gwynn unleash a guttural cry and fire her weapon twice more, in quick succession. Sparks and flying dust erupted twice near Claudette's limbs on the floor, but she was unscathed. She heard Tabitha cry out, and then the girl rushing, barefoot and dazed, to aid her bleeding aunt. Claudette knew this would be the only chance she would have to peek back and fire at the girl, or to finish the job with Gwynn. She had no desire, nor need, to take out the girl, however, and she knew Gwynn would not survive the injury she had already sustained.

Claudette looked over at Devon as he hid, crouched behind a stack of wooden crates. All of the crates were covered in thick black candles, dripping animal fat, and who knew what else, down the sides, staining the wood blood red. He looked back at her, not shaken in the least. *Good boy*, she thought. Under the light of the flames, he was quite hidden in shadow while she was not. She wanted to ask him what he could see but knew she wouldn't be able to read his lips in the darkness. She had no choice, she'd have to stand and see for herself. If Gwynn so much as twitched, she'd have to shoot her again. She mouthed to him that she was going back, and motioned for him to stay put when she saw him begin to rise to go with her.

Claudette crawled out, as silently as she could while still keeping her shooting hand available. The circle was well lit by the candles, like the stage of a tragedy with no audience. Gwynn was lying on the floor, naked, and surrounded by an immense puddle of blood. The gun was inches from her hand and the girl was bent over her, stroking her hair. Claudette witnessed the long breath released by the death of her sister. She held her own for a moment, pausing to acknowledge the passing of a soul. A quiet sob came from the girl.

"Tabitha," Claudette said, intoning the girl's name. "Tabitha, stay calm for a moment yet. We need to talk and to clear things up that you don't understand."

Tabitha looked up at the tall woman in the cotton robe with waves of mahogany colored hair. The woman was mesmerizing, but she had just killed her Aunt Gwynnie. "You killed my aunt," her voice squeaked out, tears streaming down her cheeks.

"I know, Tabitha." Claudette continued to move slowly toward the women on the floor. "There is a reason for that, and I assure you it was not something I wanted to do, but it did have to be done, in the end."

Claudette reached Gwynn's body and crouched down to meet Tabitha eye-to-eye. She slid Gwynn's handgun behind her and left hers there, as well. "I know you loved your aunt, Tabitha, but there are things you don't know. That ritual tonight could not be allowed to happen. You don't know any better, but your Aunt was a dark woman who would have brought about the destruction of the world."

Claudette reached around Gwynn's neck, unclasped the chain and brought the necklace up in one graceful motion. Both women looked into the deep red stone. It seemed to absorb light, almost creating darkness around it. Claudette fastened the clasp behind her own neck and let the cold twisted metal rest against her skin. She'd worn this trapping many times before, but now it felt heavy and alien. Claudette could clearly see, in Tabitha's eyes, the yet unvoiced surprise and all of the questions that would follow.

She looked back at the lifeless face of her sister, and tried to see some hint of the little girl she grew up with. "Gwynn was my sister Tabitha. This amulet belonged to our mother." There was so much to explain to the children, Claudette thought. She looked back at the girl for a hint of understanding, but Tabitha was still in a silent state of shock. A scuffling noise came from behind Claudette. Devon knelt down beside his mother, and offered his hand to Tabitha. His eyes were ablaze with questions as well.

"Wait," he said. He looked at Claudette with a mask of utter confusion. "Does this mean that she and I are cousins?"

Tabitha's eyes grew wide. "You're his *mother?*"

First things first, as they say, Claudette thought. The beginning was the only place to start, and the young woman would need a home and healing after her loss.

"No, Devon, you're not, but we have much to discuss and we can't do it here and now." Claudette touched each of them sympathetically on the shoulder then stood to survey the scene around them. "Come, children. Let's go eat and rest. We can talk more elsewhere. I'll have this place cleaned up, and we will handle Gwynne's death appropriately and as she would want."

Tabitha rose slowly and unsteadily, but her hand still tightly gripped Devon's. Realizing her need of him, Devon instinctively wrapped his arm around her. Claudette gathered up Tabitha's discarded blouse and helped her into it, enjoying the sight of her son as the strong lover-hero. *It would all be fine*, she thought. Taking one more look at the pair to make sure they were both presentable to be outdoors, she couldn't resist the thought, *yes, these two will make beautiful babies.*

About Laura Price

Laura Price is the imaginary person behind the eyes of her favorite character. She has had multiple short stories and poetry published, and is always filing little pieces of life in her mind to be later threaded into a new web. She lives in her own personal paradise on the beaches of Florida, where she works, plays, writes, and raises her prodigal progeny. Providing care and council for patients, Laura's work revolves around human interaction and conflict resolution. The subtle connections between people present a sort of magic which is the greatest inspiration to her writing.

Connect with Laura online:
www.AuthorLauraPrice.com
twitter.com/AuthorLPrice
facebook.com/laura.price

The Particular Man

By Desiree Matlock

Jim was busy with his yearly ritual of sitting on the park bench. It was just like any other day, but it wasn't. He'd set aside the day, their anniversary, to honor Edith. With no real income and no transportation, it was impossible to visit her grave. So, he came here and it was good enough. He had the ability to walk anywhere he could reach from the home, and he could reach this park. It was a good remembrance place. It had been part of his life, of Edith's life, since they were very young.

He'd proposed here, and sat on this very spot every anniversary since Edith's death, staying out until it got late enough that the bones complained. The warm spring sun was buffered by the dappled leaves above, the breeze was pleasant enough to keep any bugs away, and he was content. The bench was comfortingly cool just beyond the reach of his skin, and he felt snug in his spot.

His thoughts had begun to meander when a man simply appeared near the fountain, startling him out of his remembrances. The man stood still, apparently taking stock, and for several seconds Jim forgot everything else and just watched. The man stared at his own clutching hand and then the ground. After a time of doing nothing at all, the man's hands went in the pockets, shuffling contents. Jim planned on asking questions, or calling out to the new fellow to explain himself, but stopped when he saw how weary and worn the man seemed. Better to let him be. Appearing out of nowhere was probably stressful.

Jim wasn't moving from his spot though, and only adjusted his legs against the wood of the bench to ease the creak in his bones, uncomfortable, but still glad to be there. Any break from monotony was good. Not being in the home today was good.

As Jim watched, the apparently magical man pulled a perfectly ordinary notepad from one pocket and a pencil from the breast pocket. He wrote something down quickly and returned both items to their pockets. Huh. Not much of a magic show.

Jim had sat on this spot through each of their anniversaries since Edith's death and wasn't planning on skipping out early, magician or no. The magician hadn't paid any notice to Jim since arriving, so he closed his eyes, put everything out of his mind and immersed himself in a memory of Edith.

> *They walked through this park, on a soft spring day. Trees swayed in a light breeze, blossoms dancing. She smiled, making her apple cheeks bloom and her eyes gleam. "Jim, it's really not necessary. Let's just keep walking."*
>
> *"Yes it is, Edie. Let's just sit. We need to sit for a moment." She looked at him oddly, as his words blundered their way out of his mouth in the wrong order and not nearly as smoothly as he'd planned. He swung her around at arm's length to position her on the bench so that she could see to the west and plopped himself down next to her. He hoped he had timed this right.*
>
> *She looked at him, and he looked back, with no idea of how to keep her sitting there. They just stared at each other. What should he say? This was harder than he'd imagined. He looked down, then up again, and she could tell he wanted to say something.*
>
> *Suddenly, her eyes skittered off to the sky above him. She'd seen it, and was watching.*
>
> *"Look, Jimmy, a sky-writing plane." Edith pointed lightly.*
>
> *"Huh," he tilted himself that direction some and watched with her, waiting for his life to begin. The words began to form.*
>
> *"WILL," the plane wrote. Edith looked at Jim suspiciously and then smiled.*
>
> *"You silly man. Of course."*
>
> *Jim looked right at her, deadpan. "Yes, aren't men silly? I wonder what this one's up to. Perhaps his client is looking for a young man named Will? What else could it be?"*
>
> *"YOU," the plane wrote, and she laughed.*
>
> *"Doubt it. How about 'Will you clean your room up, please?'"*
>
> *"Maybe it's 'Will you leave me be?'" Jim was*

grinning.

"Could it be as romantic as 'Will you be mine?'" she responded.

"MAR...," the plane wrote, and she stopped looking. Her eyes locked on Jim.

"No, of course not. It's much bigger than that."

Jim touched the fabric of the right knee of his pants as he remembered dropping to it, and recalled how much work it had been to just push out the breath required to ask her the all-important question.

His heavy chest breathed in deep, but something was missing. The smell didn't match the memory, so he chose which air to pull into his lungs and dove back into the memory...

"I already told you," she had said, as she fell to her own knees as well, hands clasped around his, "'of course'. Didn't you hear me?"

"Yes, I suppose you did, Edie."

Jim had laughed and reached for her, for the most perfect embrace they would ever have. Pure of the complexity of later years, of wedding stress, simpler than the hurried pecks of early years with small children, warmer than the eventual comfortable routine that every couple settles into. Free from all that would later mold their mutable love over time. Nothing wrong with those embraces, they were good in different ways. Changed ways. There simply had to be a most pure, and it was that one. Every detail of that kiss was scoured into Jim's memory. He sat with his hands on his knees and held himself in place as he relived it. They had risen alone and sat together on this very bench, slowly letting the world reappear around them. Eventually, that same world had stolen her from him.

The breeze felt cool on his cheeks, pulling him back to the here and now. He squared his shoulders, letting go of his knees.

The magician was closer now, standing at the walking bridge between the fountain and the bench, looking out at the water. As Jim watched, the magician looked over and appeared to take in the older man's existence. A small nod.

Jim didn't know why he offered when he wanted to be alone

with his memories, but he didn't think there was any harm in it. "Want to sit down?"

"Why not?" The man worked his way over and sat down. They stared out at a perfectly beautiful spring day, neither looking very happy about it.

"Leo."

"Come again?"

The man chuckled. "Indeed. Uhm, sorry for the shorthand; job hazard. Name's Leo."

"Jim."

"How old are you, Jim?" He hastily tacked on, "If you don't mind my asking."

"I'm 89. Today would be my 64th anniversary."

"Wow. Congratulations!" Leo smiled, and then it faded. "Would be? I suppose she's passed."

"Yes," Jim responded simply. "Edith was the best person I have ever known."

"I had that once. It's precious. You don't realize."

Jim looked over and smiled. "No, you don't. Not until after."

"So you were married in what year?" Leo leaned toward the older man intently.

"Well, 64 years ago. So '07."

"Huh." The young man thought about it but seemed dissatisfied. His head lifted. Eyes closed into the dappled sunlight of the tree above, he listened to leaves rustle in the breeze.

The young man spoke, breaking the reverie.

"There is so much comfort in what doesn't change. Trees, sunlight, green and blue. It never changes. I didn't realize how crucially I would need that. It's almost primal. Nature."

"Not almost. It's nature. That's why us old farts love walking in the park. Everything changes. Everything goes. But not that." Jim smiled at him to lighten the words, his eyes crinkling, and Leo chuckled.

"Well, then I guess I'm an old fart, too."

They sat, side by side. Leo immersed himself in looking around again and shifted his weight restlessly.

Jim thought about his kids, grown now. Something about Leo reminded him of his youngest. Mark had been a late surprise, when they were in their fifties. He never wrote home, but on the occasional unexpected visit, he looked happy and that was good. The older two were still in touch. Judy was a professor at the college, Laura had had her troubles but seemed happy now in that artist's colony, painting sunsets into her golden years.

Leo the magician suddenly sniffed. "Smells different, though."

"Different than what?"

"Last time I was here. Something's different about the smell."

"They took down the old jasmine, maybe that's what you're noticing." Jim pointed to a gazebo partially visible through the trees behind them. It was the brilliant white of freshly painted outdoor furniture and free of overhanging boughs.

"Huh. You're right. That's got to be it. Looks like the fire hydrant colors changed, too. I thought they were red. That one there was looking pretty chipped up."

"The law changed. They've been green since..." Jim was too surprised to finish the sentence.

"Oh, yeah, I forgot." Leo's eyes skittered away oddly.

It dawned on the older man that maybe what he had here was a... No. Couldn't be. But, fire hydrants had gone glow-in-the-dark green some 50 years earlier, when his children were young, and the hydrant in question had been pretty sad indeed.

Well, it would explain the sudden appearance. There was no denying it and Jim had seen the movies. It all added up. It was possible. There wasn't any particular reason it shouldn't happen here, to him. It had to happen to someone.

Leo watched Jim's face throughout this train of thought.

"What's it like?" Jim blurted out.

Leo looked at him oddly, and the corner of his mouth crept up a bit. "I'm not sure what you're saying..."

"What do you think I'm saying? You appear out of thin air. Poof. You're carrying paper, and a pencil. A pencil!" Leo touched his pocket automatically when Jim said this. "You're remembering things I haven't seen in years."

"You're obviously imagining things..."

"You know I'm not. You're a time traveler. That's all." The old man got enough people pandering and talking to him like a child every day at the home. He looked the problem straight in the eyes.

"There's no such thing as time travel," Leo deflected.

"Look." Jim turned to face him. "I've been through a lot in life. I've survived every single one of my friends, and every second of my life has been spent one after the other, clockwise precise. I'm here now to celebrate my anniversary, not be dicked around. Edith deserved to be spoken to in plain truth. I think I do, too. I hope I do." Jim lost his steam and looked away. So did Leo.

"I'm sorry. I just - I don't know if I can start talking about it. I might not be able to stop."

"Let's cross that bridge when we come to it." Jim knew when to stop talking, and that was it. He sat back, and thought about the kids again.

Both men stayed silent while the sun rose a touch higher in the sky.

Leo spoke first. "It's not time travel."

"So? What is it?"

"Look, I'm a particle physicist. When you get down that small, well, time doesn't matter. Time is...," he grasped at nothing with his left hand, then pointed at the buildings across the park, "...a lie, like those buildings. A construct, a way to interpret and control what we don't understand."

"Okay, but that doesn't change things if you used to be in some other section of it."

"Yes, it does. It's hard to explain. The truth of the matter is that time isn't the problem. The insurmountable part of the phrase 'time travel' isn't time, it's the travel bit. I know it's a letdown, and a thousand film plots have been nullified, but it's impossible. It can't be done."

Jim scratched at his nose and let the young man keep speaking.

Leo went on, deep in the well of his own thoughts, sounding like Judy lecturing at the podium. "So, we know that time isn't real. It's a construct, it's a myth. You cannot travel through a myth. We just believe in it, like... hope," Jim's eyebrows rose as Leo continued, "...but it's no more real. We need its utility, but like all constants, time exists only to serve the forward march of our scientific formulations." Leo took a moment and then shrugged. "There is no such thing as a constant."

"Hope? Do you really think *hope* is a myth?"

"Yes--No. A useful construct more than a myth. Now, it is

helpful to us to calculate with time, but again - not real. The only part of time that is real is change. You're actually measuring change. So, there is only one way to travel through change; in an endless, forward march at the same speed as everything else, give or take a little relativity here and there. Right?"

Jim nodded, chewing on the new thoughts he was being presented with.

"I found a way to cheat it." Leo bit his lower lip. "I thought, we thought, we were so clever. Beating time travel."

"That is pretty clever, kid."

"The point is to put *yourself* into the future, right? So, forget travel. The universe has a different way. There is no need to move the original you anywhere."

"What do you mean, the 'original you'?" Jim asked. "You're a copy?"

"I don't think so, but..." Leo said as he chewed his cheek. "I know that all the other copies of me that I've been also didn't think like copies. So...I don't know." His shoulders slumped.

"I don't get it. Why not just send the real you?"

"Because you can't. The original you - the original me, the original anyone - exists already in a set course that changes in a set way, nothing can alter that. But, because of a loophole in quantum physics, down below the point where the universe makes any logical – any ordinary – sense, subatomic particles can behave sympathetically in different spaces and times."

"What? Like sympathetic magic? Sympathetic math?" Jim laughed.

Len's brow crinkled up. "Yeah, kind of. Almost 50 years before I was born, a physicist worked out that you can wiggle a particle here and make another particle in a distant place wiggle along. Then someone worked out that the particles at the other end might actually not have been there to start with, might have actually been pulled into position by the experiment. Someone else worked out how to get sympathetic action across a short gap in time. I published a paper on theories in controlling the resonance in the sympathetic action to cause an intentional spontaneous rearrangement of as many of those particles as you wanted. No traveling involved at all. Just move some of the universe around at the level beneath time, beneath motion. You could make a sympathetic you out of the particles already present in that time. Pop."

"Amazing," Jim interjected. Leo looked up in surprise, as though he'd forgotten he was talking to anyone but himself.

"Yes. So, the underlying theory was that one of me always would stay in that moment, and one of me must pop into existence in a different time."

"That's incredible." Jim's barn doors were bursting on his head. "Almost too much to process. It must be so strange to pop up in totally new places and times."

"No, we were able to control the place, but the time we couldn't do much about. We chose this park, because of proximity to the college and because it is protected. We figured it would be here for a good long while."

"Who's we?"

"Jessie and I. We devised this experiment together."

"Another one like you, huh?

"No, she didn't come with me. We wanted to keep the experiment's complicating factors down to a minimum. But, yeah, she was something. No one else was thinking that way at the time, either. I was the only person at my particular greaseboard, until she showed up." Leo's eyes grew sad. "The perfect partner to work out how to get it to actually happen. We made the device that could do it. We actually did it." He sounded surprised.

"Well, that's big," Jim said. He scratched at his eyebrow and asked, "Do you mind it? Does it hurt?"

Leo looked even more tired than before. "Coming into being feels exactly like already existing. Although...there is a momentary blankness and for that brief fraction..." he held his hands close to his face and stared past them, "I know nothing. And everything."

Jim shuddered. His gut told him what Leo meant. He hoped Edith would be there to make it easier when the time came for him.

"And then I realize that I'm new. Even though I never feel new. I mean, everything's there." Leo wrapped his arms around himself and then let go. "But I look down upon a brand new me, wrought one subatomic particle at a time and all at once. I've just been ripped from the fabric of the future and shaken into existence."

Jim chuckled. "Damn the rules."

"Yeah, but what's weird is that it doesn't even tingle. If my atoms vibrate before the split, I don't know it. My mind just goes completely blank. I'm prepared for something to happen each time, and it's a bit of a letdown when nothing at all happens except a split second of vacant stare."

Jim looked at him. "That's too bad, that breaking the rules isn't more exciting."

Leo's face opened up wide. "Exactly! Shouldn't there at least be a shiver? A spark? But no, it feels exactly the same. In that moment, I'm the newest thing in the entire universe, I've broken every universal law. But it feels totally normal."

"Better than exploding. Or being dead."

"Yeah. I shouldn't complain."

"So what next? What do you do when you get here? Aside from talk to strangers."

"I never talk to strangers." Leo looked at him oddly. "I'm breaking my routine. I don't know why."

"Well, that's fine. I'm willing." Jim settled back in his seat and watched a squirrel run along the ground. "What do you normally do?"

"It's so strange. The first thing I do every time I materialize is look down onto the same spot, the thumb of my left hand. Damned if I can work out why I do it. But I do. Every time."

Leo sat back and ran his fingers through his hair. "Then the second thing I do is realize I've done the same damn things again and then had the same damn thoughts again in the same order. After I am feeling settled, I take a look at my surroundings. I usually spot a difference or two. This time, it's that the park bench looks different than it did before. A new coat of poly told me I made it this time."

"Yup, they went with a darker green."

"I liked the old color."

"It'll fade." *Everything did*, Jim thought. "When you split apart, how does that work?"

Leo thought about it. "I suppose the effect is something like cell division. Boom! There are two of me, with the exact same memories up to that point. The first few times I popped, I thought to myself about destiny, about scientific history. I recorded my notes. How many thousands of notebooks have all the iterations of me filled by now? I even made a few jokes to myself about going rogue, being the only real, verifiable anomaly in the universe, but you give up on jokes when there's no one to smirk, no one listening to your sarcasm. Your stupid little quips. Except the notebook. And it's turning into more of a journal."

"I'm listening, Leo."

"Yes, you are," Leo paused. "For now." He fidgeted in his seat. "I mean, until the next jump."

"That's got to be rough. Why don't you just stay?" Jim asked.

Leo explained, "The terms of the experiment. The one who jumps forward needs to jump forward again. It was grand at first. By about the tenth jump, I stopped feeling special. By the hundredth, I stopped bothering with trying to form an opinion of any part of the experience at all. Now I arrive, make my notes, come to grips with existence. Sometimes I take a quiet walk, but usually I repeat the experiment the next day. Well, the next day relative to me. Sometimes I wait a while. I'm not sure why. At some point, I manage to eat and sleep each day, but not as much as I used to. I've been the one to pop forward for 247 consecutive jumps. I'm close to running out of a few minor supplies."

"I've got some things at the home, if you want to head over to the "peaceful valley' with me?" Jim offered politely

"No, I'm not there yet, old man. Give me time." They chuckled.

"No, I've got enough for now." Leo slowed down and looked at the ground. "The only thing I'm all the way out of is patience. I'm done. I am so sick of doing this." He laughed, a sad, scary laugh that hurt Jim to hear.

"But your experiment is a huge success, Leo. You're a time traveler. That's pretty amazing."

"Yeah, whatever," Leo said. His eyes closed and rolled back open. "I make it to the future every time. And that's the problem." His hand slid into his pocket and back out. Leo looked down and saw a small silver device. "I hate it."

Leo stared at it for a long time. It made Jim uncomfortable, but he just returned to his thoughts. Leo would speak when he wanted.

"I built this in the lab with Jessie's help, hundreds of years ago now, relatively."

Leo rubbed his shoulder and then slumped down on the bench.

"Almost a year without her. I feel so tired. No, not tired... empty. What am I going to do? Walk aimlessly through the park, probably. I have a day to kill until tomorrow's jump. There is always a way to make it to the next day. That's not a problem. It's tomorrow's jump, I loathe it. Every day, I come to hate it more. And I know, I just know, that I'm going to be the one who ends up having to jump again."

Angry wet eyes bored into Jim. "The scientist in me understands that my fear simply isn't grounded. That scientist says I'm just going to duplicate myself into the future. That I am actually the 247th duplicate of the original me. But I know the truth in my gut. I know! I'm the original." He calmed down, and then wiped his eyes. "I'm me. Of course I am. We all are," he finished quietly.

"But why do you have to do it? Why not just quit? Surely the experiment must be over by now," Jim pointed out.

"I promised Jessie. It was for a stupid contest. Jessie and I teamed up to beat the yearly time travel contest at the university." Leo waved in the general direction of the distant brick walls behind them.

"We were in such an infantile rush to impress the professors that we didn't really think it through. We snickered and sneered at the other contestants as I talked up my theory as the only way that the universe had to get it done. She was thoroughly impressed by my paper. She loved thinking nonlinearly with me about sympathetic action through quantum entanglement. While I explained known theory, her eyes sparkled with ideas of how to actually create it. Flesh it out. Turn my ideas into reality. She was the only one who felt my ideas were sound, and with her skills, it came together like magic. The device - this device," he looked at the thing in his hand with revulsion, "sparked into existence."

"'Create a Time Machine!' the contest said. We had no idea. The rules of our experiment became an afterthought to the creation of the device."

"You are young," Jim added helpfully. "You don't always think things through when you're young."

"I don't feel young."

"Didn't you just say you're the youngest thing in the universe?"

"Ha."

They sat again for a while and watched a boy and his dog play in the distance.

"Maybe I am still young." He paused and then continued with his story, "Jessie and I felt like we were running a trick, a gag."

Jim thought about the man across from him. How sad it would be to feel like everyone you have ever known actually knew someone else. "You miss her? This partner of yours." It almost wasn't a question.

"Every damn day. The morning of my first jump, she touched her fingers to my temple, and said, 'Remember this: Change is a constant. It doesn't matter when you are, for there you are and that is that.' I remember it when I miss her." He added her name almost like a prayer, "Jessie."

"There you are and that is that," Jim intoned. "True. Fitting." He raised his arms up and indicated their surroundings. "At least it's a nice day out, right?"

"Yeah. There's that." Leo watched a young mother ride by with a pram. Jim watched him and waited for him to speak again.

"I ran into another me a couple jumps ago," Leo said, almost guiltily, "we'd jumped to nearly the same moment by happenstance. He told me that everyone back home eventually gave up on the idea of time travel. Even me, apparently. Some prior iteration of that me went back to the college and found that I never amounted to anything at all. He, I, must have thrown the device in a box after a few attempts thinking it didn't work because nothing happened. It makes sense."

"That explains why I've never heard of you. But why don't you go back there and tell them it worked?"

"I can't go back."

"No, I mean, to the college, not the time."

"Oh." Leo thought. "That's not my job. I'm the one who jumps. Remember?"

"Well then, why didn't that other guy do it?"

Leo looked surprised, like it hadn't occurred to him. "I can't answer that. I'm not the other me." Jim didn't think he'd ever seen a man look more forlorn.

"I am always the one who jumps ahead. It feels..." his eyes rolled almost comically, "wrong! I'm fed up with it. In the crazy world I live in, I'm the asshole whose particular coin always lands on heads. Always." His hands pressed the sides of his face, like the thought was unbearable.

Jim placed his hand on the young man's back sympathetically. "But, I mean, someone has to. Right? The only reason I'm talking to you is that you're the only you who *could* have made it here to talk to me. I have to be talking to the guy who always jumped. Some other you, who got to stay, well he's somewhere else. Am I right?"

Leo looked at Jim with respect. "You got it. That's me. The asshole who has the misfortune to have jumped hundreds of time. Mr. Heads."

Leo started to stand slowly, his words almost rushed.

"You know, before I started this I briefly theorized that the problem would be with the guy who always lands on tails, and it looks like I was right, because that guy threw the device away, or whatever. He's the guy who sits home while all the other hims get to explore other times. I knew that eventually the guy that *didn't* pop into the future would want to stop trying. What's in it for him? I imagined, of course, some incredibly strenuous process of combustion, instead of the anticlimax that occurs. I imagined he'd quit because it's all pain, no gain. He's not getting any fun. Right?"

"Sure, I guess." Jim was tired of thinking. Leo was nearly standing, having raised himself off his seat. The poor boy must have been busting at the seams thinking like this for so long, Jim thought. He was on a roll though, and he might never get a sympathetic ear again.

"But no. I didn't in a million years think about what it would feel like to be this particular me. I'm the patsy who has to keep jumping, never staying any*when* long enough to get used to it. Never getting to be the guy who stays sucks."

Jim turned and waited until he felt he had Leo's full attention. "So stay."

Leo plopped back down into his seat. "Huh. You might be right. It could be that simple."

Jim pulled himself off the bench. "Of course it is. Walk with me."

The two men walked back to the pedestrian bridge and stood over the rushing water. They watched the light glint off the rippling waves.

"How much impact do any of us have on this world, really?" Leo looked disturbed.

Jim thought about it. "Edie would say that all we can do is live well, love well, and try to be good to each other."

"Yeah, Jessie was kind to people. I outlasted her without meaning to. I didn't realize." Leo closed his eyes, flicked his fingers away from himself, "Gone."

"Maybe not gone. If time is just change, maybe they're just stopped. Just...waiting for us." Jim laughed. He ran his fingers over the rough texture of the paint on the railing. "Tell me about her, about Jessie."

Leo smiled, and Jim knew that Jessie'd been this boy's Edie. "God, she was perfect. You know? Smart, sexy smart, and beautiful without knowing it. I knew from the moment I met her that she was going to make her mark, leave an indelible impact on the world. No mistake, she was brilliant. I couldn't have done this without her." He breathed in, back out, and continued, "And those eyes. The way she flicked them up at me when she brushed hair out of her way when she was working." He laughed, his eyes glazed in memory. "My stomach still does flips. There are countless other mes in unknown other times, and those mes are very likely getting on with things. They probably don't miss Jessie, but maybe they do. Maybe I'm not unique in this."

Jim thought how to answer. "So you're not unique. Does it matter?"

"Maybe." They watched a leaf float briskly by on the current below. "I want my own life back. I want to try to figure out how to get back to her. I can't handle this constant popping about. I've learned my limit. She wanted me to try to do this a thousand times. Testing degradation."

"Degradation?"

"Whether I become... less. She was positive there would be zero degradation."

"You seem pretty whole to me. She's probably right," Jim said.

"Maybe."

"I'll bet she is, she sounds pretty smart. And plus, you're not see through or anything."

They laughed.

"I like you, Jim."

"Leo, you're not what I expected out of today, but I like you. Edith would have liked you."

"Thank you." He looked genuinely touched.

"Look kid. Just stop if you want to stop. Simple."

Leo gripped the railing. "This is what I do. This is what my life is about."

"If you want to call that living. Doing something you don't want to do every single day because you feel obligated to do it. I can get you a job at a shoe factory if you want that kind of work."

"You have a point."

Leo held the device in his hand and opened the battery pack. "This is a simple lithium ion battery. Easy enough to find in the past, at a price, but completely antiquated here." He handed it to Jim.

Jim didn't recognize the power source. He weighed the tiny battery in his hand; it reminded him of a large coin. He gave it back to Leo, who clutched it to his chest. He was obviously torn. Then his eyes changed and hardened. His hand darted out and flew past Jim as he flung the battery out and away. It fell into the water below without a splash.

They both stood, surprised. Jim felt like he'd just blown out the candles on a birthday cake, breathless with the excitement of possibility.

Then Leo laughed. "Jim! Can you believe it? I couldn't even hear it hit the water. My life is forever changed and it's just...gone. Not even a little 'ploop' noise. Talk about anticlimactic."

"You'll be fine." They started walking further into the park.

"What the hell. We'll see, I guess." Jim watched Leo methodically tuck the small silver device back into his pocket. "For whatever reason, I'm still following procedure."

"So what? You chose no more Mr. Heads. Stop second-guessing yourself. Go live."

Leo pulled the battered notebook and pencil from his pocket and sighed. He scribbled a bit inside it. Jim figured it was probably about how today's jump went, with a few candid words about the human element, or about meeting Jim. Who knew?

It wasn't Jim's business. The old man recognized he was already far too interested, too involved. He took a deep breath and could almost smell the jasmine that should have been there. His bones were starting to get tired of walking around and he wanted to go home, back to waiting to be with Edie.

A thought struck him. "Maybe Jessie tried it out?" Jim suggested. "You know, before you guys scrapped the experiment."

"Wow, there's a thought. I can see me handing it to her, if I thought it wasn't working." Leo's eyes sparked at the thought. They both made mental notes to spend more time in the park, and maybe see who the universe ripped into existence.

"A man can hope."

About Désirée Matlock

Désirée Matlock presently lives in a beach town with her beau, twin daughters, two cats and a dog, where, whenever she gets two seconds to rub together, she writes by a window overlooking a lake. She loves to travel and play the piano, although never at the same time. She won't bore you further with the mundane details of her simple life unless you visit her blog.

Connect with Désirée online:
www.DesisTwoCents.com

Other books by Désirée Matlock
Into the Abyss (Anthology)

Destiny

By Angel Woolery

You

are

a

force

over which,
I have no control.

You lead me
doggedly
down a path,

toward an end

I cannot foresee.

My eyes kept wide,
still the mystery remains.

Be it
the path of virtue?

Is it wrought
of primrose?

It is of no import.

I must
follow.

I am
susceptible
to you.

Your slightest whim
compels me.

Your softest whisper,
my command.

When you hold back
nothing,

I am your casualty.

My heart left
in a million

jagged,

tragic,

little pieces.

But when you love me,

when
you
really
love
me,

your gentleness
is
my undoing.

Your caprice can find me

spent

from passion

or

bathed in anguish.

You care not
how I receive
your will

as long as you are the brace
upon which I arc.

So,

I will let you
have your way with me

more times
than seems prudent.

I can do no differently.

You are as certain
as moonlight.
As inescapable
as life.

Destiny.

Without you
I cease to exist.

You are both
rogue
and
cherished friend.

Your caustic wit

oft
sears me.

Your generosity,
sweet
balsam.

I trust you.

I must
be
mad.

About Angel Woolery

Angel's work has been described by other poets as "gritty" and "sweetly sensual". Poetry in particular is gratifying for her as a writer as it is a personal, yet formal, artistic exercise. She finds the intellectual challenge of shaping thought into a predetermined format, a pleasurable way to while away some hours. Though what intrigues her most is that the emotional intent behind each piece is transmuted beautifully into something different by each reader, allowing the creation to become as meaningful and personal to them as it is to her.

Connect with Angel online:
Facebook.com/AngelWooleryPoet

Other books by Angel Woolery
The Taste of Innocence
Into the Abyss (Anthology)

Thank you for taking the time to enjoy our creative works. Look out for more books from the Ink Slingers Guild, both as a group and as individuals!

If you enjoyed any or all of the stories in this book, we would love it if you could take a few minutes to share it on Amazon or Goodreads. Your opinion really does make a difference!

May your world be filled with adventure and the stuff that dreams are made of.

Cheers!

The Ink Slingers Guild

www.InkSlingersGuild.com